GOBLIN
QUEST

Philip Reeve was born in Brighton and worked in a bookshop for many years before becoming a bestselling author and illustrator. His debut novel, MORTAL ENGINES, the first in an epic series, was published to great acclaim around the world. He has won the CILIP Carnegie Medal, the Smarties Gold Award, the Guardian Children's Fiction Prize and the Blue Peter Book of the Year. He lives with his wife and son on Dartmoor, where the wildest places are probably full of boglins, dampdrakes and other mysterious creatures.

www.philip-reeve.com
www.mortalengines.co.uk

By Philip Reeve

Mortal Engines
Predator's Gold
Infernal Devices
A Darkling Plain

Fever Crumb
A Web of Air
Scrivener's Moon

No Such Thing As Dragons

Here Lies Arthur

Goblins
Goblins Vs Dwarves

In the BUSTER BAYLISS series:

Night of the Living Veg
The Big Freeze
Day of the Hamster
Custardfinger

GOBLIN QUEST

Philip Reeve

MARION LLOYD BOOKS

First published in the UK in 2014 by Marion Lloyd Books
An imprint of Scholastic Ltd
Euston House, 24 Eversholt Street
London, NW1 1DB, UK
Registered office: Westfield Road, Southam, Warwickshire, CV47 0RA
SCHOLASTIC and associated logos are trademarks and/or
registered trademarks of Scholastic Inc.

ISBN 978 1407 13832 9

A CIP catalogue record for this book is available
from the British Library

Printed and bound by CPI Group (UK) Ltd, Croydon, CR0 4YY
Papers used by Scholastic Children's Books are made from
wood grown in sustainable forests.

1 3 5 7 9 10 8 6 4 2

www.scholastic.co.uk

For SAM, with luv an
KiSsiz from oRL tHe GOBbLinZ

Here be Cushions (?)
Far Penderglaze
Grundy
The Western Ocean
Wedge
Hoonish
Near Penderglaze
Floonhaven
R. Floon
Lusvenn
Choon Head
Choon
R. Choon
Calchoen

The Cold Hills

Porthstrewy

Bonehill Mountains

WASTES
of ULAWN

Oethford

Stag Headed
Oak

Clovenstone

Oeth Moor

N

W

E

S

To
Coriander

To
Porthzafron
Hindhaven
Croke
and the
Woolmark

Contents

A Visitor Drops In

"Aaaaaaaaaaaaaargh!"

The sound that echoed across Clovenstone that morning was one which Skarper had often heard before. In fact, it was one that he had often *made* before, usually when he was being chased by something, or falling from a great height towards Certain Death. But nothing was chasing him today, and he was not falling from anywhere. He was just ambling about in the sunshine, looking for mushrooms.

Summer had come to Clovenstone at last, after a long, hard winter and a cold spring. The snow that had shrouded the ruins of the old fortress-city for so long had finally melted, although it still lingered on the lofty summits of the Bonehill Mountains which loomed beyond the eastern wall. Woken by sunbeams poking into his nest up in Blackspike Tower, Skarper

1

had remembered suddenly how much he liked fried mushrooms for his breakfast, and he had come scampering down from the Inner Wall to this flattish, grassy part of Clovenstone to see if any had pushed their heads up through the earth there.

He had found some, too. They were the fat, yellowish-white puffballs which the goblins of Clovenstone called urth grobbits. These were Skarper's favourites, and he had just stuffed his pockets with them and was turning for home when he heard that strange new noise.

"AAAAAAAAAAAA. . ."

It seemed to be growing louder.

Skarper looked around, but there was nothing to see. Only the grass moved, blowing in the spaces between the crumbling, ancient buildings.

". . .AAAAAAAAA. . ."

Skarper looked up. What was that, right in the very top of the sky? That black speck, hard to make out in the dazzling sunshine, especially to goblin eyes which preferred the dark. Was it an insect? Was it a bird? It seemed to have two flailing arms, and two frantically kicking legs. It seemed to be a man. . .

A falling man.

". . .AAAAAAAAAAARGH!!!"

"Oh, bumcakes!" said Skarper.

He started to run one way, then changed his mind and ran the other. That was a bad decision. With a massive THWUMP the man landed on him.

The goblin name for human beings was "softlings", but it turned out they didn't feel very soft when they were being dropped on you. Skarper would have been squashed flat if the bit of Clovenstone he happened to be standing in had not been so soft and boggy. As it was, he was driven deep down into the oozy moss.

"Ow!" said the softling, after a while. "Ow, my head!" he added. "And my ribs. And my elbow."

"What about me?" asked Skarper in a squashed and bitter voice from somewhere underneath him. "What about my. . . What about *all* of me?"

The softling had not realized until then that the hard, lumpy thing he had landed on was a goblin. With a cry of, "Ow, my knee!" he sprang up and drew his sword.

"Unhand me, foul goblin!" he shouted.

Skarper climbed out of the Skarper-shaped crater he had made in the wet ground. "My hands are nowhere near you, and anyway, they're called paws," he said. He looked ruefully at his tail. It already had one kink in it where it had been broken and set badly: now it would have two more. "Who do you think you are, anyway?"

he asked. "Dropping on people like that. What's your game?"

"I am Prince Rhind of the Woolmark," said the softling, drawing himself up tall and proud and sticking out his chin as if he thought Skarper should have heard of him and ought to be impressed. He was a handsome sort of softling, Skarper supposed, though slightly on the chubby side. He had a pinkish face and sandy-coloured hair. Underneath all the mud he was very expensively dressed, in richly embroidered felt clothes and a shining coat of fish-scale mail.

"As for what brings me here," Prince Rhind went on, "that is a long and fascinating tale. . ." But before he could get any further a plump white cloud dropped out of the sky and started to whizz about at head height.

"Yoohoo!" said the cloud.

"I might have known!" groaned Skarper.

It was not really the cloud that had said "yoohoo" of course (that would be silly). It was the cloud maidens, the wispy, vaporous young sky-spirits who sat on top of it, looking worriedly at Prince Rhind.

"Are you all right, sweet prince?" they twittered. "When we said that you would see Clovenstone if you leaned over the edge, we did not mean for you to lean quite that far over!"

"Be of good cheer, sweet maidens of the skies," said the prince. "I am unharmed. Happily, this goblin broke my fall."

"It wasn't happy from where I was standing," said Skarper. "What did you bring him here for?" But the cloud maidens just sniffed and looked snootily the other way. They didn't like goblins.

"I have come seeking the fell fortress of Clovenstone," announced Prince Rhind, "where I have heard tell there resides a treasure which will be of aid to me in my perilous quest. These good maidens were kind enough to offer me a lift."

"Well, this is Clovenstone all right," said Skarper. "It isn't really a fell fortress any more though."

"No, indeed. . ." Prince Rhind looked about him at the ruins. His handsome young face was a little downcast. The cloud maidens drifted overhead giggling and showering him with tiny heart-shaped hailstones inscribed with messages like "BE MINE" and "DREAMBOAT".

"You do have treasure houses here, don't you?" he asked. "I was told there were treasure houses. . ."

"Oh, they're all inside the Inner Wall," Skarper told him. "We don't keep much treasure in them these days though."

"What do you keep in them then?"

"Cheese, mainly."

"Cheese?"

"Cheese. Haven't you heard of Clovenstone Blue? We make it here. It's very popular." Skarper wrung some bog water out of his shoes and looked at Prince Rhind of the Woolmark with his head on one side. He didn't seem a bad sort of softling. Probably he wasn't really dangerous except when he fell on people, and he probably didn't make a habit of that; it seemed to have been more in the way of an accident.

"You'd better come and meet Henwyn and everybody," he said, doubtfully.

Prince Rhind nodded, though he looked doubtful too. "Everybody? Yes. . ." He seemed wary of saying too much to Skarper. Perhaps, like most softlings, he mistrusted goblins. At last he said, "Take me to this Henwyn, goblin, that I may share with him the great matter of my quest. I only hope that the thing I seek still resides here, for it is clear to me that much has changed at Clovenstone."

Prince Rhind

Prince Rhind of the Woolmark was not often right about things, as Skarper and his friends would realize when they came to know him better, but he was right about that. Things had changed and changed again at Clovenstone. Once, long ago, it had been the castle of an evil sorcerer called the Lych Lord, who had used his goblin armies to try and conquer the whole of the Westlands.

Now his high black keep was gone, and the goblins who remained, living in the ruined towers of the Inner Wall which used to ring it, couldn't really be bothered with conquering anybody. Indeed, the previous summer, when the dwarves of the north had tried to do some conquering of their own, it had been the goblins who helped to defeat them. People in the Westlands were starting to realize that goblins were not all bad, after all.

The cloud maidens' cloud trailed after Prince Rhind like a lovestruck balloon as he followed Skarper up the roads between the ruins, towards the gate that led through the Inner Wall. "It is not *entirely* what I was led to expect," Rhind admitted, glancing at the giant molehills which the dwarves had left behind. The huge skull of a diremole grinned down at him from the wall above the gate as Skarper heaved on the knocker and shouted, "Open up!"

"Who is it?" yelled a sleepy goblin voice from one of the windows high above.

"It's Skarper, you idiot."

"Well, why can't you come in the underneath way, the same you went out?"

"I've brought a guest," said Skarper, pointing at Prince Rhind. "Guests come in the front way, that's polite."

"Oh, all right," said the voice, a bit peevishly. "Hang on. I'll come down."

Skarper and Prince Rhind stood outside the gate and waited. After a few moments Prince Rhind said, "The person I really need to see is your queen."

"We haven't got a queen," said Skarper. "There used to be a king – King Knobbler – but we laughed at his pants and he had to go off and live in Coriander. They don't laugh at people's pants in Coriander. Well, not so much."

Rhind's handsome forehead was creased by a princely frown. "My court sorcerer told me that Clovenstone was ruled by a wise and kindly lady who would help me on my quest."

"Oh, he must mean Princess Ned," said Skarper, and his ears drooped. Ned had been wise and kindly, and although she had not exactly ruled Clovenstone – she was more interested in gardening than ruling things – all the goblins had looked to her for guidance. Also for scones. But Ned was dead. She had died quite unexpectedly the previous year, at the end of that business with the dwarves, and there had been nothing that the goblins could do for her except to tend the flowers that grew upon her grave in a corner of the pretty garden she had made inside the Inner Wall.

"I see grief on your face, goblin," said Prince Rhind. "Don't tell me that the Lady of Clovenstone is dead?"

"All right," said Skarper. "But I 'spect you'll hear all about it sooner or later."

Rhind's frown grew approximately fifteen per cent frownier. "That is sad news indeed. I had looked to her to aid me in my quest, you see."

"There's always Fentongoose and Dr Prong," said Skarper. "They know all about quests and stuff. I 'spect they'll help you."

A noisy rattling of keys and undoing of bolts had

begun behind the huge gate, and at last it creaked open a little way. An ugly head poked out through the gap and looked the visitor up and down. The head belonged to Libnog, Skarper's batch-brother (which meant that he had hatched from the same batch of eggstones, coughed up like hairballs by the magical slowsilver lake beneath Clovenstone).

"What do we have to be polite to him for?" Libnog asked.

"Because he's a prince, you ignorant goblin!" shouted the cloud maidens, who had been hovering about above, writing CLOUD MAIDENS + RHIND LOVE 4 EVER on the gatehouse wall with icicles. (They had a thing about princes.)

"He's Prince Rhind and he's come all the way from somewhere called Woolmark on some sort of quest," said Skarper.

Libnog looked Rhind up and down again. Then he tried looking him down and up. Goblins aren't easy to impress, and Libnog wasn't. "I suppose he'd better come in then," he grumbled.

And so it was that Prince Rhind of the Woolmark came to Clovenstone, striding through the dank and dripping tunnel behind the gate and out into the broad central space on the summit of the crag called

Meneth Eskern. Once the Lych Lord's Keep had stood there, safe in the circle of the Inner Wall and the six and a half goblin-haunted towers. Armouries and guardhouses stood there still, but all that remained of the Keep itself were mounds of shattered masonry. Among the dark stones, Ned's little garden shone like a trove of treasure, jewelled and gilded with the flowers of spring. The bluebells that grew so thickly there had been planted by Ned herself. They were the magical bluebells of Oeth Moor, and they thrived in the soil of Clovenstone, so rich in slowsilver. Each time the breeze stirred the flowers they actually rang with tiny, pretty, tinkling notes.

Prince Rhind stood listening a moment, then sniffed.

"Why is there a smell of cheese?" he asked.

"That's from the cheesery," said Skarper. "Didn't I tell you? We make cheese here at Clovenstone now. It gives us something to do, now that we've all stopped fightin' each other all the time."

"It is most . . . pungent," said Rhind, wrinkling up his nose. "In the Woolmark we eat only the cheese of sheep, which does not smell quite so . . . interesting."

By that time, the news that a visitor had arrived was spreading fast. From doors and windows all around, the ugly figures of the goblins came creeping. Prince

Rhind looked at them nervously. They were not waving weaponry or shouting war cries, like the goblins that he'd heard about in stories, but they still looked pretty ferocious with their fangs and claws and beady eyes, their spiky armour and their studded leather jerkins. He started to wonder if it had really been such a good idea to accept the cloud maidens' offer of a lift and leave his travelling companions to make their own way to Clovenstone.

Then he saw humans pushing their way through the goblin throng – two old men and one young one – and that calmed him a little. The young one stepped out in front of him and grinned. "Welcome to Clovenstone, stranger!"

"I am Prince Rhind," said the Prince, drawing himself straight and tall again, as if he was posing for his own statue. "You must be . . . Fentongoose?"

"No, I'm Henwyn," said the young man. He shielded his eyes against the sun and peered up at the cloud that was hanging overhead. "Hello, cloud maidens!"

"Whatever," muttered the cloud maidens. They had been very taken with Henwyn once, but that had been before they found Prince Rhind. Henwyn was handsome enough, but he was only a cheesewright who had blundered into Clovenstone seeking adventure; he wasn't an actual *prince*.

"I am Fentongoose," said the less shabby of the two older men, squeezing between two fat goblins to stand at Henwyn's side. "And this is my friend and colleague, Dr Quesney Prong."

"Greetings," said Prong – who was not just shabbier than Fentongoose but taller, thinner and sterner looking.

"What brings you to Clovenstone, Prince Rhind?" asked Henwyn. "I heard the goblins saying something about a vest?"

"He's on a quest," said Skarper.

"Oh, a *quest*? That makes a bit more sense, now I come to think about it. What sort of quest?"

Rhind frowned quite hard. "I was supposed to speak of it only to the Lady of Clovenstone. But your goblin Skarper tells me that she is no more."

Henwyn hung his head sadly. Prong and Fentongoose looked glum. Some of the goblins burst into tears.

"Alas," said Henwyn, "Skarper spoke the truth."

"Then I am not sure what to do," said Rhind, scratching his head. "Perhaps I should wait for my companions to join me, so that I may seek their counsel."

"There're more of you?" asked Libnog.

"Oh yes! My sister Breenge, my cook Ninnis, and my sorcerer, the wise and mighty Prawl."

"Prawl?" Everyone perked up at the mention of

that name. Even the goblins who had been most upset by the reminder of Princess Ned stopped sniffling and blew their noses with loud trumpety sounds on one another's sleeves.

"Prawl?" said Fentongoose. "Not *the* Prawl? From Coriander? Youngish fellow with spectacles and sort of sticky-out ears? Why, he was with me and Carnglaze when we first came to Clovenstone, foolishly believing that we could awaken its old power. I wondered where Prawl had got to! So he travelled all the way to Tyr Davas, did he? But what's all this wise and mighty business? Prawl is not a sorcerer! He's no more a sorcerer than I am!"

"Then this must be a different Prawl," said Prince Rhind coldly. "For my Prawl is a great and learned sorcerer, wise in the lore of the Westlands."

Faintly, above the chatter of the goblins and the tinkling of bluebells, the sound of a far-off horn came echoing over Clovenstone from the south.

"Aha! I expect that will be them now!" said Rhind.

"It sounds like they're at Southerly Gate," said Skarper.

"Then let us go and meet them," Henwyn declared. "We'll soon find out if this wise and mighty Prawl is *our* Prawl or not!"

The Sheep Lords

It was almost five miles from the towers of the Inner Wall to the crumbling Outer Wall which ringed all Clovenstone, but quite a procession set off down the old straight road through the ruins to meet the new arrivals. Nothing much had happened since Ned's funeral, and the goblins and their softling friends were all eager to see these travellers who came from a land so far away that few of them had even heard of it.

"The land of Tyr Davas, also known as the Woolmark, lies east of Hindhaven and south of the Forest of Croke," explained Dr Prong as they went tramping south through the ruins. "It is a wide and rolling land of green hills, and the folk who live there are famed for their skill with sheep. The Sheep Lords, men call them. Their king, Raun son of Efan, rules over flocks ten thousand strong from his golden hall at Dyn Gwlan."

15

Dr Prong was very keen on educating the goblins, but as usual none of them were listening. They hurried along with the cloud maidens' cloud bobbing above them, and Henwyn went ahead with Prince Rhind because he felt that, now Ned was gone, he was sort of responsible for Clovenstone, and he wanted to stop the goblins from making too bad a first impression on these visitors if he could.

Near the edge of the woods which filled the southern portion of Clovenstone they met with Zeewa, the girl from Musk who had come the summer before to cure herself of a curse and stayed on partly because it was too cold to travel home and partly because she had grown to like the old place and the people who lived there. She did not seem too pleased to see them now, however. The chatter and clatter of the approaching goblins had scared away the deer she had been stalking. She waited, leaning on her spear, at the place where the road plunged into the trees, and called out, "What's happening? Are we under attack?"

"Just welcoming some visitors," said Henwyn. "Come with us!"

So she did. She was as curious about the newcomers as any of the others, although she did not much like the look of Prince Rhind. Too proud and sure of himself, she thought. She had been like that once herself, for

her father was Ushagi, King in the Tall Grass Country west of Leopard Mountain. Her curse, and the curing of it, had changed her, and she thought the change had been a good one. She hoped this snooty-looking young princeling would find something at Clovenstone that would change him, too.

Down the long stair to the River Oeth they all went striding, tramping, scampering. Carefully, carefully they crossed the old stone bridge – but they need not have worried. The troll who lived beneath it was away upriver, hunting with his new friends, Torridge, Cribba and Ken. He had been showing those three urban trolls how proper trolls hunted in the wilderlands, and in return they had persuaded him to stop trying to eat anyone who set foot upon his bridge.

Henwyn and Rhind had just reached the top of the long stairway on the far side of the river, and were waiting there for the others to catch up, when they heard a silvery horn-call. Henwyn saw the bright clothes of the travellers and the harnesses of their horses shining among the trees ahead. He had assumed that they would wait at Southerly Gate, but the goblins who had been on guard there must have fallen asleep or gone off hunting rabbits as usual. The Sheep Lords had ridden straight in, and were making their way up Clovenstone's main road as bold as brass.

When they saw the big crowd of goblins swarming towards them they grew a lot less bold. The two riders reined in their horses and drew swords, and a plump woman who had been strolling along beside a little brightly coloured wagon leaped up on to its seat and made ready to defend herself with an outsized frying pan. Henwyn hurried to meet them, shouting, "Don't be afraid! Welcome to Clovenstone! There is nothing to fear!"

And from amid the little bunch of worried riders a voice replied, "Henwyn! Henwyn! I say, it is me, Prawl!"

So it is *our Prawl*, thought Henwyn, as the former sorcerer slithered down off his horse and came running over to hug him. He looked very different from the shabby conjurer who had arrived at Clovenstone two years before. He was splendidly dressed in robes of purple felt, with a travelling cloak to match, all embroidered with stars and moons in gold and silver thread. His greyish hair had been trimmed and curled and oiled by someone who knew a lot about trimming and curling and oiling. Henwyn might not have recognized him at all had it not been for his ears, which still stuck out like jug handles, and the pair of spectacles he wore, two little windows in a horn frame, which flashed cheerfully in the sunshine.

"So it's true!" said Henwyn. "You are working for the Sheep Lords now?"

"Oh yes," said Prawl, waving at Fentongoose and at those goblins whom he recognized. "I set off by sea for Barragan last spring but a storm drove my ship ashore near Molscombe, on the coast of Tyr Davas. When the good people there heard that I was a sorcerer they took me straight to their king at Dyn Gwlan. He was looking for a new wizard, you see. The previous one had accidentally blown himself up when one of his spells backfired. There was nothing left of him but two smoking boots and an unfortunate stain on the ceiling."

"But you're not a wizard!" said Fentongoose, shaking his friend's hand. "You're no more magical than I am! Ow!" he added (for Doctor Prong had just kicked him on the shin). "What did you that for, Prong?"

"All sorts of strange things have been happening in the world since that Slowsilver Star passed by," Prong whispered. "It is quite possible that your friend with the ears has developed magical powers. And if he hasn't, and he is just tricking these Sheep people into believing that he is a sorcerer, then I don't suppose he wants you shouting about it all over Clovenstone."

"Oh!" said Fentongoose. "Fair point. Er, Prawl, allow me to present Doctor Quesney Prong, and Zeewa, from the Tall Grass Country, and . . . well, you already know Prince Rhind!"

"Greetings, brother," said the other rider, also dismounting. Pulling off her hat and shaking out her long, fair hair, she revealed herself to be a young woman – a rather hefty young woman, wearing the same sort of felt clothing as Prince Rhind. It was she who had been blowing the horn they had heard. It hung at her side on a crocheted baldric, the long, curling horn of a prize ram. A long bow was slung across her back, and a quiver of arrows with felt flights hung from the saddle of her horse.

"That's Rhind's sister, Lady Breenge, shield maiden of Dyn Gwlan," whispered Prawl. "She is not just a pretty face. She is a bold warrior, and her bow has slain many a sheep rustler on the borders of Tyr Davas. Don't you think she's the most beautiful girl you've ever seen?"

"Er. . ." said Henwyn, who hadn't realized that Breenge was a girl at all, she was so big and tough looking. (The goblins, of course, could barely tell male softlings from female ones at the best of times.)

"I am in love with her!" confessed Prawl, blushing. "I was going to turn down King Raun's offer of a job until I set eyes on her, and then I just knew that she was the one for me."

"And does she return your feelings?" asked Fentongoose.

But it didn't look as if the shield maiden of Tyr Davas did, because she scowled at Prawl and said, "What are you whispering about, sorcerer?" Then, before he could answer, she spoke again to Rhind. "I am glad to find you here, brother. When those sky creatures made off with you, I feared it was all a trick, and that we might never see you again."

"We're not creatures!" shouted the cloud maidens from above. "He was far safer riding through the sky with us than plodding along behind you on that horse."

Lady Breenge glanced up at the cloud, which quickly rose a bit higher, in case she threw something at it. It seemed that she did not like the cloud maidens. (Not many people did.)

Prince Rhind, who had not heard anything that Prawl had said, introduced his sister, who nodded briefly at Henwyn and the others. Then he quickly named the third of his companions. "This is Mistress Ninnis, my cook."

Ninnis was a jolly-looking person, as round as a robin and with the same bright eyes. She put down her frying pan and waved at the goblins. She bobbed a curtsey and beamed. She seemed delighted to meet them.

"Now, Prawl," said Rhind, "it seems we have a problem. When we set out on this noble quest of ours, you told me that we should seek the help of the Lady of Clovenstone and that she would give me . . . that which I need to complete the quest. But it turns out that she's dead."

"Dead?" Prawl looked shocked. "Princess Dead, Ned? I mean, Princess Ned—"

"As a doornail," said Rhind, who cared far more about the inconvenience to his quest than about some dead princess he'd never even met. "Stone dead. Popped her clogs, turned up her toes, pushing up the daisies. Well, bluebells. The point is, can we trust these friends of hers? Goblins, strange old men, a Muskish wench and, er. . ."

"He's a cheesewright!" called the cloud maidens helpfully, seeing him pause and look at Henwyn.

"Trust them?" Prawl had still not come to terms with the sad news about Ned. His ears flushed pink with emotion. "Of course we can trust them!"

Henwyn decided that enough was enough. He didn't like this Rhind, and he wished that he and his sister and his cook would just hurry up and go off on this quest he kept banging on about. But he didn't

22

want them telling everyone they met along the way that they had received no help or welcome from the goblins of Clovenstone.

"Why don't we all go back to the Inner Wall?" he said. "You can rest your horses, and we'll have a feast, and you can tell us what it is that you are questing for."

The Legend of the Drowned Land

"Oh, how . . . quaint!" said Breenge, when they showed her into the big hall at the foot of Blackspike Tower where the goblins held their rowdy council meetings and entertained visitors. Its walls were bedecked with skulls and shields and ancient, rusty weapons, the furniture was a ramshackle mishmash of stuff from every corner of Clovenstone, and the flagstones of the floor were cracked and grimy. Bits of old meals lay mouldering in the gaps between them, and other bits were stuck to the walls. (Goblins are messy eaters, and they hate doing housework. They had met and entertained in the hall at the foot of Redcap Tower before, but it was pretty much full of dirty plates and old fish heads now, so they had switched to this one rather than tidy it.)

But Henwyn and Skarper were determined that

Clovenstone should show proper hospitality to these wanderers from afar. They let Rhind's company graze their horses on the sward outside the main gate, and had some of the goblins bring the best chairs and arrange them around a table large enough for all the humans and a lot of the goblins to sit around. Skarper's batch-brother Gutgust and a few of the cleaner goblins went bustling off to the kitchens to see about some food.

"Now," said Henwyn, looking at Prince Rhind. He did not think he liked the young Sheep Lord any more than Skarper did, but he knew that first impressions could sometimes be wrong – he had not liked Skarper when he first met him, but they had soon become the best of friends. "Why are you here?" he asked. "What do you seek? And how was Princess Ned supposed to help you?"

"Very well." Rhind looked about him at the ugly faces of the goblins, and then behind him at his sister and Ninnis. He lowered his voice and said dramatically, "We seek the Elvenhorn."

"The what?" said Henwyn.

"What's that?" asked Skarper.

All the goblins looked at each other and shrugged. What was an Elvenhorn when it was at home?

Prawl broke in. "The Elvenhorn," he said, "is one of the treasures of Clovenstone. It was stolen by the Lych

Lord himself from Elvensea, the ancient kingdom of the elves, which lies drowned now beneath the waters of the Western Ocean."

"And how do you know it wasn't squashed when the Keep collapsed?" asked Skarper.

"I doubt the Elvenhorn can be destroyed," said Prawl. "I am sure it must be here. And I knew that when Princess Ned heard of our need for it, she would be keen to help us find it."

"But there's no such thing as elves!" Skarper pointed out. "Everyone knows they're just made up."

"There are some who say the same about goblins," said Breenge.

"But elves?" said Henwyn. "I mean . . . really?"

Prince Rhind stood up. The sunbeams shafting through the chamber windows lit his golden hair and shone in his blue eyes as he spoke. "You are right, goblin. There are no elves. There have been no elves for a thousand years. Once they walked upon the hills of the Westlands, and wandered singing in the woods. All we know of them is a few fragments of old tales. They were beauteous, immortal, and very wise. When men arrived, the elves departed, and lived upon their island of Elvensea, out in the Western Ocean. But the Lych Lord – the same Lych Lord who raised this foul old castle of yours – hated and feared the elves. He knew that he could not grow strong in any world that held such wisdom and such beauty. So he tricked and defeated them, slew them all, and hid their land of Elvensea beneath the waves. Only the Elvenhorn can raise it again."

"Clovenstone isn't a foul old castle," said Zeewa in the silence which followed this speech. "It's a bit smelly, maybe, but. . ."

"Elvenhorn, Elvenhorn," Fentongoose was muttering. "No, I can't place it." He had carefully catalogued all the magical treasures which had been salvaged from the rubble after the Keep fell. "I don't remember any Elvenhorns," he said.

"Perhaps it's one of the items which our friend Carnglaze has carted back to Coriander to sell in his antiques shop?" asked Prong.

"Statues for rich softlings' gardens is more in Carnglaze's line," said Skarper. "He doesn't really do enchanted musical instruments. I s'pose it is a musical instrument, this Elvenhorn thing?"

"I have a picture," said Prawl, rummaging in his bag. "I found it in one of the ancient scrolls in the library at Dyn Gwlan. King Raun has an excellent library, but it is not much used. Apart from a few works on sheep breeding, I don't believe anyone has read any of the books and scrolls for a hundred years."

"Reading is boring," said Breenge. "Who but

27

a halfwit would want to sit in a dingy old library, straining their eyes to read words some other halfwit scribbled down? Give me a good horse under me, and the sun on my face, and the wind in my hair, and a bow in my hand!"

"Oh yes!" agreed Prawl. "That is much more healthy! The outdoor life, fresh air and exercise and so forth. I completely agree!"

"You do?" Fentongoose looked startled. "When we lived in Coriander it was all Carnglaze and I could do to get you out of the reading room. You always had your nose in a book! You said you couldn't *stand* fresh air or exercise! You— Ow!" (It was Prawl who had kicked him this time, quite painfully, under the table.)

"Nevertheless," said Prawl, pulling a scroll from his bag and unrolling it to reveal a lot of writing in some ancient language. "I did nose about the library at Dyn Gwlan a bit, on rainy days, and it was there that I found this. It is a description of the Elvenhorn, written by a sage of old, and it has a picture. Look."

Everyone looked. A lot of the goblins didn't really understand the idea of pictures, but they looked anyway, not wanting to appear stupid in front of their visitors. There on the scroll was a drawing of the Elvenhorn, just as Prawl had promised. But it wasn't the beautiful object that Henwyn and Skarper had been expecting. Henwyn had been imagining a golden trumpet. Skarper had been picturing an ivory horn, perhaps off a unicorn, bound round with bands of slowsilver. Instead, the picture showed something that looked like the houses which caddis fly larvae build for themselves in the mud at the bottom of ponds. A roughly shaped cone of stones and grit, studded with barnacles and bits of rusty metal.

"Oh," said Henwyn.

"That's nice," said Skarper, sounding as unconvinced as Breenge had when she called the dining hall quaint.

Prince Rhind said loudly, "According to legend, the first elves used this magical horn to raise Elvensea from the depths, and then cast it into the depths of the sea to stop anyone using it against them. But the Lych Lord bribed the people of the sea to swim down and find it for him, and once he had defeated the elves he hid it away in Clovenstone. I mean to take it and ride north. A fast ship waits for me at Floonhaven on the Nibbled Coast. I shall sail in it beyond the Autumn Isles to where drowned Elvensea lies. There I shall sound the horn. Elvensea will rise again, and we shall learn the lost secrets of the elves."

Everyone was still staring at the picture. Fentongoose was shaking his head sadly, because he knew that he would have to disappoint Prawl and his friends: he was quite certain that he had never come across anything like that among Clovenstone's treasures. But before he could speak, a goblin named Grumpling butted in.

"'Ere," he said, pointing at the picture with a grubby claw. "That's my scratchbackler!"

"Your what?' asked Prince Rhind.

"My scratchbackler!" Grumpling was a large and lumpy goblin, and quite startlingly stupid. His ugly face twisted into a confused but angry frown as he glared at the scroll in Prawl's hands. "I gets an itchy back," he explained, "so I scratches it wiv that there scratchbackler."

"He means a 'back scratcher'," explained a smaller goblin sitting next to him, and then added, "Urf!" as Grumpling sat on him.

"I know what I means," growled Grumpling, menacingly. "I means my scratchbackler. It's mine. I found it in the ruins so it's mine. How did you gets hold of it, softling? Give it here!"

He made a snatch at the scroll. Prawl flinched backwards and fell off his chair. Skarper and some other goblins grabbed Grumpling by his belt before he could leap across the table. Fentongoose said, "Now, now, Grumpling, do you remember that conversation we had about the difference between pictures of things and the actual things themselves?"

"Give me back my scratchbackler!" roared Grumpling.

"I knew he hadn't really understood," whispered Fentongoose.

Grumpling was one of Clovenstone's Problem Goblins. There had been loads like him when Skarper was a hatchling. Big, brutish bullies, who got their own way by beating up the others. Most of them had perished in the furious fights that raged after the goblins finally found their way into the Keep, or been squished shortly afterwards, when it collapsed. For a while, the smaller and quieter goblins had been left in peace, and they had had Princess Ned to help them work out new ways of getting along together. Now Ned was gone, and Grumpling, who had been barely more than a hatchling himself when the Keep fell, had grown almost as big and strong as old King Knobbler.

He was a Chilli Hat, part of the tribe who lived in Redcap Tower. The differences between the goblins of the different towers had not mattered much in Ned's time, but Grumpling seemed to want the old days back. The gang of bullies he had gathered round him wore their red caps with pride, and were filling their tower with trinkets pinched from other goblins, who were too scared of Grumpling to complain. Fentongoose and Henwyn were very worried about Grumpling and completely unsure of what to do about him.

"Grumpling!" said Skarper, as the angry Chilli Hat made another lunge for the parchment. "That's not your scratchbackler! It's just a drawing of it! Like the drawings Zeewa did to show us what the animals of her homeland look like? Remember?"

"Animals!" said Grumpling, and a glimmer of understanding flickered in his stupid eyes. Zeewa was good at drawing, and during the winter she had decorated the walls of Fentongoose's study with lions and leopards while telling the goblins tales of the Tall Grass Country. Grumpling had often tried to spear and eat those charcoal creatures. Eventually even he had had to accept that, although they *looked* like animals, they weren't *real* animals.

"Go back to your own tower, Grumpling," said Skarper. "You'll find your back scratcher lying wherever you left it."

"And perhaps you'll consider giving it to Prince Rhind?" suggested Henwyn. "That would be a friendly thing to do, wouldn't it?"

Grumpling looked at him and curled his lip, baring a couple of off-white fangs.

"You know?" urged Henwyn. "For this quest of his?"

"Not flibbin' likely!" growled Grumpling. "It's my scratchbackler, softling, and it stays mine, understand?"

And with that he turned and went stomping from the hall, with a bunch of his red-hatted mates close behind him.

"Sorry," said Henwyn.

"Grumpling is more of your traditional sort of goblin," said Skarper.

Prince Rhind seemed confused. "And are you just going to leave it at that? Aren't you going to make him hand over the Elvenhorn? The most important magical artefact in all the Westlands, the key that may unlock the secrets of the elves and begin a new golden age – and you're going to let that scaly freak go on scratching his back with it?"

"Well, it is his," said Henwyn helplessly.

"But you are his king! Or is Fentongoose his king? Who is king here? I'm confused."

"Nobody is king," said Skarper. "Not any more. We sort of look after ourselves."

"How absurd!" snorted Breenge.

"How ridiculous!" snorted Rhind. "I insist that you fetch the Elvenhorn here and hand it into my safekeeping!"

33

"Sorry," said Skarper.

"But without it, my glorious quest cannot succeed!"

"Sorry!" said Fentongoose. "Sorry!" chorused the goblins.

Rhind had already turned red in the face. Now he turned very pale instead. His voice, when he spoke, was tight and thin.

"Then we shall go to this Redcap Tower," he said, "and take the Elvenhorn by force!"

The goblins chortled, and a few threw their hats and helmets high into the air with glee. "Good luck with that!" they shouted. The one whom Grumpling had sat on earlier said, "Grumpling loves that scratchbackler of his. He sleeps with it tucked under his pillow. You softlings won't get it away from him without a fight, and if you fight, he'll win."

"And if he doesn't," said Libnog, "we'll have to fight you too. Because Grumpling may be horrible and stupid but he's a goblin, and so is we. So we'd have to avengle him. An there's loads of us an only, er, one, two, three . . . not very many of you."

The Sheep Lords stood silent, scowling, while goblin laughter racketed all around them. Prawl looked embarrassed. Breenge's hand strayed to her bow.

When the merriment finally subsided, Prince Rhind

said grimly, "So, it seems that my quest shall end here. I shall tell the world that we had a chance to raise drowned Elvensea, but that it was denied us by the goblins of Clovenstone."

"Tell it to the sheep!" shouted a goblin.

"They're the only ones who'll listen to you lot!"

"Moo! Moo!"

"That's cows, you idiot. . ."

"Oh. Baa! Baa!"

Rhind looked at his companions, and they all stood up and made their way through the throng of jeering goblins to the door. Henwyn hurried ahead of them to open it. "I shall lead you back to your horses," he said, still trying to be polite.

Henwyn was the only one who had been troubled by Prince Rhind's threat. He had travelled outside Clovenstone, and he knew that goblins had an evil reputation down in the softlands. Their defeat of the dwarves had done a lot to change that, so he did not want people to start thinking ill of them again. These were strange times, with all sorts of old powers and magics stirring, and they could never know when Clovenstone might need the help of its neighbours. So it worried him that they had managed to offend Prince Rhind, and he felt the least that he could do was to show him out, like a proper host.

35

Skarper, sensing what his friend was thinking, went after him. When they had gone, and the door of the hall was swinging shut behind the Woolmark folk, Doctor Prong said to Fentongoose, "Perhaps it is for the best. I'm not at all sure it would be a good idea to raise the lost island of the elves."

"Why not?" asked Fentongoose.

"I can't say for sure," replied Dr Prong. "We know so little about it. But it seems to me that some things are better left lost."

Hostage of the Sheep Lords

Skarper and Henwyn hurried with their visitors out of the doorway at the base of the Blackspike and down the steep street that led to the gate through the Inner Wall. Prawl kept trying to make conversation, but Rhind and his sister were silent and angry-looking. Only Mistress Ninnis still seemed cheerful, smiling at Skarper when he glanced at her, but she was just a cook so her opinion scarcely seemed to matter.

Skarper had a feeling that this was not over yet. Perhaps, if they couldn't get the Elvenhorn just by asking, they would come back with an army. Prince Rhind could probably command a host of men; warriors of the Woolmark, mounted on vicious war-sheep. They might have all sorts of weapons and siege engines down there in Tyr Davas. They

37

would probably bring battering
rams which were actual rams. . .

He felt sorry that Prince Rhind
and his companions had ever come to Clovenstone.

Then they rounded a corner, and he saw a sight
which cheered him up no end. His batch-brother
Gutgust and a bunch of smaller goblins were just
emerging from the cookhouse behind the cheesery, and
they were carrying an enormous dish, as big as a good-
sized rowing boat. It held a cheese cobbler, Gutgust's
speciality, and the delicious scent seemed to perfume
the very air.

"Are you quite sure you won't stay for a bite to eat
before you leave?" asked Henwyn, still hoping that
the goblins and the Sheep Lords might part as friends.
"Perhaps if we talk things over some more. . ."

By way of answer, Prince Rhind simply picked
Henwyn up by the scruff of his neck and hurled him
at the oncoming goblins. He crashed headlong into the
cobbler dish, and the goblins who had been carrying
it fell like skittles. Skarper had a glimpse of Henwyn
sledging down the street on the vast dish, covered
in cheese. Then Breenge grabbed him. He squeaked
in surprise, and kicked her hard in a soft spot that her
fancy felt armour didn't quite cover. "Ow!" shouted
Breenge, and then, "Catch him, Prawl!", but Prawl

just dithered, not wanting to take sides, and Skarper scrambled out of reach, up some stone stairs and on to a narrow parapet that overhung the street.

Gutgust and the other goblin cooks were running for safety, too, alarmed by the sword which Rhind had drawn, and by the bow which appeared in his sister's hand – goblins hated arrows.

"No matter, Breenge!" called Rhind. "We have the other one!"

Henwyn had come to a sudden stop when the cobbler dish hit a wall and overturned. As he scrambled out of the wreckage, dazed and cheesy, Rhind had snatched hold of him again and now held him upright by his hair.

"Ha!" shouted Prince Rhind, looking up at Skarper. "We have your friend, goblin! This human traitor deserves to die for throwing in his lot with the likes of you!" And he held his sword-point close to Henwyn's throat.

"Eep!" said Henwyn.

"Don't!" shouted Skarper.

"Oh, don't fear for him," said Prince Rhind. "I will not harm him. Not if you bring me the Elvenhorn. We shall camp tonight outside the southern entrance to this fell place. Bring the Elvenhorn there at dawn, and we shall release your friend."

"You're mad!" said Skarper. "There's bloomin' loads of us! We'll rescue Henwyn easy!"

"Attack us and your friend dies," said Prince Rhind. "Bring us the Elvenhorn, and he goes free. That is the only way that you will see him alive again."

And he dragged Henwyn away down the street and out through the gate to where their horses grazed, Ninnis and Prawl trailing after him, Breenge going last, walking backwards with an arrow nocked to her bowstring and her eyes on the goblins.

As he vanished through the gateway Henwyn glanced back at Skarper with a look that seemed to say, "I'm sorry!" and also, "Help!" and, "I wish I wasn't covered in cheese!"

Gutgust and a few of the other goblin chefs started to go after them, but Skarper called them back. He knew that Prince Rhind had meant what he said, and that it would take him only an instant to kill Henwyn. The goblins might kill him and his sister afterwards, but what good would that do if Henwyn were dead?

"No," he said. "We need a plan of some sort."

"Oh, we're really good at them!" said one of the chefs eagerly. "Princess Ned taught us everything she knew. Quick, we'll need some eggs, flour and butter..."

"Not a *flan*," said Skarper wearily. "A *plan*."

"Oh."

"Are you any good at plans?" he asked them hopefully.

"Not really," admitted the chefs.

"Anchovies!" said Gutgust. But "anchovies" was the only thing that Gutgust ever said (no one knew why).

Skarper wasn't very good at plans either. He had come up with a few which he'd been quite proud of in the past, but he couldn't think of any way to get Henwyn back from the Woolmarkers with all his different bits still attached and all his blood still inside him. And while he stood pondering, there came a faint rumble of hoofbeats from outside as the Woolmarkers cantered away with their captive. They would collect their wagon, which they had left on the far bank of the Oeth, and then go south through Southerly Gate, he thought. Perhaps the guards there would try to stop them – but why should they? They would not know that Henwyn was not riding with them of his own free will.

He glanced up at the sky, wondering if the cloud maidens could be persuaded to take a message to Southerly Gate. But it seemed the cloud maidens had grown bored of waiting outside while the mortals talked, and gone in search of other princes to pester. The sky was empty. The sun, sinking westwards now, piled purple shadows in the hollows of the hills.

Skarper and the chefs trudged back towards the Blackspike to tell the others what had happened.

A Robbery is Planned

Everyone was horrified when they heard what Prince Rhind and his people had done.

"I knew we shouldn't trust those woollen-headed Sheep Lords!" said Doctor Prong.

"Poor Henwyn!" said Fentongoose.

"We must rescue him!" vowed Zeewa.

"It's a tragedy!" wailed Libnog. "All that lovely cheese cobbler! Ruined!"

But it turned out that there was quite a lot of cobbler left, smeared on the cobblestones of the street and in the abandoned dish, and the goblins didn't mind that it was a bit trampled. They carried it up to the hall and ate it while they discussed their plans for getting Henwyn back.

"We could use the Bratapult to shoot ourselves into the middle of their camp!"

"We could disguise ourselves as washerwomen!"

"We could train a badger to creep in and nibble through Henwyn's bonds!"

"Anchovies!"

But though they talked till the sky beyond the hall's high windows blushed red with evening, there still seemed to Skarper to be only one solution.

"Why not just give them the Elvenhorn?' he asked. "We've got no use for it ourselves. We didn't even know we had it till Rhind and his friends showed up. Let them have it. Then they can go off to raise Elvensea and they won't never have to bother us again."

"Grumpling won't like that," said Spinch, who was the goblin Grumpling had sat on earlier.

"Grumpling will just have to scratch his itchy back with a different priceless mystical relic," said Fentongoose.

"But he won't let you take it!" said Spinch. "He's like that. When my batch-brother Flegg borrowed his favourite toothpick without asking, Grumpling chucked him down the pooin hole. He'll never let you have his scratchbackler."

"What if we just borrowed it?' asked Libnog. "We could pretends to give it to the softlings an then when they let Henwyn go we can slaughter them all an take the scratchbackler an give it back to Grumpling. They

44

won't need it any more if they're dead, so we'll be doin' them a favour, in a way."

"That's not very sporting," Fentongoose objected.

"We's GOBLINS!" said Libnog. "HELLO?"

Spinch was shaking his head so hard that his crumpled red cap slipped down over his eyes. "Wouldn't work anyway," he said. "Grumpling won't let you have his scratchbackler even for a borrow."

"Not even to save Henwyn?" asked Zeewa.

"Specially not to save Henwyn," said Spinch. "Grumpling hates Henwyn. Grumpling says he wishes there weren't no softlings in Clovenstone at all. He says fings was better in the old days when we had a proper goblin king. I reckon he finks he'd make a good goblin king himself."

The other goblins shuffled nervously. None of them fancied having Grumpling as their king.

Skarper stood up. "I've had enough of this!" he said. "That Elvenhorn doesn't belong to Grumpling anyway. It belongs to all of us. And if we need it to save Henwyn then we ought to just take it."

"Take it?" The goblins looked worried. The older ones were remembering the furious and deadly battles which used to break out when goblins from one tower raided another, trying to steal their neighbours' treasures. Some of them still bore the scars: missing eyes and teeth and legs and paws and tails. A Growler called Spikey Peet still had a short spear sticking right through his head from some long ago dust-up with the Grimspike Boys. (Luckily it had missed his brain.)

"But Grumpling is bigger and stronger and tougher than any of us," said Libnog.

"Then we'll have to use the one thing we've got that Grumpling hasn't!" Skarper shouted.

The goblins looked blank. They weren't good at this sort of clever talk. What could Skarper mean?

"I've got a bunion," somebody suggested. "I don't think Grumpling's got one of them."

"I'm not talking about BUNIONS!" shouted Skarper. "I'm talking about BRAINS!"

"Oh, those," said the goblins, disappointed. (They thought that brains were overrated.)

"You mean we should outwit the brute?" asked Fentongoose. "An excellent idea!"

"We shall devise a strategy," promised Dr Prong.

Skarper shook his head. The goblins didn't have enough brains, but Prong and Fentongoose between them had far too many. If he were to let them start inventing strategies they would make everything far too complicated, and still be talking and drawing little maps when the sun rose.

"Leave this to me," he told them. "Henwyn was

my friend before he was any of yours, so I should be the one who steals the Elvenhorn and gets him back. I've got an idea about how to do it, too. But I'll need Zeewa's help."

Ill-Met
by Poolight

"This isn't going to be very nice," said Skarper, half an hour later.

He and Zeewa had slipped out of the Blackspike through one of the secret snickets which led beneath the Inner Wall. Now they were standing at the foot of Redcap Tower, which reared up into the night above them, looking tall enough and pointy enough to poke the moon's eye out, if the moon wasn't careful.

"Why do we have to go in this way?' asked Zeewa, wrinkling her nose as Skarper carefully slid a flat stone slab aside to reveal a dark hole, an entrance into one of the tunnels which radiated outwards from Redcap's basements. A horrid smell emerged from the hole, along with a faint, eerie glow.

"Grumpling will be expecting us to try and nick his back scratcher," said Skarper. "He'll have set sentries on all the stairways. They'll probably be asleep, because they're goblin sentries, but we still can't risk it. We'd probably have to clamber over them, and even goblins usually wake up when you clamber over them. We don't want to wake up nobody, not if we can help it."

"And if we do. . ." said Zeewa. She took a firmer grip on the haft of her broad-bladed stabbing spear, patted the oxhide pouch which hung from her belt, and said, "Lead on, Skarper."

Skarper swung himself over the edge of the hole and lowered himself in. He dangled there for a moment by his fingertips, blinking at the horrible smell. Then he let go and dropped. There was a faint, wet SPLUDGE. Then another, as Zeewa dropped down behind him.

The basement of Redcap Tower was full of poo. All the basements of all the goblin towers were at least partly full of poo, because the goblins of long ago had sawed holes in the floors of the rooms above and used them as toilets. The Chilli Hats of Redcap Tower – who got their name from their habit of eating the fiery red chillis which they grew in the Lych Lord's old glasshouses – did more poos than most, and all the poos of all the goblins that had ever lived in the Redcap were heaped up in its basement, or dribbling away down that tunnel into which Skarper and Zeewa had just jumped.

"Eww!" said Zeewa.

"Not as bad as I was expecting," said Skarper.

"It's up to my knees!"

"Think yourself lucky then. I'm a lot shorter than you, remember."

They started to wade along the tunnel. It was night in the world above, but down here they could see their way quite clearly because the mounds and slicks of poo through which they floundered were glowing with a soft light. Either it was a property of all those fierce red chillis in the Chilli Hats' diet, or their poo had been mixed with the luminous droppings of the blind white bats which nested in holes in the tunnel roof and flapped silently out sometimes to startle the two intruders, battering their flimsy wings in Skarper's face, tangling in Zeewa's hair.

At last they emerged from the tunnel into the basement itself. There the poo was even deeper.

"It's up to my waist now!" whispered Zeewa.

"I know! It's up to my chin!"

"Now it's up to my chest!"

"Not far to go now. Look, there are the pooin holes, right above us. . ."

"Eugh! Now it's up to my shoulders!"

"Glubbubble glug blug blub. . ." said Skarper.

Zeewa unwrapped the rope which she had wound

around her waist. There was a hook on the end of it, and she began to swing this around her head. When it was moving fast, whooshing through the stinky air, she launched it upwards towards those dark openings that showed in the ceiling above her like the holes in a very old and mouldy cheese.

There was a faint clunk as the hook hit the edge of the holes, but it did not find a purchase there. It fell back into the morass below.

Zeewa, trying not to breathe, reeled it in and tried again. Again the hook whooshed round and round; again there came that clunk from above; again the moment of hope – would it catch this time? Would it hold? – and then the disappointment as it fell. But this time, instead of a simple splat as it dropped into the poo, there came a distinct bonk, and a muffled "Ow!"

Skarper had managed to get his head above the surface. "What was that?" he hissed. Glowing poo he felt he could cope with, but *talking* poo? That was just weird.

"Who's there?' asked Zeewa, raising her spear.

Over on the far side of the chamber two eyes glinted in the faint glow of the poo. "It's me," said a whiny sort of voice. "Flegg."

"You're the one Grumpling chucked down the pooin holes for nicking his toothpick!" said Skarper.

"I was only borrowin it," said Flegg bitterly.

"How long have you been here?' asked Zeewa.

"Ages!" said Flegg. "I can't get out! The only way out is down that tunnel, and it only leads to worse places: great caves of poo, deep underground. There are *things* down there. . ." He shuddered, and smelly ripples spread through the swamp of poo. "Please, Skarper – you've got to get me out of here!"

"We're not going out," said Skarper, and pointed at the ceiling. "We're going up."

Zeewa swung her grappling hook for a third time. This time it hooked on something above, and held firm. She tested the rope, then hauled herself up it, through the pooin hole, and reached back for Skarper.

"Come with us!" Skarper told poor Flegg. "You can help. Then we can all leave together."

"Help with what?" asked Flegg suspiciously.

"We're going to borrow something from Grumpling ourselves. I expect you'd like to get your own back on him?"

"But Grumpling is the king of this tower," said Flegg doubtfully.

"We don't have kings in these towers no more," said Skarper. "We're finished with all that nonsense. It's high time somebody taught Grumpling a lesson, and we're the ones to do it."

While he spoke he was scrambling hand over hand up the rope, till Zeewa caught him and dragged him through the pooin hole.

Flegg watched him go. Then he called nervously, "All right! I'm coming! Wait for me!"

The room above the poo lake was almost as dingy and stinking as the lake itself. Old books, looted from Clovenstone's ancient libraries, lay about in heaps, where pooing goblins could grab them to use as bumwipe if they were feeling particularly civilized. Zeewa, Skarper and Flegg picked their way between the rotting volumes, careful not to trip over any and go plunging back down another of the pooin holes which were dotted at random all over the floor.

At last they found their way to a door and out into a passage. Up a long spiral of worn stone steps they went. Now and then they passed a sleeping goblin. From open doorways drifted sounds of snoring.

"Where is Grumpling's bedchamber?' Skarper asked Flegg. He was glad they had found this small poo-caked goblin: he would save them a lot of searching.

"Keep goin' up," said Flegg.

Up and up. Once they passed a room where firelight glowed and dice rattled, but the heavy door was half closed, and they padded past it and on up the stairs, unheeded by the goblin gamblers within.

At last they reached Grumpling's chamber, right at the top of the tower. It was a chilly place, with big gaps in the stonework through which the moonlight shone and the night breeze blew. Skarper was glad of that; the moonlight let him see where he was going, while with a bit of luck the breeze might blow away some of the smell of poo. Even so, there were a few sleepy sniffs from Grumpling's henchmen, who lay sprawled about on the floor. "Who farted?' asked one of them, as Skarper tiptoed over him.

Zeewa followed Skarper into the big room, but Flegg seemed to think he had done his part just by leading them there. He stayed cowering in the doorway, watching with wide, watery eyes as they crept towards the sleeping Grumpling.

No nest on the floor for the King of the Chilli Hats! Grumpling had found himself a proper bed. It was a huge four-poster with moth-eaten curtains and a carven headboard, which he had made his Chilli Hats drag up all the twisting, turning stairs of their tower. He lay snoring in it, half covered by a heap of furs and throws. Under his lumpy pillow, Skarper could just see the tip of the Elvenhorn poking out into a handy moonbeam.

He turned to Zeewa. As silently as she could, the girl set down her spear, reached into the bag she carried and drew out a sheet of parchment and a stick of charcoal.

Skarper crept closer to the bed. Floorboards squeaked and squoinked beneath him, but Grumpling never stirred. Carefully, carefully, Skarper lifted the edge of the pillow. Carefully, carefully he slid the Elvenhorn out. It was bigger than he had expected, and even more encrusted with shells and stones and barnacles. Some of the stones shone in the moonlight like precious gems, which they probably were.

Meanwhile, Zeewa was drawing the thing in as much detail as she could manage, standing there in the half-dark. As soon as she was finished, she passed her picture to Skarper, who handed her the Elevenhorn in exchange. Carefully, carefully, he slid the drawing under Grumpling's pillow.

Grumpling muttered something in his sleep and half-opened one dull yellow eye, but Skarper whispered, "There, there," and he settled into his dreams again.

With luck, thought Skarper, he would find Zeewa's drawing under his pillow when he woke and think it was the actual Elvenhorn. Hopefully he wouldn't work out that he'd been robbed for hours and hours.

Chuckling silently at his own cleverness and Grumpling's stupidity, he started tiptoeing after Zeewa back towards the door.

But he had reckoned without Flegg. The little Chilli Hat had been watching everything from the shadows beyond the door, and suddenly he shouted, "Grumpling! They're robbing you!"

"Ssshhhh!" hissed Skarper. "You'll wake him!"

"I wants to wake him!" yelled Flegg, at the top of his squeaky voice. "Wake up, Grumpling! Traitors! Thieves! Intrudlers!"

All the goblins in the chamber were waking up, groping for the weapons they'd laid down beside them when they went to sleep. Moonlight jinked on notched old sword blades and the spikes of maces. "Wossup?" the goblins grumbled, and, "'Oo's 'air?"

The huge bed groaned as Grumpling rolled over on it and sat up blinking. "Eh?" he said. His eyes focused on Flegg. "It's him, boys! It's that toofpick-nabber. Somebody grab 'im! Chuck him out the window!"

"No, Grumpling!" wailed Flegg, as a dozen dirty paws reached for him. "I am loyal! Look how loyal I am! I've climbed all the way up here from the pooin holes just to tell you about Skarper and this softling. Them's the traitors! Them's the nabbers! They's stolen your scratchbackler!"

Grumpling grunted. He lifted his pillow, and his eyes narrowed as he peered beneath it.

"My scratchbackler's still right here where I left it," he said.

"It's a trick!" wailed Flegg, as Grumpling's boys seized him and started to drag him towards the nearest window. "It's only a picture! Skarper nabbed your scratchler and that softling done a picture of it!"

"Picture?" Grumpling was getting annoyed at this business of the difference between things and pictures of things. It was confusing softling rubbish, that was what it was. Why couldn't things just be things? He picked up Zeewa's drawing. He sniffed it. He turned it this way, then that. He tried to scratch his back with it. "It *looks* like my scratchbackler," he said suspiciously. "But it *feels* different. Like it's gone all *papery*."

He turned the drawing over. The blank back of the parchment glowed in the moonlight.

"Aaaargh!" screamed Grumpling. "It's distrappeared!"

"It's in the softling's pouch, Grumpling! Seize the softling! Search her pouch! Then chuck her and Skarper out the window!"

But Skarper and Zeewa were not hanging around to be seized or chucked out of windows. Quite early on, while Grumpling was still peering at the drawing, Skarper had whispered to Zeewa, "Run!", and now they were hurtling down the stairs, Skarper leading the way, Zeewa close behind him like a long shadow.

Goblins spilled out of the doors of their lairs, woken by the voices from above. "What's going on?' they asked.

"Bad dream!" said Skarper, scampering past.

"Grumpling had a nightmare!" explained Zeewa, following him down.

Grumpling's fierce bellow of rage came rolling down the stairs behind them, shaking plaster from the old walls, like the tolling of some huge, cracked bell. "I bin ROBBLED! Stop them! STOP THEM ROBBLERS, I SAYS!"

Skarper and Zeewa had had a good start, and the goblins further down the tower were slower to wake and last to hear the angry roarings from above. But they could all tell that something was amiss. A few grabbed at Skarper and Zeewa as they passed. The flight was beginning to turn into a fight – not deadly yet, but furious, the goblins using fists and fangs, teeth and tails, while Skarper elbowed goblins in the belly and Zeewa laid about her with her spear-shaft. The constant scuffles delayed them, and all the time, filling the stairway behind them, they could hear Grumpling's angry howls.

"I BIN ROBBLED!"

Even so, they had almost reached the exit by the time they were finally caught. There was a doorway which led out on to the Inner Wall, and all the guards there had left their posts to come and see what the racket was about. The door stood unguarded, but four thick bolts sealed it, and as Skarper was opening the third of them he heard Zeewa shriek, then felt the rough paw of one of Grumpling's henchgoblins close upon his ear. Zeewa slammed her spear-shaft down on the goblin who had caught her, but his skull was thick, and the shaft snapped. Skarper's captor used his ear as a handle with which to lift him, kicking and struggling, into the air.

Goblins crowded round them. One had a torch. The flames cast their yellow light over a sea of ugly, inquisitive faces.

The sea parted as Grumpling came stomping through to stand before his captives, scowling. He pointed a trembling claw at Zeewa. "I knew it was asking fer trouble, lettin softlings into Clovenstone," he said. "What's in her bag?"

"I'll show you if you like," said Zeewa, and she twisted free of Grumpling's friends before they could snatch it from her. While they watched, she plucked another charcoal stick and a second sheet of parchment from the bag and began to draw.

"What are you drawing?" asked Skarper. "Not the Elvenhorn? He won't fall for that a second time. Well, not for long."

But although the picture that was taking shape on Zeewa's parchment was long and pointy, it was not the Elvenhorn. With a few swift, simple strokes she drew a sword. She held the drawing up in Grumpling's face.

"She's got a sword!" shouted Grumpling, and he and all his goblins scrambled backwards, out of reach of the sharply pointed blade. "Where'd she get that from?"

"I am challenging you to a duel, Grumpling," said Zeewa.

Grumpling, like most bullies, was a coward. He didn't like the idea of fighting the girl one bit, but he didn't want his Chilli Hats to see that he was afraid of her, so he stretched a big goblin grin across his face and said, "All right, softling." One of his mates passed him a huge old broadsword, gleaming sharp. He tested its edge with his thumb. "Ouch! I mean, Ha! I'm gonna chop you up easy."

"Not if I chop you up first," said Zeewa. She was drawing again, her charcoal swooshing over the parchment. When she held up the new picture the grin dropped off Grumpling's face. For there in the girl's outstretched hand was his own head! He recognized it from that time old Fentongoose had made him look at a thing called a mirror and explained what his reflection was and why he didn't need to keep hitting it. There were his own handsome cauliflower ears, his noble cauliflower nose, his unripe-gooseberry eyes, and his mouth, open like a knife drawer, all sharp fangs and astonishment.

She was holding his head! How could she be holding his head? She must have cut it off without his even noticing! And how pale it was!

Grumpling went weak at the knees. "I don't . . . I don't feel too good, boys," he croaked.

"Grumpling's head!" the other goblins were muttering. "She's beheaded Grumpling!" And their panic and amazement was so great that even the cleverer ones among them, who didn't usually have any trouble telling the difference between things and their pictures, were caught up in a sort of panic, and believed that they, too, could see their leader's head dangling from Zeewa's hand. A few were asking how come Grumpling still had a head attached to his shoulders. "That's just the ghost of his head," others explained, and soon all their voices were drowned out in the rising panic as Grumpling crumpled to his knees and then collapsed backwards into the arms of his henchgoblins.

For a moment Skarper was afraid that their fright and confusion would turn into anger, and that they would rush Zeewa and avenge their king by lopping her into the tiniest pieces they could manage. But they were all far too scared of this strange Muskish girl who had produced a sword from nowhere – a powerful magic sword, no doubt, so sharp that she had been able to slice Grumpling's head off without them even seeing her move!

The goblin who had been holding Skarper dropped him and ran. Skarper wasted no time. He scrambled back to the door, opened that last bolt, and pushed his way out into the lovely, cool, moonlit, Grumpingless night.

"Come on!" he shouted back to Zeewa. But Zeewa was making one last drawing.

The previous year, when the dwarves had attacked Clovenstone, they had brought all manner of strange and cunning weapons with them. Some that had particularly alarmed the goblins were the little black metal balls they threw, filled with some mysterious powder, and which exploded with a bang and a flash upon landing. Fentongoose claimed that these were called "bombs", but the goblins all called them "booms", after the noise they made. It was one of these that Zeewa sketched, complete with its fizzing fuse.

When she was finished, she set it down on the floor of the passageway, just inside the door.

The eyes of the Chilli Hats widened as they recognized it. "It's a dwarf-boom!" they wailed. "She got a dwarf-boom! Run! RUN FER YER LIVES!"

And run they did, dragging their possibly headless king behind them, to seek shelter from the explosion around a bend of the passage.

Zeewa grinned at Skarper. "Now let's go!" she said.

Skarper sniffed the air as they ran out on to the battlements. The moon was sinking. The ruined roofs of Clovenstone stuck up like rocky islands from a sea of mist.

"I can't wait to get back to the Blackspike and wash this stink off me," said Zeewa, as they started down the long stairways of the Inner Wall.

"Wash?" said Skarper with a shudder. "Ew! There's not time, anyway. Not if we're goin' to get this Elvenhorn to Southerley Gate by the time the sun peeks up."

Henwyn's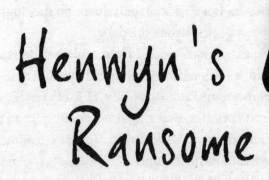
Ransome

Henwyn had had an uncomfortable journey to Southerley Gate, draped over the back of Prince Rhind's horse as the Woolmarkers galloped through the twilight. When they passed into the green shadows of the woods he had thought, *Perhaps the twiglings will come to my rescue.* But the creatures of the trees stayed hidden.

As they descended to the bridge across the Oeth (the riders dismounted, Henwyn's face bashing against the horse's sweaty flank as Rhind led it down that long stair) he had almost hoped that the old troll would be back in its lair under the bridge: a troll attack might give him just the diversion that he needed to stage a Daring Escape. But the troll was still in the uplands with Torridge, Cribba and Ken: they were cooking trout around a campfire and singing cheerful trollish songs, and had no idea of what was happening to Henwyn.

He spent that night bound hand and foot, dumped in the grass on top of a low hill about a mile south of Clovenstone's Outer Wall. The horses of the Sheep Lords were tethered nearby, and he could hear them shifting sometimes in the dark. Breenge slept in a little felt tent, above which the flag of the Woolmark flapped: a white sheep on a green field. Prawl, wrapped in his cloak, slept under the wagon. Rhind paced around the hill's summit, keeping guard.

The little cook, Ninnis, was awake too. She was the only one of the party who seemed to feel sorry for Henwyn. She had brought him a cushion to rest his head on, and a blanket to cover him, and, while Rhind wasn't looking, she had fed him one of the dumplings she had made to go with the stew she had served for supper. It was a bit embarassing for Henwyn, being fed like a pet, but he didn't mind too much, because the dumpling was delicious.

"It is a pity you had to go and start an argument before we'd eaten," she said to Rhind. (She had been his father's cook since he was little, so she was allowed to speak to him like that, even though he was a prince.) "I'm partial to a nice cheese cobbler myself. I'd have liked to taste some of that Clovenstone Blue."

"Cheese made by goblin paws?" scoffed Rhind. "It would be as foul and as squalid as everything else that goblins touch."

"Oh, those goblins seemed friendly enough to me," clucked the cook. "And the prisoner smells lovely, all covered in their cheese."

"Smells like stale socks to me," snorted Rhind.

"Well, you never did appreciate fine cooking, Your Highness."

The cook sat comfortably on the seat of her wagon, but the prince was constantly on the move, one hand resting on his sword hilt, patrolling the edges of the little camp. The hillside sloped down gently towards a river, and the laughter of the distant water sounded very loud in the still and silent night. Beyond the river, the Outer Wall of Clovenstone showed pale as bone whenever the moonlight brushed it.

"If the goblins try anything before dawn, we'll see them coming," said Rhind, when his sister came out of the tent to take her turn at sentry duty sometime in the middle of the night.

But they didn't try anything, and Henwyn started to feel resentful. Were his friends not even going to attempt to rescue him? He was ashamed at having let himself be taken prisoner so easily by these Sheep Lords, and the shame soon turned to anger. It was much easier to blame Skarper and the others for not rescuing him than to blame himself for getting captured in the first place.

But angry or not, he eventually grew sleepy, and sank into restless dreams. He was woken by a sudden shout from Breenge.

"Rhind! Awake, my brother! They come!"

Henwyn sat up and tried to rub the sleep out of his eyes, then remembered that his hands were tied. He blinked a bit instead. The little tent was shaking and bulging as Prince Rhind got his boots and armour on inside. There was a loud thump and a muffled "Ow!" from the direction of the wagon as Prawl woke and sat upright, forgetting that he was underneath it. Eastwards, beyond the spiky outlines of the Bonehill Mountains, the sky was red, and a line of fiery gold showed along the world's rim. Clovenstone still lay in darkness, but not deep enough to hide the two figures who had come out through Southerly Gate and were walking up the slope towards the Sheep Lords' camp.

The tent shuddered some more, and Rhind emerged. He stole around the hilltop, trying to look commanding, but the effect was spoiled by the way that his hair was all mushed up on one side from his night on the ground. He glanced at his sister and said,

"Stay by the prisoner, Breenge. If those goblins try to trick us, kill him."

Breenge nodded, and drew a knife from her belt (an awfully sharp and long knife, it looked to Henwyn).

"I say, er, steady on now, there's no need for unpleasantness," said Prawl, as tousled as Rhind and as blinky as Henwyn.

"Be silent, sorcerer," said Breenge.

"Sorry."

The two newcomers were close enough now for Henwyn to see that they were Skarper and Zeewa, and his heart lifted at the sight of them. As they drew closer, Zeewa took something from her belt. Rhind must have thought it was a sword, because he drew his own and shouted loudly, "You were supposed to come unarmed!" But Henwyn knew that Zeewa didn't approve of swords, which she thought were clumsy, foolish things, and no match for the spears of her own Tall Grass Country.

"She is unarmed, Rhind," he said. But by that time the first long rays of the rising sun were fingering the hill and even Rhind could see that the thing Zeewa held out as she strode towards him was no sword.

"The Elvenhorn!" he said, in a strangled sort of whisper intended for his companions. In a louder voice he commanded Zeewa, "Bring it here!"

"That's exactly what we are doing!" said Skarper grumpily. "We've spent the whole night getting it and bringing it here, too, when we should have been curled up snug in our own nice nests. Hello, Henwyn! Are you all right?"

"Yes," said Henwyn. "A bit stiff, that's all. And covered in cheese."

"Believe me, there are worse things to be covered in," said Zeewa.

"Let him go, Rhind," said Skarper. "Then we'll give you the Elvenhorn and you can be off on your quest, and good riddance to you."

"Careful, my brother," said Breenge. "Does not the old proverb say, 'Trust not the word of a goblin'?"

"Does it? I haven't heard that one."

"Well if it doesn't, it ought to. They're bound to try some trick or other."

"Good point, Breenge," said Prince Rhind. "I say, goblin. How do we know you won't just run off with the Elvenhorn as soon as your friend is free? Give us the Elvenhorn, and we'll give you your friend."

"And how do we know you won't run off with Henwyn as soon as you have the Elvenhorn in your hands?" demanded Zeewa.

"Why would we do that?" asked Rhind, bewildered. "He's no earthly use to us, and he smells like socks."

"Free him then," said Zeewa. "And I shall give you the Elvenhorn. You have my word that there will be no tricks, and I am no goblin, but the daughter of Ushagi, Lord of Ten Thousand Buffalo and King of the Tall Grass Country, west of Leopard Mountain."

"I've never heard of any King Ushagi," said Breenge. "Or the Tall Grass Country either."

But Zeewa had drawn herself up to her full height, the sunrise shone in her eyes, and although she was weary and still a bit pooey, she was so clearly a princess and a daughter of kings that there was no point in arguing. Quickly, Breenge sliced through the ropes that bound Henwyn's wrists and ankles. He stood up, and then immediately fell over again because his legs were all wobbly from having been tied all night. But he managed to stand again, and to stumble downhill to where Skarper stood waiting, and Zeewa came past him carrying the Elvenhorn, which she gave to Prince Rhind.

Rhind held the horn high in the gathering light, as if he were hoping some passing artist might notice him and stop to do a massive painting entitled, *Prince Rhind Finds the Elvenhorn*. (In fact, he was wishing he had thought to ask an artist as well as a cook along on his quest.) The light of the new day caressed the ancient instrument and glimmered in all the semi-precious stones that studded it, and it looked rare and wild and magical.

Then, before anyone could stop him, Rhind put the horn to his lips, and blew.

It made a high, thin sound, like a far-off sheep with indigestion, or the squeaking of a mystical kazoo. But, thin though it was, the sound travelled. It rolled away across Oeth Moor and Clovenstone into the far blue distances, and Skarper had the strange feeling that it would keep on rolling until it reached the very edges of the world.

"No!" shouted Prawl. "Stop! You're meant to blow it when we reach Elvensea, not here!"

Rhind lowered the horn. "I had to try it," he said. "I mean, we want to know that it works, don't we? We want to be sure that they haven't palmed us off with just any old horn. I was just checking that it actually is magical."

Echoes of the horn blast still seemed to hang in the bright air as if they were rebounding from mountains so far off they could not be seen.

"Seems all right to me," said Breenge.

"*One blast shall part the waters*," said Ninnis, in a strange, dreamy voice.

"And so our quest begins in earnest," said Prince Rhind. "Soon all the world shall know our names.

Our tale shall be told in song and story. The beauty and bravery of Breenge and the perspicacity of Prawl shall be legendary, and I shall be one of the heroes of the Westlands and dwell in the Hall of Heroes at Boskennack."

Henwyn snorted. He had met the heroes of the Westlands, and a very disappointing bunch they'd been, but that spring the High King had summoned the old warrior Garvon Hael back to Boskennack to take charge of their training and knock some sense into them. Henwyn didn't think that Garvon Hael would have much time for Prince Rhind. "You will need to lose some weight and gain some sense before you enter the Hall of Heroes, Rhind," he said.

Prince Rhind ignored him. He took from a pouch on his belt a baldric, much like the one on which his sister's war horn hung. It was made from green wool and decorated with the forms of running sheep. He attached the Elvenhorn to it, slung it across his chest, and mounted his horse, which Breenge had already untethered. Breenge followed suit, while Prawl hurriedly took down the tent and stowed it in the back of the wagon.

"North, to Floonhaven!" shouted Rhind. "North, to Elvensea!"

None of them said a word more to Skarper, Henwyn

or Zeewa. "Not so much as a 'thank you'," as Skarper would say later, "or a 'sorry for being such rotten, thieving hooligans'." Only Prawl managed to give them an awkward little wave as the company rode away, Rhind far out in the lead, cantering across the heather towards Clovenstone's Westerly Gate, from where the old road led north and west to the harbours of the Nibbled Coast.

Echoes of the Elvenhorn

The cry of the Elvenhorn had been heard all over Clovenstone. In the mires north of the Inner Wall the clammy boglins of the marshes heard it and looked up, listening. In the woods near Westerly Gate the old giant Fraddon lifted his head, and the twiglings who had been chasing one another through his hair went stiff and still as bunches of mistletoe, waiting for the sound to fade.

All winter Fraddon had been lost in his memories. He had been thinking about his friend, Princess Ned, and how he had brought her to Clovenstone, and how sad and strange it was that she was no longer there. He had barely noticed the thick snows of winter as they fell and drifted and thawed around him. He had not noticed the snowdrops or the crocuses or the bluebells as they pushed their way up between his giant toes.

But he noticed the sound of the Elvenhorn. It came into his memories and dragged him back to the real world for a moment. *Something is going to happen*, he thought. *Something new*. And then, as usual, he thought, *I must tell Ned about it*.

But of course he couldn't, because she had gone beneath the grass. And what was the point of any new thing happening if Ned was not there to see it?

The horn's cry sang among the crags and corries of Meneth Eskern. It echoed around the towers of the Inner Wall and set their old stones trembling. It woke Flegg, who had fallen asleep in Grumpling's chamber up at the top of Redcap Tower. He didn't know what it meant, that faint and far-off tooting noise, but he knew that he was very happy not to be trapped down the pooin holes any more, and very pleased with himself for the clever way he'd found to weasel his way back into Grumpling's good books.

Wondering if Grumpling and the others had managed to get the Elevenhorn back, and whether they had chopped up Skarper and Zeewa, he went scuttling down the stairs. He had not descended very far before he could hear the voices of the other Chilli Hats grumbling and complaining somewhere below him.

Grumpling's lumpish henchgoblins were all clustered together at a bend in the little passageway which led out on to the wall. Flegg squeezed past them, and peered around the corner of the wall. The door on to the wall was open, but no one was going out.

"What's happenin'?" asked Flegg, tugging at the tail of Grumpling's second in command, a large goblin named Widdas.

"Grumpling's had his head chopped off!" said Widdas.

"Ooooh," groaned Grumpling, who was sitting in the middle of the knot of goblins with his back against the wall. A couple of the other Chilli Hats were fanning him with their red caps.

"That Muskish softling did it," said Widdas. "We wants to get after her, but we can't, because look what she left in the doorway!"

Cautiously, Flegg peered around the bend in the passage again. There was something lying on the floor there, just inside the door. A scrap of parchment with some marks on it. . .

"Careful, Flegg!" said Widdas. "It's a dwarf boom! It could go off bang at any moment!"

"How long has it been there?" asked Flegg.

"Hours an' hours! So it must be goin to eskplode really soon! Be quiet! Even our voices might set it off!"

Flegg sighed. Sometimes his fellow goblins were so stupid it depressed him. He strolled along the passage and picked up the parchment.

"No!" and "Aaargh!" and "Get down!" squealed the other Chilli Hats, sticking their fingers in their ears and bracing themselves for the explosion.

Flegg crumpled up the parchment into a tiny ball. He tossed it from paw to paw, while the goblins winced and gasped. Then, to their total astonishment, he batted it high into the air with a flick of his tail and opened his mouth wide. The parchment ball dropped in, and Flegg swallowed it with a loud gulp. For a moment he looked thoughtful. Then he lifted his tail and let out a long, satisfying fart.

"There," he said.

"Wow!" said the few goblins who hadn't run away when he started his juggling act.

Flegg patted his tummy. "Dwarves!" he scoffed. "They haven't made a boom yet that can get the better of a Chilli Hat's belly. Don't you lot know that?"

The Chilli Hats shuffled their feet and looked ashamed.

"Flegg," said Grumpling, "you saved my life! At least, you would have done if my head hadn't already got chopped off."

"Yes," said Flegg, "I was just coming to that, O King. You see, you does still seem to have a head."

Grumpling felt his face suspiciously: his ears, his fangs, his snout. "That's just my imaginingings," he said sadly. "Remember when Beaker got his leg chopped off in that fight with the Sternbrow crowd? He could still feel it for years afterwards."

The Chilli Hats all nodded wisely. "The mind can play strange tricks," said Widdas.

But Flegg said, "Yes, but we couldn't actually *see* Beaker's leg, could we?"

"Course not! It had got chopped off."

"So how come we can see your head?"

The goblins all looked puzzled. One called Gove started to explain that it was an after-image, like you got when you looked at a candle flame for too long and then looked away and you could still the candle flame for a bit, but that was too scientific for the Chilli Hats and they shushed him by kicking him and sitting on his head. Slowly, as if Flegg's words had broken a spell, understanding was starting to dawn.

"You mean, I'm NOT dead?" asked Grumpling.

"You is very much alive, O King of the Chilli Hats," said Flegg.

Grumpling stood up. He tilted his head from side to side a few times, just to check that it really was attached. Then he started walloping the goblins who stood around him. "You idiots!" he roared. "Why din't any of you lot work that out what Flegg just said?"

"But we didn't. . ."

"You said. . ."

"Don't blame us, Grumpling!"

"We're goblins, not doctors!"

"Ow!"

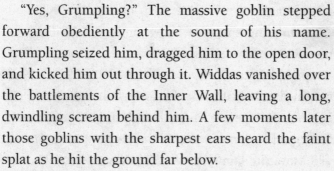

"An how come none of you had the nerve to eat that dwarf boom like what little Flegg here just did?"

"But. . ."

"We. . ."

"Please stop hitting us!"

"Widdas?" said Grumpling.

"Yes, Grumpling?" The massive goblin stepped forward obediently at the sound of his name. Grumpling seized him, dragged him to the open door, and kicked him out through it. Widdas vanished over the battlements of the Inner Wall, leaving a long, dwindling scream behind him. A few moments later those goblins with the sharpest ears heard the faint splat as he hit the ground far below.

"Oh dear, it looks like I is needin a new second in command," said Grumpling. His evil little eyes swept across the faces of his burly goblin warriors, and then looked down at Flegg.

"Flegg. He'll do. He's twice the goblin any of you rubbish lot is!"

Brilliant! thought Flegg. *Go, Flegg! From the pooin holes to Grumpling's right paw in the space of one night!*

"An the first fing he's goin ter do fer me," said Grumpling, "is he's goin ter get my scratchbackler back what Skarper and that softling robbled."

Which was not so brilliant, thought Flegg, cos it was probably going to end up in a fight and if it ended up in a fight he, Flegg, as Grumpling's second in command, would be expected to be right in the thick of it. But he didn't want to follow Widdas on a one-way flight to the land of splat, so he grinned and said, "I will, O mighty and magnificent Grumpling! You can rely on me!

Grumpling smiled a fangy smile. "Magnifificent," he said. "That's me."

Up on the high tops of the towers the echoes of the Elvenhorn lingered yet, as though the old stones held the sound, or the towers themselves were tuning forks, still vibrating faintly to the horn's high note. Human ears, or even goblin ones, could not detect it now, but the birds heard it, and so did the dragonets which nested in the charred rooftimbers of Sternbrow Tower.

Sternbrow had burned out in a goblin versus goblin

battle two years before, shortly before the Keep fell. The Blackspike Boys had made an alliance with the Chilli Hats and the Sternbrow Crew and launched a wild raid on the eastern towers. During the fighting, some goblin had dropped a burning brand down Sternbrow's pooin holes, and the gas which had built up over the centuries in the thick layers of poo in the basement had ignited. A great belch of flame had rushed up through the heart of the tower and blown the roof off. The Sternbrow goblins referred to this dreadful event as the Apoocalypse, and they had never returned to their tower since.

So the dragonets roosted there undisturbed, up among the charred timbers and the blowing weeds. Little things in dragon form they were, like miniature versions of the evil fire breathers that haunted the Westlands' oldest legends. The dragonets did not breathe fire, and they were not evil, although one of them was called Nuisance. Henwyn had given it that name because it was fond of him, and often it would seek him out and show its affection by biting his earlobes, or his nose, or sharpening its claws on his head.

The other dragonets were shy of humans and goblins. They kept themselves to themselves, up in that blackened chimney of a tower, and it was easy to forget that they were there at all. But that morning the music of the Elvenhorn seemed to have roused them. They burst from their roosts and went whirring and whirling in ever-wider circles around the tower's heights, calling out to each other in their high voices, which sounded a bit like the calling of buzzards. Far out over the ruins their wild flights carried them, until the goblins at work in the cheesery and in the fields outside the Inner Wall looked up at them in wonder.

At long last Nuisance spied something moving on the long, straight road that ran from Southerly Gate to the Inner Wall. He left his brothers and sisters to their circling and dived, folding his wings and dropping like a golden dart, down through the sunlight and the new green leaves of the trees.

Henwyn, Skarper and Zeewa were making their weary way home. They had just crossed the troll bridge and were climbing the stairs on the Oeth's northern bank. Here the goblins had once fought a terrible battle against the twiglings and Fraddon the giant. It seemed strange to remember it now, thought Henwyn, as he climbed wearily up the mossy steps. Nowadays, with Clovenstone at peace, the twiglings had put away their withy spears and their wild wood-magic. They were content to no more than flick a few acorns down

at travellers who passed beneath their trees.

Deep in thought, he didn't notice the little dragonet until it landed on his shoulder and bit him painfully on the ear.

"Ow!" he shouted. "Why, you little—"

Nuisance took wing again and whirled around Henwyn's head. Then he whirled around Zeewa's head, and finally around Skarper's. "Prriiiiip!" he chirruped. "Prrriiiiiip!" It was the dragonets' alarm call.

"It's as if he is trying to tell us something!" said Zeewa.

"I'll be telling him something in a minute!" grumbled Henwyn, rubbing at his punctured earlobe. "I mean – ow!"

"What does he want, do you think?" asked Skarper.

The dragonet was doing all sorts of acrobatics, and still making that frantic "Priiiip! Prrriiiiip!" But what did it mean? Henwyn sighed, and shook his head in frustration.

In the stories of adventure which he had loved to listen to before he came to Clovenstone and found adventures of his own, the hero would often have a clever dog (or horse). "Woof, woof!" it would say (or "neigh", if it were a horse). Then it would stamp its paws (or hooves), and toss its noble head. And the hero would say, "What's that Rover/Dobbin? Someone's in trouble? At the old silver mine?" And together they would go running (or riding) to the rescue.

But in real life it wasn't always that easy to tell what a dragonet meant when it started doing loop-the-loops in front of your nose and going, "Prriiiip!"

"Maybe there are some more eggs hatching?" suggested Skarper, because the eggs of dragonets were so thick-shelled that the hatchlings often couldn't break their way out without the help of someone on the outside with a hammer.

"Is that it, Nuisance?" asked Henwyn. "Do your hatchlings need our help? Can you lead us to where the eggs are?"

But that didn't seem to be it. Nuisance just bit him again, on the other ear this time, and took off through the trees like a golden arrow, straight up into the sky, where the rest of his little brood could be seen calling and circling.

Too weary to worry much about dragonets, the three travellers trudged on up the long road, and came at last to the gate in the Inner Wall. Skarper's batch-brother Bootle was on duty that morning, and before they passed inside Skarper asked him if there had been any trouble with Grumpling after the excitements of the previous night.

"Nuffin," said Bootle. "He's just shut up inside the

Redcap with all the other Chilli Hats."

"Maybe he's forgotten about the Elvenhorn," said Zeewa hopefully. "Maybe he's found something else to scratch his back with."

"I hope you're right," said Skarper. "I hope we never hears another word about that rubbish old horn."

But he was out of luck, because they had no sooner passed inside the wall than Fentongoose and Dr Prong came running out to meet them.

A "Hello, Henwyn," might have been nice, Henwyn thought. Or even a "Henwyn, how pleased we are that you are still alive!" But the two old philosophers had no time for pleasantries of that sort.

"Skarper! Zeewa!" they shouted. "Do you still have the Elvenhorn?"

"Tell us you do! Tell us you did not give it to the Sheep Lords!"

"It is vitally important that, whatever happens, we must *not* let Prince Rhind take it!"

Goblin Quest

While Skarper and Zeewa had been fetching the Elvenhorn and exchanging it for Henwyn, Fentongoose and Doctor Prong had been hard at work in Fentongoose's library. This was an old guardhouse near the cheesery, its walls lined with badly made bookshelves on which the former sorcerer had arranged all the books and maps and scrolls and papers that he had been able to salvage from the goblins' bumwipe heaps. The Lych Lord, back in the days when he ruled Clovenstone, had gathered books from all the lands that he had conquered; so many books that, even though the goblins had been ripping them up to wipe their bottoms on for the past hundred years, the ones which were left still formed a collection bigger than any other in the Westlands.

Fentongoose delighted in his library. When he was

not too busy trying to teach manners to the goblin hatchlings, he would spend his time reading and rearranging the books. Sometimes he arranged them alphabetically by title, sometimes by the name of the writer. Sometimes he grouped them by subject.

At present, they were arranged by age. The newest volumes – fine leather-bound folios and grimoires no more than a few hundred years old – were at one end of the long stretch of shelves. Beyond them lay older books – handwritten, with pages made of parchment and vellum instead of paper. Then came the tight-rolled scrolls, dating from a time before books had been invented, and the bundles of clay tablets, baked in the book ovens of Barragan in days of old. And stacked on the floor in the furthest, darkest corner of the library lay the stone books, which were not really books at all, just leaves of slate or black marble on which some long-ago scribes had scratched crude word-pictures.

Not many of these stone books had been gathered into the libraries of the Lych Lord, for they were rare. But the ones which had, had all survived because they were tougher by far than the books of baked clay, parchment or paper, and because the goblins never, ever used them for bumwipe – they were not very absorbent.

It was on one of these ancient stones that

Fentongoose had found a reference to the Elvenhorn. "I knew I had seen it mentioned somewhere before," he said, while Skarper, Zeewa, Henwyn, and a few goblins who were not still asleep came clustering round the big table in the middle of the library.

He and Dr Prong had spent all night trying to translate the ancient letters on the stone. They were faint and faded, and to untrained eyes they looked like rows and rows of tiny diagrams of different types of gate. Scrumpled and scribbled scraps of paper scattered on the floor showed what a struggle Prong and Fentongoose had had trying to tease out their meaning. But they had succeeded at last. What they had learned made everyone unhappy.

"*Chronicle of the Autumn Islands, Recounting Our Salvation from the Great and Terrible Cushions,*" read Dr Prong, his face close to the stone, the tip of his finger running along the lines of scratchy letters.

"I am not at all sure that 'cushion' is the right translation for that word," said Fentongoose. "We are still working on it."

Dr Prong read on. "*For many years the peoples of these Isles have lived in terror of the dreadful Cushions which come from across the ocean from the land in the west.* There is a bit missing here – we could pick out only a few words – 'fire', 'death'. . ."

"I am almost *sure* that word cannot be cushion," said Fentongoose.

"And 'west' can't be right, either," said Zeewa. "There is no land west of the Autumn Isles. The ocean stretches on for ever. Unless. . ."

"West of the Autumn Isles, down the path of the Setting Sun," said Henwyn. "That is where Prince Rhind said Elvensea once lay."

"*They came,*" said Dr Prong, impatient at all the interruptions, "*across the sea. And wherever they went, death and fire did follow.* But then it says, *In this year, in the month of Trevas-Billas* – the harvesting of the oats – *there came from the east in black ships seven wozzards.*"

"I'm sure that says wizard, actually," said Fentongoose. "There is no such thing as a wozzard."

"Wozzard is quite definitely what it says here," said Dr Prong firmly. "It must be an old-fashioned form of the word."

"Well, it's a very silly one," said Fentongoose. "But have it your own way."

"Now, where was I?" said Prong, scowling at him. "Ah yes: *black ships . . . seven wozzards. . .*"

"You see?" asked Fentongoose excitedly, turning to the listeners. "these wizards. . ."

"Wozzards!"

"These *wizards* must have been the Lych Lord and

89

his six fellow sorcerers, the ones who helped him raise the Black Keep and build the seven towers of Clovenstone!"

Skarper and Henwyn both knew that story, which Fentongoose had first told them while they sat with Princess Ned in her old ship, balanced on Westerly Gate, on the evening of Henwyn's arrival at Clovenstone. Long ago, seven sorcerers had tamed the power of the slowsilver lake which lay beneath this place, and they had grown great and powerful and set out to right the wrongs of the world, until one of them had argued with the others, and cast them down, and become the Lych Lord. So this stone book came from a time before that happened – a time so long ago that it made you feel dizzy just imagining such a depth of years.

"*Seven wozzards*," said Dr Prong, going on with his reading in a loud voice, as if daring Fentongoose to interrupt again. "*These seven vowed that they would defeat the Cushions.* (Perhaps it says pillows? No, that still does not make sense. . .) *So they sailed into the west, despite our warnings, and we feared that they would be*. . . (Now, this word means, 'to render something into a paste, or purée, by jumping up and down on it whilst wearing stone-soled sandals', but I do not think it is meant to be taken literally, I think it just means that they feared the seven wozzards would be killed. It is certainly a rather colourful way of putting it.) *However, seven nights later* (or possibly nine, or thirty six) *we beheld a mighty fire upon the western sky, as of a terrible battle raging. And the sea was troubled, and the sun grew dark. And soon after that, the wozzards in their seven ships returned to tell us that, by their magic, the Queen of Elvensea has been cast down, and her Cushions had been scattered. . ."*

"So they were scatter cushions?" asked Skarper.

". . .and her land was sunk beneath the waves. Many of our ships have sailed there since, and our sailors report that there is nothing to be seen of it, only a wild waste of waters restlessly rolling.

"The wozzards told us that they achieved all this through the use of a magical trumpet. This trumpet, having done its work, was cast into the depths of the sea, there to remain hidden until the world ends. Do not try to seek it, reader! One blast of that horn will part the waters, two shall raise the drowned land, and then the world will tremble again before the terror of the Cushions."

"Elves," said Skarper. "That's what that word must mean. Nobody's scared of cushions, not really. They mean elves."

"I am certain it is not elves," said Dr Prong. "It is something else. . ."

"The land that the Lych Lord and his wozzard friends sank with this magic trumpet business," said Henwyn, "that must be Elvensea, mustn't it? There can't be two sunken continents out in the Western Ocean."

"But elves are good, aren't they?" Zeewa asked. "I mean, it was the Lych Lord who defeated them, and he was evil, so. . ."

"The Lych Lord was not always evil," said Fentongoose. "Even if he was, you should not fall into the trap of thinking that his enemies were always good. There was wild magic in the world in those days. Perhaps the Lych Lord and his fellow sorcerers saw Elvensea as a threat to themselves – another land of magic, far out there in the Western Ocean, but not far enough for comfort. Perhaps the people of Elvensea – these elves, or cushions, or whatever we choose to call them – were really their bitter rivals? This old stone recalls a war between two powerful bands of magic-users. Clovenstone defeated Elvensea. But we must not imagine that the sorcerers of Elvensea were any less power-hungry or dangerous than them. Why else would the folk of the Autumn Isles have been so afraid of them?"

"I wish we'd never even heard of that blimmin' Elvenhorn," said Skarper.

"But we have heard of it," said Zeewa. "And now

Prince Rhind has it, and he imagines the masters of Elvensea were good and kindly folk, and that everyone will thank him for waking their magic again."

"Well, we must stop him!" said Skarper. "We don't want a load of blimmin' elf magic all over the place – it'll be a proper bother."

"Rhind can't have got far," said a small goblin called Spurtle. "He only set off at sunrise."

"His horses are faster than any we have in Clovenstone," said Henwyn.

"Goblins go fast!" said Yabber.

"Goblins can hunt!" said Libnog.

"Goblins can follow softling scents through marsh and moor and mountains," said Spurtle.

"We ought to have a quest of our own!" said Skarper suddenly. "Why do only softlings and princes and such get to go on quests and have songs sung about them an' stuff? I say we should have our own goblin quest to fetch this Elvenhorn back and smash it, or plop it back into the deepliest depths of the sea, whichever is most convenient."

Around the table, goblin eyes shone. They liked this idea. It had been brilliant last year when they had biffed those stupid dwarves and all the softlings had said what heroes they were. Now they would be heroes again.

"I'll go!" yelled Spikey Peet.

"An' me!" shouted Libnog.

"Me too!" said a dozen more.

"Steady!" said Fentongoose. "You can't all go – that wouldn't be a quest, it would just be chaos."

"Seven sorcerers once set out from Clovenstone to defeat the power of Elvensea," said Dr Prong. "Perhaps seven of us should go to make sure that it stays defeated. Also, seven is a very auspicious and magical number, and it will sound good if anyone writes songs about us."

"I should go," said Henwyn, "because it is sort of my fault that he was able to take the Elvenhorn in the first place."

"Me too," said Skarper. He could not say why, exactly; it was just a sudden, wild feeling that he had, a need to see lands he had never seen, and sail the seas he had read about while he was a hatchling in the bumwipe heaps. But it would be impossible to make his fellow goblins understand that, so he just said, "Me an Henwyn always go together. An Zeewa should go, cos she's a brilliant hunter. And what about Libnog? He's cunning and brave."

"Hear that?" asked Libnog, looking round proudly at the other goblins. "Cunning and brave, that's me."

Henwyn shook his head. "Libnog will be needed

here." He knew that Libnog was one of the few goblins with any brains; without him, the others could not be trusted to keep doing all the things that needed doing to keep Clovenstone running – they would just muck about.

"Awww," said Libnog.

"But we'll take Spurtle," said Henwyn, "because Spurtle is small and good at thieving things, and may be able to fetch the Elvenhorn out of Prince Rhind's camp without a fight. . ."

"Unless it's full moon of course!" jeered the other goblins. "Then Prince Rhind can have a nice sit down on him!"

Spurtle snarled at them. He had once fallen into the Slowsilver Lake, and although the effects had almost worn off, he still had a relapse once a month, on the night of the full moon, when he turned into a small but quite comfortable sofa. "I'll go," he said.

"And Gutgust!" said Henwyn. "He may say nothing but 'anchovies', but he is mighty in the thick of battle, and we shall need him if we *do* have to fight."

"Anchovies!" said Gutgust happily, and Skarper realized that it was too late to argue, although Gutgust wasn't the goblin he would have chosen – Gutgust wasn't just mighty in the thick of battle, he was mighty thick.

"And who else?" asked Zeewa.

"Oooh, me, me, me!" shouted the other goblins, leaping up and down with their paws in the air.

"Won't you need a philosopher to help you?" asked Fentongoose.

"Help us with what?" said Skarper. "We know all about the Elvenhorn already. We just need to grab it. That doesn't take brains."

"Besides," said Henwyn hurriedly, "you and Dr Prong are needed here at Clovenstone, to keep an eye on things."

"So who shall be the sixth and seventh members of your company?" asked Prong.

"Me an' Grumpling!" said a voice from behind him.

It was the voice of Flegg. He had come in unnoticed while they were all busy talking. Behind him in the open doorway stood the hulking form of Grumpling. Flegg strode boldly across the library to stand beside Henwyn. "Why should you get to pick everyone who goes, softling? The Elvenhorn was stolen from Grumpling by those Woolmarkers and their accomplices." (He shot a sharp look at Skarper and Zeewa.) "It's only right that Grumpling should join the quest to recover it."

"No!" said Skarper. "Don't listen to Flegg! He's up to something! He betrayed me and Zeewa even though

we helped him out of the pooin holes. And as for Grumpling, who'd want him along on a quest?"

Henwyn was inclined to agree, but Zeewa said, "No. Let Grumpling come. Flegg is right, a Chilli Hat should come with us."

"I'd rather he went with you on your quest than stopped here causing nuisance for the rest of us," said Libnog.

Grumpling beckoned Flegg back to him and whispered loudly, "What's this thing I've got to go on?"

"A quest, O mighty Grumpling," Flegg whispered back.

"What's that?"

"It's my way of getting back your scratchbackler."

"Oh. . ." Grumpling looked dimly satisfied, but Flegg wasn't.

"I shall come too," he announced.

Henwyn shook his head. "Sorry, Flegg. We need strong, brave goblins for this business, and you are neither."

Flegg looked horrified. He liked being Grumpling's favourite. If he was left here alone, the other Chilli Hats would make his life a misery, and quite a short misery. Not only that, he was forming vague plans about getting this powerful Elvenhorn for himself. It sounded much too useful to be chucked into the sea by goody-goodies or used as a back scratcher by an idiot.

"Ah, but I am Grumpling's servant and advisor. And think how useful I will be if poets and people do write songs about us, and they need something to rhyme with 'egg' or 'leg'. Besides, I am clever and wily."

"Cunning and slimy, more like," said Skarper. "What if Flegg betrays us again?"

"Why would I do that?" asked Flegg, all innocence. "I'm a goblin, Skarper, same as you. I don't want this old elfy magic woken up any more than you do."

"Well, I suppose. . ." said Skarper.

"Don't worry," said Zeewa softly, and she fingered the blade of the spear which she had been repairing. "If he tries to double-cross us, my spear is thirsty."

"So be it!" said Henwyn. "Let us make ready! We shall not take horses, because goblins go faster on foot, and I always fall off. But we shall need travelling garb, and provisions for a long journey. Some of those little cheesy biscuits would be nice. We shall leave before sundown!"

The room emptied, people and goblins swirling out through the small doorway like water down a drain. Soon only Dr Prong was left, still stooped over the ancient stone on the table.

"It is not 'elves'," he muttered to himself, staring

at the ancient scratches. "And it cannot really be 'cushions'. So what *is* that word? What waits at Elvensea?"

Setting Off

Remember that horn blast that had woken the giant, Fraddon, startled the boglins, and upset the dragonets? Its echoes had faded now from Clovenstone. But, like a ripple spreading in a clear pool where a bird has brushed the water's surface, the sound kept travelling onwards and outwards. It was just a whisper now, faint beyond the hearing of any mortal thing. It had trembled the veins of ore in dwarf mines on the Nibbled Coast, and merged for a moment with the cry of the gulls where the white surf surged and splashed upon the beaches of the Autumn Isles. Far out across the Western Ocean it flew, over the sea's great silences and the slop and ripple of the big, slow waves.

And at last it came to the place where, all those long centuries before, the island of Elvensea had foundered like a vast stone ship.

There was no ear there to hear it. There was nothing but the empty sea and the empty sky and the silent music of the Elvenhorn. But the sea was listening. Slowly the waves began to change – not their shapes, but their motion and their direction. If you had been out there in a boat (and you are very lucky that you were *not* out there in a boat) you might not have noticed what was happening for a long time. But if you had been hanging high above the sea, perhaps as a guest aboard a handy cloud, you would have been able to watch as the waves rearranged themselves into a spiral, and began to turn; slowly at first, and then faster and faster, as if a gigantic, invisible spoon was stirring that part of the ocean. A whirlpool was forming, its centre dipping down and down through the fish-filled fathoms until right at the bottom of it, in the heart of a pit of rushing water, a domed roof appeared, and around it stone towers, and below it the shapes of other walls and turrets all blurred with barnacles and shining mounds of weed.

Nothing else happened. The whirlpool whirled, the drowned towers stood silent in its depths, and that was all. Elvensea was waiting for the second horn blast.

Henwyn and Zeewa prepared carefully for the quest, loading their packs with the things they thought would be most useful: ropes, maps, tinder boxes, spare socks and drawers, bread, dried fruit, and a wheel of Clovenstone Blue. The goblins packed carelessly, slinging any old thing into their packs, forgetting things they'd need and weighing themselves down instead with trinkets that would be too heavy to carry far, and which they would lose interest in and sling into the roadside bushes before they'd gone five miles from Westerly Gate. They all made sure they had good weapons with them, though the short, sharp swords that goblins loved best, and, in Grumpling's case, two massive old battleaxes, which he strapped crosswise to his back.

Henwyn was still not happy about bringing Grumpling and Flegg on the quest. Who would be? They were horrible. He was glad to be taking them away from Clovenstone, but he wished he had a few larger goblins who could help him deal with Grumpling if Grumpling made trouble on the way. Gutgust was the only one big enough to fight Grumpling, and there was only one of Gutgust. He wished the trolls were around, but they had still not returned from their camping trip.

When everything was ready at last, and the goodbyes had been said, and the company was setting off along the road to Westerly Gate, he went on ahead of them and made his way to the place where Fraddon had stood all winter, in the clearing where Princess Ned's first garden had been. The garden was almost invisible now, and you had to look quite hard to make out the shapes of flower beds and beanpoles among the thick weeds and young trees. Fraddon was vanishing too; as tall and still as the trees around him, with ivy growing up his legs and moss hanging from his woody hair. Young twiglings peered down at Henwyn from his beard.

Henwyn sat down on a mossy stone beside the stream and looked up at the old giant. Fraddon was smaller than he had been two years before, when they'd first met. Giants grow down, not up; they dwindle as they age, like mountains. Once, long before Henwyn's time, Fraddon had been big enough to scoop the ship carrying Princess Ned out of the sea and carry it home under his arm. Now, his head did not reach higher than the highest trees. But he would still be able to pick up a goblin of Grumpling's size and stuff him in his pocket, if Grumpling misbehaved.

"Fraddon," said Henwyn, "a new peril has arisen. Skarper and Zeewa and me and some of the goblins are going to try and stop it. Will you come with us on the quest? Your great long legs could catch up with Prince Rhind in no time. If you came, we wouldn't need a quest, probably."

Fraddon's eyes were closed. There was no telling

whether he had heard or not, or whether he was even awake. He swayed gently as the wind blew across the treetops. The twiglings skittered and giggled in his beard, peeking down at Henwyn with their black button eyes.

"Old Fraddon doesn't hear you, human being," said one of the twiglings. "You talk too fast for him. Move too fast. Think too fast. Live too fast and die too soon. He listens to the trees now, not you humans and your little buzzing voices."

"Is this peril you're talking about a peril to trees?" asked another.

Henwyn didn't think it was. Elves liked trees, didn't they? In the stories they were always wandering around in woods, tending the young saplings and punishing anyone who tried to cut them down. If Prince Rhind woke the elves' magic, the twiglings would probably be grateful. Fraddon would probably be glad. Maybe the peril that Fentongoose and Dr Prong believed was coming was only perilous for people, and goblins.

He missed Fraddon, though. He missed his big, rumbly voice, his giant kindness. He sat on the stone and watched him, and wished there was something he could say or do that would make Fraddon happy again. But he knew the old giant's heart was broken, and broken hearts take ages to heal, even normal-sized ones.

And then, through the trees, he heard Skarper and the others making their way towards the gate. Goblin voices raised in song echoed through the woods, making the twiglings hiss and quiver, then sending them scampering into hiding.

> *Goblin Quest!*
> *Goblin Quest!*
> *From Clovenstone into the west,*
> *We'll show them goblins are the best.*
> *From mighty Clovenstone we come,*
> *We'll kick Prince Rhind up his woolly bum.*
> *Our blades are bright,*
> *Our songs are fine,*
> *Though we do sometimes try to fit far too*
> *   many syllables into one line.*
> *Goblin Quest!*
> *Goblin Quest!*

Henwyn sighed. *If I were a proper hero*, he thought, *I could make a rousing speech and Fraddon would wake up and come with us and all would be well. But I'm not, and I can't, and he won't.*

So he slipped down off his rocky perch, and went to join the goblins.

The Perilous Wood

Prawl had never been a very good sorcerer, and he had never been a very good rider, either. The mare on which he was mounted clearly thought he was a fool. As Prince Rhind's company made their way into the wild country north-west of Clovenstone she kept wearily trying to knock him off against each tree and boulder that they passed, as if he were an annoying burr that had got caught in her coat. Whenever they stopped to let the horses drink at a stream or river, she would lower her head with such suddenness that Prawl would go somersaulting over her neck and land with a splash in the water.

After the third time it happened, Prince Rhind made him ride in the wagon.

"Your clever brain must not be harmed, Prawl," he said. "We shall have need of your wisdom when we reach Elvensea."

But Prawl didn't feel very wise as he joggled along on the wagon's seat next to Mistress Ninnis. He would sooner have been riding ahead with Breenge and her brother, and he sighed wistfully as he watched her draw further and further ahead.

"She must think I'm an idiot," he said.

"Who, Lady Breenge?" asked the cook, cheerful as ever. "Oh, she has always thought you are an idiot; she didn't need to see you falling off a horse to convince her of it."

It was evening. Long shadows stretched across the heathland. The road they were following wound along the top of the steep, wooded valley of the River Oeth. On either side bare hills of heather and gorse stretched to the horizons. The smoke of a few distant farms rose straight up into the windless air. The bowl of the sky was deep blue, waiting for the first stars.

"They are following," said Ninnis suddenly.

"Who are?" asked Prawl, who had been lost in thoughts of Breenge.

The cook turned her head and looked at Prawl with her twinkling, bird-bright eyes. "The boy and the girl and a bunch o' them goblin friends of yours from Clovenstone."

"How can you possibly know that?" asked Prawl. He twisted round to look back, but there was no sign of anyone following the wagon, only the pale road unwinding behind it into the evening hills.

"I have the sight," said Ninnis softly.

"The what?"

"The second sight. I should have thought a mighty sorcerer like you would know all about it. I see things that are happening far away, and sometimes things that haven't happened yet."

"Oh, *that* sort of second sight."

"Your friends are just setting out through Westerly Gate. They have not brought horses with them, but goblins are quick on their feet and won't mind travelling by night while we are resting. They'll catch us sometime tomorrow, I reckon."

Prawl shook his head. "I cannot see any of that! You should be Rhind's sorcerer, not me!"

Ninnis chuckled. "Why, he'd not want an old biddy like me as his court sorcerer! Besides which, I prefer pies to potions."

"But at least you have some magic about you. I have none at all."

"Well, don't tell His Highness that, or he will fire you and I shall have no one to talk to on this journey but proud Lady Breenge." She nudged him and winked. "I tell you what! If you want to impress the prince and that sister of his, you catch up with him and tell him what I just told you. Only make out it was you that had the vision, not me."

Rhind and Breenge were about half a mile ahead of the lumbering wagon. They had reined in their horses at a place where the road dipped steeply down into a dark wood. Rhind had dismounted and gone down into the trees on foot, as if to spy out the way ahead. When Prawl ran up to where Breenge waited he saw why. Nailed to a birch which grew beside the road was a board, and painted on the board was a depressed-looking skull and the words RODE CLOSED and DANGER.

Many travellers had already taken heed of that sign; Prawl could see where horses and perhaps a wagon or two had struck off on a different route which led around the wood, through the rock-strewn heathland behind. But the detour looked difficult, and Rhind was an impatient sort of prince. He wanted to be sure that some danger really lurked among those trees before he took the trouble to go around them. That was why he had gone on ahead to check.

He was climbing back up out of the tree-shadows as Prawl arrived. His face was grim. "There are bones among the trees," he said. "I reckon something lives down there. Troll, maybe, or something worse. There

109

are probably all sorts of strange things in these hills since the Slowsilver Star came."

"Well, blast!" said Breenge. "Then I suppose we must take the other path, and rejoin the river road further on."

"T'would be best, sister," said Rhind. "I fear no mortal enemy, but against these magical creatures I'd sooner not fight unless I have to. Not with night coming on."

Breenge noticed Prawl waiting nearby. "What do you want?" she snapped.

Prawl blushed. Stammering, he told Breenge and her brother about the party that had left Clovenstone.

"There!" said Breenge, when he had finished. "We shall have mortal enemies to battle after all! We shall lie in wait for these goblins and their friends, and kill them all."

"I say," cried Prawl, "that's a bit extreme! (Though ever so brave and spirited of you, of course, Lady Breenge.)"

"No, sister," said Rhind. "Why would we waste our time and risk our lives to ambush a parcel of goblins? They are fickle, feckless creatures who will probably lose interest in pursuing us after a few miles. And if they do make it this far. . ."

He leaned over and used the hilt of his sword to

knock the warning sign free of the two rusty nails which held it to the tree. Then he tossed it away down the hillside where the thick bracken hid it from view.

"We shall ride as far as the edge of the trees down there, then turn uphill to join the new path. By the time those creatures get here it will be dark, and they will think our tracks lead into the trees. The thing in the woods will deal with them."

"Trolls do eat goblins, I suppose?" asked Breenge.

"It might not be a troll," said Rhind. "But from the look of all those bones down there I'd say it eats just about anybody."

Night had fallen by the time the travellers from Clovenstone arrived at that place. Even the goblins, with their sharp, twilight-loving eyes, did not notice the warning sign that Rhind had cast into the bracken. Only Skarper sensed anything wrong. Looking ahead at the pale ribbon of road dipping into the trees he said, "Why don't we camp here tonight, and go through those woods tomorrow when the sun is up?"

The others wouldn't hear of it.

"It is only a little wood," said Henwyn.

"Why don't we keep walking all night," said Spurtle, "and sleep in some shady place when the sun comes up? Dark suits goblins better, and we might overtake them softlings that way; they'll be snoozin' an' snorin' by now, I 'spect."

"Anchovies!" said Gutgust, and that seemed to settle it. They started down the sloping road into the trees with Henwyn saying, "Maybe we won't want to keep walking all night. But at least let's get this wood behind us before we make camp. Maybe we'll see the light of Rhind's campfire from the top of that next hill."

"Here!" said Spurtle, who was scampering ahead. "This is weird. The softlings' tracks turns sideways here, off the road and up the hill."

"Why would they do that?" asked Zeewa.

"Maybe there's something wrong with those trees," said Skarper.

But by that time Henwyn had already strolled past them and into the wood.

The shadows of the trees closed over him, and with them came silence. The noises of the world outside – the evening wind, the chuckle of the river, and the bickering of the goblins – were muffled here. The trees overhanging the road were dark and solemn, and scraps of mist veiled those that stood deeper in the dell. And what was that strange noise?

"Aaaaah-aaaah-oooooooh-aaaahhhh-aahhh. . ."

"Someone's moaning," said Zeewa, entering the

woods behind him.

"Someone's got a bellyache," said Flegg.

"No, someone's singing," said Henwyn, holding up a hand for silence so that he could hear the weird song more clearly. "Goblins have no ear for music."

"Aaaaaah-aaaaah-oooooooh-aaaaaahhhh-aaahhh," went the lonely voice, drifting between the trees like mist.

"I like sumpfing wiv more of a tune to it," said Grumpling.

"We have happier music in the Tall Grass Country," said Zeewa. "Music that makes you want to dance."

"It's beautiful!" said Henwyn.

He left the road and started downhill towards the source of the sound. Tree roots tripped him, and pale bones snapped like dry twigs underfoot, but he did not notice them. Something was shining faintly in the trees ahead, where the shadows pooled the deepest, and it seemed suddenly very important that he should reach it. A slender figure, it seemed to him to be, glowing with its own soft light there in the wood's gloom. At home in Adherak when he was growing up he'd heard the tales of wood nymphs who wandered at dusk, singing for their lost loves. He had never thought to see one with his own eyes. Perhaps the sounding of the Elvenhorn had woken this one.

"Henwyn!" shouted Skarper, left behind with the others. He wanted to run after his friend, but he felt wary of leaving the road, which seemed the last solid thing in this shifting world of mist and shadows.

"There's something white down there between the trees," said Zeewa.

"Prob'ly a bone," said Spurtle. "There's loads of them here. They're crunchy." He had picked up a long white bone from the leaf litter beside the road and he was cheerfully sucking out the marrow.

"Lots of softlings died here," said Grumpling, booting a skull downhill like a bony football. "Not long ago, neither."

Zeewa said, "There is magic here. I can feel it in the air and the ground."

"Henwyn!" shouted Skarper again, but there came no answer, only that unearthly, tuneless singing from the heart of the wood.

Typical, thought Skarper. *We haven't been away from Clovenstone for even one day yet, and already Henwyn's got himself in Mortal Peril. Well, if he thinks I'm going to go and help him he's got another think coming.*

But of course he was going to help. He always did. He drew his short sword and started down through the trees, and the others came after him – some, like Zeewa, because they wanted to help him, some, like Grumpling, because they were hoping for a good fight, and the rest because they did not want to be left behind in that eerie place.

At the bottom of the hill stood Henwyn. He had his back to them and he was so still that Skarper was afraid he'd been enchanted or something until he turned at the sound of their footsteps crunching through the dead leaves and said, "Shhh!"

"What is it?" whispered Skarper.

"Look!" Henwyn pointed through the twilight to a place where a ring of black trees grew. They were not gnarled old yews like the rest of the wood – too slender, too thorny. Through the narrow gaps between their trunks there flickered a ghostly, faintly glowing figure. It seemed to be swaying from side to side, and as it swayed, it sang.

"Aaaaah-ooooh-aaaahhh-oooohhh-aaaahhhh. . ."

"A wood nymph!" whispered Henwyn.

"A g-g-ghost!" whispered Spurtle.

"Anchovies!" whispered Gutgust.

"It's a flower," said Zeewa.

"A what?" the goblins chorused.

"Some sort of strange flower. . ." Zeewa went forward, crunching over the litter of bones, and Henwyn went with her, afraid she might scare away the beautiful singer. "A flower?" he said peevishly.

"Who ever heard of singing flowers?"

But Zeewa had been right. As soon as they stepped into that circle of slender trunks he could see that his wood nymph was nothing of the sort. What he had taken for her gown was just a tightly folded bud of massive, waxy petals; what he had thought was her face were just a few darker patches near the top. In the dark it had looked like eyes, a mouth, and a nose. As for the singing, he could tell now that it was just the night breeze keening through the trees. This flower must give off some natural magic the same way that others gave off scent, and it had tricked him into hearing singing.

"Aha!" he said, trying to make it sound as if he had suspected something of this sort all along. "A tree that mimics the appearance and song of a wood nymph. Fascinating."

"Why would it do that?" asked Zeewa.

"Who knows?" said Henwyn. "It's not very good, though. Didn't fool me for a moment."

He reached out and prodded the fleshy petals of the flower. Instantly, creaking like a ship in high seas, the ring of trees folded inwards, closing on him and Zeewa like a trap.

It was a trap, of course. A natural trap, like those plants in tropical forests that give off a smell like rotting meat and then snap shut on all the flies that arrive expecting a tasty snack. What Henwyn and Zeewa had taken for a ring of trees was really just the many limbs of one, and when Henwyn prodded the bloom at the centre of them he had released some vegetable spring which caused them all to jerk inwards, trapping them both.

If Fentongoose had been there he could have told them that they had fallen victim to a mantrap tree, of which, in the old days, there had been whole forests in the night valleys of Musk. What one was doing growing on the hills of the Westlands in the present day was a mystery. Perhaps some servant of the Lych Lord, hastening home to Clovenstone from the harbours of the north with seeds and cuttings for his master's gardens, had dropped a seed upon this lonely road, and it had lain there ever since until the light of the Slowsilver Star conjured it into life.

How it had come there was actually not of much interest to Henwyn at that moment. How to get out of it; that was what he would have liked to know. At first, as the black trunks sprang inwards to pinion him and Zeewa, he had been afraid that they were going to be crushed, but in fact the trunks just made a prison; a cage just large enough to contain the pair of them.

"Help!" he shouted, squeezing a hand out through a gap between two of the trunks and flapping at the

goblins outside.

Skarper, running round the tree, saw the hand reach out. He grabbed hold of it and pulled, but the gap was not wide enough to pull a whole Henwyn through.

"What's it doing to you?" he asked.

"It's not doing anything," said Henwyn, from inside his woody prison.

"It's waiting," said Zeewa. "I have seen plants in the swampland at the foot of Leopard Mountain which trap flies and spiders in this way. It is waiting till we die and rot and our juices trickle down into the earth to feed its foul roots."

"Eww!" said Henwyn.

"Don't worry," Skarper told him. "It might trap lonely travellers like that, but not ones who have a whole load of goblins outside to help them. We'll soon have you out of there!"

He tugged at the trunks. They felt about as bendable as wrought-iron railings.

"Grumpling?' he asked. "Can your strength help us?"

Grumpling unshouldered one of the two huge axes which he had brought with him. "No problem," he growled. The others scattered out of range as he lifted the axe high above his head and then swung it at the nearest of the mantrap's trunks.

118

There was a loud thunk. The tree shuddered, tightening its grip on Henwyn and Zeewa. The axe head dropped to the ground in two halves, leaving Grumpling staring at the useless handle.

"Stupid tree!" he said. "That was one of my best axes!"

Behind him in the darkness Flegg's eyes gleamed. "Oh dear. What a pity. Grumpling has tried, and since no one is as strong as the mighty Grumpling there is no point in any of us trying. Henwyn and Zeewa are doomed. It's sad, but there it is. We'd best leave them here and be on our way. We can't delay our quest for the sake of these two softlings, and we should not linger here. Who knows what other nasty dangers these woods hold?"

"Anchovies!" screeched Gutgust suddenly, as if to prove Flegg's point. He had just trodden in what turned out to be a baby mantrap tree, a sapling no larger than an egg basket. It had snapped shut on his foot like an actual mantrap. "An-cho-vieeeeeeees!" he wailed, hopping around, knocking Spurtle over in his efforts to wrench it off.

"But we can't just leave Henwyn and Zeewa here!" shouted Skarper.

"I'm sure Henwyn would agree that our quest is more important than his life," said Flegg. He was already shoving a bewildered Grumpling back up the dark hillside towards the road. "Every moment we linger here, Prince Rhind and his friends carry the Elvenhorn further from our reach."

"But. . ." Skarper gave another despairing tug at the mantrap's trunks. He could see about half of Henwyn's face peering out at him through one of the gaps between them, and Zeewa behind him, stabbing the floor of their prison with her spear.

"We won't leave you here," Skarper promised. "We'll think of some way to free you!"

"Best think of it soon, then," said Zeewa. "The stench of this flower is muddying my wits!"

It was true. The thick, sweetish odour of the unearthly flower had not been so noticeable before the tree closed. Now it filled the cage of trunks like a velvet fog. Henwyn was finding it difficult to keep his eyes open.

"Perhaps we could poison it with something?" he suggested sleepily. "Or just forget to water it; I used to be forever killing my mother's geraniums like that when I lived in Adherak. . ." His head nodded and his eyes closed. He shook himself awake with an effort, and said, "Fraddon? Princess Ned?" But of course Fraddon was far away and Ned was gone. For a moment, as he drowsed, he had imagined himself back in that other cage of trees, the one which the twiglings had conjured round him on the day he came to Clovenstone.

"Fraddon!" said Skarper. "That's it! Flegg was wrong! There is someone stronger than Grumpling! Old Fraddon could uproot this horrid shrub with his bare hands if we could call him here."

"But Fraddon is in Clovenstone," said Henwyn sleepily. Behind him, Zeewa had stopped jabbing her spear into the tree and was snoring softly.

"Clovenstone's not that far," Skarper said. "Those big ears of Fraddon's ought to hear me if I shout loud enough. I'll fetch him and come back, Henwyn; I promise!"

It was a desperate plan. He had no idea how far his voice could carry, or how good Fraddon's hearing was, or whether the old giant would even care enough to help now he was in that mossy, sleepy mood. But he could think of nothing else to do. He scurried back to the road, where Gutgust sat muttering, "Anchovies!" and Spurtle tried to pull the baby mantrap off his foot. Of Grumpling and Flegg there was no sign, so Skarper assumed that they had gone on their way. *Good riddance*, he thought. He ran back up the road the way they had come, out of the mist and the tree-dark, into good, clean starlight on the hilltop where he'd wanted to make camp earlier. Far away, the summits of the Bonehill Mountains reared up their stony heads beneath the waxing moon. Somewhere there, lost among the folds of the land, lay Clovenstone.

Cupping his paws around his mouth, Skarper bellowed, "Fraddon! Fraddon!"

HOW TO BE a Bee

Clutched in the mantrap, Henwyn dreamed. It was uncomfortable, pillowed there among the knobby, knobbly limbs of the carnivorous tree, and his dreams were uncomfortable too. He dreamed that he was lying on the stuffy floor of a cavern, and that some dwarves, whose cavern it was, were poking him with their picks and shovels in an attempt to wake him up and move him on.

Then, as he sank into a deeper sleep, that dream faded, and another came. He dreamed that he was looking out over a wide grey sea. There was no land in sight, and no clear line where the sea met the vague and hazy sky. A loud roaring filled the air. A hole had opened in the surface of the sea, and all the water seemed to be swirling down into it. Henwyn was being drawn towards it too. Wider and wider it yawned, and way down in the bottom he thought he could see dry land: roads and rooftops and fair towers rising.

He woke with a start. He was still in the heart of the mantrap tree, squashed up against Zeewa, who was murmuring some song in her own language while she slept. Something had changed, but he was so drowsy that it took him a while to work out what. Then he saw that the mantrap tree's flower was opening. No longer looking even slightly like a wood nymph, it had risen higher on its stem and opened those white, glowing petals inside the cage of tree trunks like a parasol.

Above it, out in the inky woods, a voice was going, "Buzzz."

"Fraddon!" shouted Skarper, and the echoes mocked him, bouncing back from crags and empty hillsides and the wild, wet moors that he knew would swallow his voice long before it reached Clovenstone. *Silly little goblin*, he thought. *Howling and yowling in the wilderness. You're on your own now. You've left all your wise friends behind, and you can't look to them to come and get you out of trouble.*

"Fraddon!" he shouted again, one last time, still staring at the dark eastern sky and hoping that he might make out the huge shape of the giant striding easily over the folded hills. But the hope was very small and frail now, and, as the echoes faded, it crumpled up and vanished like a leaf in a bonfire. He was too far from Clovenstone. Not even a giant's giant ears would hear his shouts. Or, if they did, they would sound no more important than the buzz of a tiny fly. . .

Fly. That gave him a new idea. It was a small idea, and perhaps a stupid one, but it was definitely an idea, and he did not have so many of those that he could afford to ignore it.

So he stopped shouting for Fraddon and ran back down into the woods, to where Gutgust and Spurtle waited. They had dislodged the baby mantrap from Gutgust's foot and they were trying to light a fire using the fragments of it and a few dank bits of fallen timber which they had found among the trees.

"Trees oughter be frightened of fire!" said Spurtle. "If we can get a fire goin' we can tell it to let Henwyn an Zeewa go or we'll burn it up. Or down. Or up."

"And it might just clunch them tighter," said Skarper, "and you might just roast them like a couple of chestnuts. And it won't listen to you anyway; it won't understand threats. I've got a better idea. What are flowers for?"

The goblins looked blankly at him.

"They looks pretty?" suggested Spurtle.

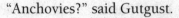

"Anchovies?" said Gutgust.

"They attract bees," said Skarper.

"And Henwyns," said Spurtle.

"Right. That tree wants Henwyn and Zeewa as plant food. But to make baby trees it must need bees. That's how flowers work. I read all about it, in the bumwipe heaps."

"That's weird," said Spurtle. "Are you sure?"

"Clever softlings have studied trees and plants and things and found out how they work," he said.

"Why?"

"Because trees and plants and things is interesting."

"No they isn't."

"They is if your friend is stuck inside them. That's probably why the softlings started studying them in the first place, and then they got a taste for it and carried on. It's a science. It's called Bottomy."

"Why?"

"I don't know. Probably because when you sit down on plants and things it's your bottom that you sit on them with."

"Maybe that's why they started studying them," reasoned Spurtle. "You wouldn't want to sit down on the prickly ones, or the ones that give you a rash."

"Anyway," said Skarper. "Maybe if this tree thinks there's a really big bee buzzing about looking for some pollen, it might open up to let it get at the flower. And then maybe we can whisk Henwyn and Zeewa out."

Spurtle understood. He nodded wisely. Even Gutgust said, "Anchovies!" in an admiring sort of way.

"So all we need to do is wait for a really big bee to come along," said Spurtle.

Skarper sighed. "We aren't going to wait for a bee," he said. "We're going to *make* a bee."

"How do you make a bee?" asked Spurtle. "And why are you looking at me like that?"

Five minutes later Spurtle was dangling over the mantrap tree, saying, "Buzzz, buzzz!" in the most bee-like voice he could manage. Skarper had painted his dark goblin clothes with stripes of pale clay from the road, and cut a spare cloak into rough wings that flapped from his shoulders. Two spindly twigs, tied round his head with string, made bee-like antennae. A rope was knotted around his waist, the other end tied to a long branch. Gutgust and Skarper held on to the other end of the branch and managed to swing Spurtle over the tree where their friends lay imprisoned.

"Buzz," said Spurtle miserably, dangling there. He didn't feel like a bee and he didn't think he looked like a bee, and he was terribly afraid that if the others let go of that branch or the rope snapped then he would drop into the tree, and the tree would think he was another helping of dinner rather than a useful pollinator. He could see the pale glow of the flower below him, inside that cage of trunks. Tiny shapes were flying in and out of the cage, their wings shining softly in the light from the huge petals.

"Moths!" said Spurtle. "Skarper, I reckon it's moths what pollentates this flower, not bees at all!"

"Try making a noise like a moth, then!" called Skarper.

"What noise do moths make?' Spurtle asked.

"Anchovies!" growled Gutgust, sweating with the effort of keeping Spurtle airborne. Spurtle was the smallest of the goblins, which was why Skarper had chosen him to be the bee, but he was still quite a weight. The long branch was difficult to control, too; it kept swaying about with Spurtle dangling from the end of it like a fish on a line, crashing into the surrounding trees.

Skarper felt that sad, deflating-balloon feeling that always came to him when a brilliant plan turned out not to be so brilliant after all. "All right," he said. "Let him down. We'll have to think of something else."

Gutgust took the words "Let him down" a bit too literally. He simply let go of the branch. The weight of the fake bee was far too much for Skarper to support alone. The branch crashed down, and Spurtle fell with a terrified squeal right on top of the mantrap tree. His sudden arrival seemed to confuse it. It opened its cage of trunks, then closed them again as if to trap this new victim along with the others. But Skarper leaped forward and threw himself between two of the trunks before they could spring back together. He wasn't strong enough to hold them apart alone, but he shouted for Gutgust, and the burly goblin joined him, pushing with all his strength against the trunks as they struggled to close. Meanwhile, Skarper darted between his legs and dragged out Henwyn, then Zeewa. Then Skarper pulled Spurtle out, and Gutgust jumped clear and let the tree crash shut.

It kept opening and closing for a while after that, creaking and snapping as if it was angry at being robbed of its prey. But the goblins and their friends were far away by then, and at last it fell still, and the woods were quiet again.

The night was almost worn out, and the goblins were weary. They scrambled up to the hilltop on the far side of the woods, dragging Zeewa and Henwyn with them, and fell asleep there in a big heap. But Henwyn did not sleep for long: he had slept enough, and as soon as the sun showed its head above the Bonehill Mountains he was up and urging the others to awake and be on their way. "There is no time to lose!" he kept saying. "Rhind will be halfway to the sea by now!" In fact he was very embarrassed by all the trouble he had caused. All he seemed to do these days was get captured, first by Woolmarkers, then by a tree. He was well aware that he had almost got himself and Zeewa eaten when they were only a few hours' march from Clovenstone, and he was determined to make amends, and to take more care on the rest of this quest.

Before they left that place, Skarper skirted back round the edge of the wood to the road on the far side. He dragged a dead branch across it to make a barricade and propped a rock against the branch on which he scratched:

DANGER!
MAN EATING TREE* AHEAD!
DANGER!
*IT ALSO EATS LADIES

When he had finished he stood back to admire his work, and that was when he noticed the corner of an old board poking out of some bracken further down the hillside. That would have made a much better sign, he thought, as he went toiling down the steep slope to fetch it. But when he pulled it from the bracken

130

he found that it was a sign already. A few moments' searching and he found the rusty nail sticking out of the birch tree where it had once been hung.

So either it fell off by accident, thought Skarper, *or someone pulled it down and hid it. And I'm guessing that someone was Prince Rhind of the Woolmark. And I'm also thinking that pulling down and hiding danger signs is not very friendly...*

"Skarper!" There was Henwyn, a tiny figure on the hill beyond the woods, waving his arms, all eager to be off.

Skarper hammered the sign back into place with a rock and went running to join him.

They set off through the sunrise, and after a few miles they found Flegg and Grumpling, asleep on a hillock by the side of the road. Small hills humped up there, and a long, pinkish outcropping of stone stuck up through the turf on the summit of the one nearest to the road. Grumpling was sitting with his back against it, while Flegg had curled up like a dog in the wet heather nearby.

"Let's creep past and leave them there," suggested Zeewa. "They're no use to us, running off like that at the first sign of trouble."

"No," said Henwyn. "This is Grumpling's quest as well as ours. And we may yet have need of his strength, and Flegg's cunning." And he left the road and set off up one of the little wandering sheep tracks that led through the heather to the stone.

Grumpling opened one eye as Henwyn climbed towards him.

"I thought you was all getting eaten," he said. "That's what he told me." And he lashed out and kicked Flegg, who went rolling down the slope into a patch of tall thistles.

"I thought so too," said Henwyn. "But Skarper and the others all worked together and managed to save me."

Grumpling didn't look as overjoyed at this happy news as he might, but it was early, and he had slept badly, propped against that hard old rock. Flegg didn't exactly seem delighted either, but that was understandable since he was full of prickles.

"We're bound for the sea," said Henwyn, holding out a hand to help Grumpling up. "With luck, we may still catch that thief Rhind before he reaches Floonhaven and takes ship."

Grumpling didn't take the proffered hand. "I don't need no softling's help just standing up," he growled. He clambered to his feet, and after a good scratch he joined the others and they set off again, with Flegg hopping along behind, trying to pick the prickles from his paws.

Giants in the Earth

Over the morning moors came Fraddon, wading through the chest-deep mist which hung in all the valleys, and setting his feet down carefully in case there were farms or animal pens down there beneath the whiteness.

He had woken with the memory of a tiny voice that called his name, "Fraddon! Fraddon!", faint and far away. He had thought at first that it must be the memory of a dream, but then, as the sun rose, he had remembered how Henwyn had sat on that rock by the stream over there and talked to him about the goblins and some peril or other, and a quest. He started to wonder if they had set out on their quest, and decided that they probably had. And perhaps something had gone wrong with it, and it had been Henwyn or Skarper he had heard calling for help in the night.

So he had lifted his big feet, one by one, out of the earth and the weeds that had grown up around them. The twiglings scurried down out of his hair and beard, complaining in their rustly voices. He had stepped over the outer wall near Westerly Gate and set off across the moor, following the course of the Oeth and the old road that ran beside it.

The mist and the goblins were both long gone by the time he reached the wood in the dip of the road. He noticed the barricade which Skarper had made, the old danger sign and the new. The tallest trees in the little wood were not as tall as him. He squeezed his way between them, running his hands over their crowns of leaves. Not a bad wood, he decided, but something had gone wrong with it – and there at its heart he found the mantrap tree.

"Poor old thing," said Fraddon. "This is no place for the likes of you to grow."

The mantrap nipped at his huge fingers as he parted its trunks, making sure that none of his friends was trapped inside. When he was certain that it was empty, he carefully uprooted it and tucked it under his arm. He knew quiet corners in Clovenstone where a tree like this could grow. The magic in the soil would nurture it, and he would bring it deer or wild pigs sometimes, and have the twiglings make a fence around it to stop foolish goblins being trapped by it.

The tree stopped struggling when he lifted it up. He shook the soil from its trailing roots and tucked it under his arm, then stepped up on to the hill beyond the wood to see if he could see Skarper and his friends.

He couldn't, but he saw something else. A little way to the north, low hills clumped close to the road, and the sun shone warmly on a pinkish outcropping of rock. It was the rock that Grumpling had slept beside, but Fraddon didn't know that: it wasn't that which drew his eye to it and made him stride north and kneel beside it.

He set the mantrap carefully aside and started to brush away the earth from around the rock. It wasn't really a rock; not quite. It was becoming something, part stone and part something else. It was warm with more than just the sun's heat.

Perhaps there was a seam of slowsilver beneath this place, thought Fraddon. He tore the roots of the grass with his big, blunt fingernails. Perhaps the magic from Clovenstone had washed down with the waters of the River Oeth and found its way into these hills. He pulled back the turf like a green blanket. He brushed away the crumbs and clods of peaty soil, and revealed not bedrock, but a huge face, whose nose was the outcropping that had poked up through the grass.

Years and years and years ago, among the northernmost peaks of the Bonehill Mountains, Fraddon had seen rock faces like this: giants freshly budded from the ground, the earth's idea of a man. He had been one himself, in times that he could barely remember, dreaming his earth dreams before the giant he thought of as his father had helped him from the ground. He had not expected to find another here.

It looked so peaceful, that huge face, that he wondered if it would be right to wake the new giant. But now that the soil had been cleared away, the new giant could feel the warmth of the sun and the breath of the wind against his stony face. He stirred his limbs, the long hills moving sleepily beneath their coverlets of grass. He opened his eyes, deep and blue, like twin tarns. He looked up at Fraddon. . .

. . .Who thought, *What now? He will need to be told things and taught things, otherwise he'll rampage about like the wild giants of old, stamping people's houses flat and stealing cows by the handful, and never knowing any better. I can't take charge of him – I'm too old, too tired, too sad. . .*

But no one else was going to do it. There was no other giant within a thousand miles of that place.

The new giant smiled at Fraddon. He half raised his head, and laughed as the song of the birds and the sigh of the windblown grass trickled into the caverns of his ears. Loose stones tumbled from the hill of his chest as he sat up; streams changed their courses as his huge limbs heaved free of the earth.

He was three, four, five times as big as Fraddon. *I had not realized how small I'd grown*, thought Fraddon. He was almost afraid of the new giant, but at the same time he felt something new beginning, just as he had all those years before when he had waded into the sea off Choon Head to pick up that lovely ship, and met Princess Ned.

He held out his hand, and the huge, stony-warm hand of the new giant grasped it, and the new giant laughed with a noise like landslides.

"Welcome to the world," said Fraddon, and then remembered that the new giant would need a name, and decided that he should be called Bryn, which means "hill" in the language of the Westlands. "Welcome to the world, Bryn!"

No Welcome in Ulawn

Henwyn, Zeewa and the goblins walked all morning, and by noon they could see the sea, which looked like a low blue-grey wall built along the northern horizon. The road swung west, running parallel with the coast through a high, bare country called the Wastes of Ulawn. What trees grew there were low and bent over by the wind, which came always from the north, bringing the salt smell of the sea with it. The people of that land seemed to spend their time building walls: long, crumbly, drystone walls which wandered aimlessly over the low hills, dividing the land up into tiny fields where squawking gangs of gulls hunted for worms.

Of the people themselves, there was little trace at first. The rare houses that the goblins passed were shut tight. Ploughs and carts stood abandoned in the fields.

At one farmstead a herd of red cows grazed, but they were the only sign of life. Grumpling wanted to kill one of the cows for snacks, but Skarper and the others persuaded him that that would not be friendly. He ate some seagulls instead, which made him do loud, feathery burps as they marched on.

And then, at last, they turned a corner and found the people of Ulawn waiting for them.

It did not look like a friendly crowd. They had made a barricade across the road with carts and barrels and old doors, and they crouched behind it, clutching pitchforks and scythes and other farm tools of the dual-purpose type that can be used for either farming or poking goblins.

"Begone, foul creatures!" shouted their leader, a large, red-faced woman with a flail. Beside her, a boy whirled a sling and sent one of the hard stones of the place whizzing through the air to hit Gutgust neatly in the middle of his narrow forehead.

"Anchovies!" said Gutgust in surprise, as the stone rebounded with a hollow thud.

Skarper and Zeewa shoved Henwyn to the front. It seemed pretty clear that these folk didn't like goblins, but everybody liked Henwyn.

"Greetings, good people of Ulawn!" said Henwyn, in his friendliest and most cheerful voice. "We are your neighbours from Clovenstone, and we are passing through this country on our way to Floonhaven. We seek Prince Rhind of the Woolmark and his companions. Perhaps they have passed this way?"

"Aye," said the red-faced woman. "That they have. And the prince warned us that you might be following behind him. Goblin raiders, come down from the Lych Lord's old towers to steal our houses and burn down our cattle."

"'Twas the other way round, Mags," said a man behind her.

"Don't matter which way round it were," said Mags, flushing even darker red. "No goblin shall cross our country! We have not forgotten the tales of olden times, when goblin gangs burned Oethmouth and Wainscott, and murdered the poor king of Porthstrewy."

"That's not fair!" said Henwyn. "That was ages and ages ago! Goblins are different nowadays. They aren't rampaging savages any more." He glanced behind him, and shuffled sideways to try and hide Grumpling, who was glaring murderously at the Ulawn folk and fingering his axe, his fangs caked with gulls' blood and feathers. "We don't want any trouble," he promised. "We need to find Prince Rhind."

"Prince Rhind told us you'd say that," said Mags, narrowing her eyes. "'There be human traitors running with these goblins,' he said, 'and they'll try to lull you with sweet words into letting them pass. But don't you go listening to them, for if you do, there will be blood and fire and death, just as there was when the King of Porthstrewy took pity on a goblin."

"Oh bother Prince Rhind," said Henwyn angrily. For, of course, it was only natural that the folk of Ulawn, living so near to Clovenstone, would still remember the dreadful things that goblins of old had done. Rhind had been clever enough to realize that, and to play upon their fears.

"Let's kill 'em all," said Grumpling. "And then we can eat their cows. These seagull birds in't very filling."

"I heard that!" shouted Mags, from behind the barricade. "I heard what that big goblin said!" A flurry of sling-stones fell upon the goblins, and also upon Henwyn and Zeewa, whose hides were not so thick. One of the people behind the barricade even had a bow, and shot an arrow which stuck through Skarper's hat. "Arrers!" screeched Skarper and Flegg and Spurtle. The travellers from Clovenstone retreated in an undignified scramble and gathered out of range to discuss their next move.

"I still say we kill 'em all," growled Grumpling.

"But there's only seven of us an' there's loads of them and they've got arrers!" complained Flegg.

"But we is goblins, an' they is only softlings," said Grumpling, fingering his axe.

"We're not killing anybody," said Henwyn. "We don't want people to start thinking that the goblins of Clovenstone are the kind of goblins who go about murdering their neighbours."

"They already do think that!" said Zeewa, ducking as a lucky slingshot ricocheted off a roadside boulder and dinged against Spurtle's rusty helmet.

"They only believe it because that rotten Rhind has been spreading lies about us," said Skarper. "Let's prove he's wrong."

The other goblins agreed. Apart from Grumpling, none of them wanted to have to fight those angry softlings, with their slings and arrers and pointy implements.

Henwyn fetched out his hanky and held it over his head as a flag of truce while he walked back towards the barricade.

"If we cannot pass this way," he said, "will you tell us of some other road that will take us to Floonhaven?"

"This is the only road," said Mags.

"Well, there is the old road," said one of the others.

"Be quiet," Mags snapped at him.

"'Tis all right, Mags. Not even goblins would be crazy enough to walk the old road."

"We are not crazy," said Henwyn. "Well, except for Grumpling. And possibly Gutgust. But our need is dire, and if this old road is the only way to reach Floonhaven, then that is the road that we shall walk. How do we find it?"

Mags looked doubtful. "Go back five mile or so, and it be the third turning on the left. But 'tis a dangerous way, Henwyn of Clovenstone. You and your goblins would be better just going home to your old towers."

"That we cannot do," said Henwyn. "We are on a quest, and we shall not turn for home till it is completed."

"Goblins on a quest?" snorted the Ulawn woman. "Whoever heard of such a thing?"

Henwyn shrugged and smiled and walked back to where his friends were waiting. He sensed that Mags was a kindly woman at heart, and he was waiting for her to take pity on him and to call after him and say that it was all right, the goblins could use this road after all. But she didn't. Prince Rhind had told his lies too well.

"There's another way," Henwyn told the goblins when he reached them. He took from his pack the map that Fentongoose had given him before they left Clovenstone. After peering at it for a long time he finally made out the old road which the Ulawn folk had spoken of, a faint, dotted line that wandered along the Nibbled Coast, a few miles north of where they stood.

"A cliff path?" asked Zeewa, who did not much like heights.

"A sea path?" asked Spurtle, who had heard that the sea could be dangerous.

"It is just what we need," declared Henwyn, rolling up the map again. "Why, if I had known it was there I would have gone that way to start with. It is probably quicker than this road, and we shall reach Floonhaven long before Rhind's gang. And the views will be lovely, and the sea air will do us all good!"

The Pebble and the Worm

The little harbour town of Floonhaven had been doing very well for itself recently. The houses which clustered on each bank of the River Floon had a plump, well-fed look, and the castle of King Hadow had recently had a new extension built.

The reason was tin. The cliffs on either side of the harbour were honeycombed with mile upon mile of old tin mines. For years, everyone had believed that they were empty, but King Hadow had recently employed some dwarvish miners, and they had discovered whole untapped seams. The ingots of tin which they mined left Floonhaven aboard merchant ships, and the money flowed back in.

Today, the little place was looking more prosperous than ever. This was because of the beautiful white ship that was moored in the harbour. When Prince Rhind began his quest he had sent envoys to Coriander with orders to charter the finest ship that the gold of the Woolmark could buy. The *Swan of Govannon* had set sail at once, and it had been waiting in Floonhaven for nearly a week when Rhind and his company finally came riding down the long road from Ulawn.

The ship was well-named, for she looked like a swan, so white and so graceful, with an elegant little castle at her prow and another at her stern. Long pennants streamed from her masthead, and more fluttered from the pikes of the little band of Floonish men-at-arms who stood on the quayside with King Hadow and Queen Harlyn and a choir of children who began singing, "Welcome, Visitors from the Land of Sheep" as soon as Prince Rhind and his companions came in sight.

Prince Rhind rode forward to accept their greetings, and many high and lordly words were spoken about friendship between Floonhaven and the Woolmark and the bold quest on which Prince Rhind would soon embark. But Prawl, waiting behind with Ninnis in her wagon, could not hear them. He sat there with the sea breeze ruffling his hair, gazing dopily at Breenge, until suddenly Ninnis tapped him on the shoulder with her wooden spoon.

"Your friends have escaped," she said.

"Oh good!" said Prawl, who had been worried about Henwyn and the others ever since Prince Rhind hid that danger sign – a most unprincely thing to do, in Prawl's opinion. He was glad to know that they had not been harmed by whatever danger it had been warning of. "How do you know?" he asked the cook. "Have you had another vision?"

Ninnis nodded. "They were turned back in the Waste of Ulawn. The farming folk would not let them use the road."

"I'm not surprised, after all those dreadful fibs Prince Rhind told about them. . ."

"But they are coming by another way," said Ninnis. "By the old road which runs along the cliffs."

"Oh!" said Prawl happily, and then, when he understood what that would mean, "Oh. . . You mean they're coming here?"

"Yes," said Ninnis.

"I'd better warn Prince Rhind," said Prawl. "He won't be pleased."

"No, he won't."

"And he can be very nasty when things don't please him."

"Yes, he can."

"He spoke very sharply to poor Breenge this morning when her horse stood on his toe."

147

"Yes, he did."

"So imagine what he'll say when I tell him we'll soon be up to our necks in goblins."

The cook beckoned him closer. She undid a little leather bag which she always wore at her belt, and opened it. Prawl tried to peer inside, but Ninnis quickly shut it again, after drawing out two little objects. One was a small pebble with the deep blue-grey colour of a stormy sky. The other seemed to be a small, dried-up worm.

"When you've given His Highness your news," she said, "go to the end of the harbour wall and drop these into the sea."

"What will that do?" asked Prawl.

"It will make Prince Rhind think that you're a wise sorcerer, working powerful magic on his behalf," said Ninnis. "I'm sure Lady Breenge will be impressed, too."

"Oh! Thank you, Ninnis!"

"Think nought of it, young man," said the cook, beaming at him. She watched as he hurried over to speak with the prince, then strode along Floonhaven's curving harbour wall. Her smile faded as he raised his hands and let the pebble and the worm fall into the sea. Her eyes were not twinkling any more in their usual friendly way; they were filled with a light of quite a different sort.

"*Winds of the wild north, do my will,*" the cook said under her breath. "*Worms of the dark deeps, heed my call. Find out the folk who dog our steps, and the cold sea take them all. . .*"

The Cliff Path

Old beyond reckoning was the road which ran along the Nibbled Coast. Once it had linked a dozen tiny harbours which had nestled in the mouse holes of the cliffs, but the sea had long since washed those harbours away, or else marauding goblins from Clovenstone in the black years had burned them, and tumbled their stones into the surf, and few used the old road any more. There was no need, anyway, since a far better road had been built inland, a road that was not forever being pounded and clawed and torn down by the wind and the wild sea.

But the old road ran there still, sometimes no more than a line in the grass on the clifftops, sometimes descending down long flights of stone-carved stairs into deep coves full of wave-boom and shingle-hiss, sometimes winding along the sheer cliff faces themselves, patched and splinted with rotten bridges of wet wood where the waves had gnawed whole sections away.

The goblins did not mind the look of it. They had all grown up bird's-nesting among the rooftops of Clovenstone, so horrible heights and rickety walkways did not bother them, but none of them trusted the sea. Even Skarper, who had seen the sea before, at Coriander, had never seen a sea like this. The Coriander sea had been blue and sparkling and playful. This northern sea was grey and fierce, a restless, snarling thing, rushing against the black rocks like some huge and hungry beast.

Zeewa did not mind the sea too much – she had crossed it in a small boat full of ghosts when she first came to the Westlands – but she was a girl of the wide Muskish savannahs, and that sheer drop on one side of the path appalled her. She was so afraid of falling that sometimes she felt a terrible urge to just step out into that gulf and get it over with.

As for Henywn, he was afraid of both the heights and the sea, but he was much too proud to admit it. Besides, this was the only road open to them; they had no choice but to walk it.

And at first it was not too bad. They had struck the old road in one of its gentler stretches. It ran over the high clifftops where foxgloves bobbed and nodded, and so long as they did not glance to the right they could pretend that they were walking in sunlit meadows rather than along the brink of precipices. When the steep stairways led them down into the coves they drowned out the surf-boom and shingle-hiss with a cheery marching song.

But as they went westward, their shadows lengthening behind them, the cliffs grew higher and the road grew worse. More and more often they found themselves creeping along ledges slick with spray and seagulls' droppings, high above the hungry breakers and the black rocks. They pressed themselves against the cliff face and edged along in a line, teeth chattering, soaked by the foam which burst high into the air each time a fresh wave broke, and which the rising wind drove hard against the cliffs.

Then, as if the ledges had not been bad enough, they came to a place where there was no ledge at all. The cliff that the road had been hewn into had fallen, and across the sheer new cliff face stretched a line of rotted wooden posts, driven into the rock like nails into a wall. These supported a ramshackle walkway of wet planks.

"We can't go along that!" said Zeewa.

"We must turn back!" said Skarper.

But the wind was worsening, and the road behind them was being lashed by huge waves. The cove that they had just come through was deep in swirling foam. There was no turning back.

"Curse them stupid softlings fer not lettin' us use their road!" shouted Flegg.

"I in't wastin' curses on them," said Grumpling. "I'm savin' mine fer the stupid softling what brought us this way instead."

Few of them dared to look down as they inched out on to the creaking plankway, but Flegg did.

"Eek!" he shrieked, pointing through one of the gaps which gaped between the boards. "Sea sperpents!"

"Sea *serpents*, you mean," said Skarper. And then, "What!?"

They all peered down, except for Zeewa, who was clinging to the slimy cliff face with her eyes tightly shut. A hundred feet below, the white sea writhed; the white sea roared; it worried and thundered at the jagged shore.

"I can't see no sea sperpents," said Grumpling.

"It's serpents," said Skarper.

"Flegg just saw a bit of driftwood, probably," said Henwyn.

"I know what I seed," said Flegg, stubbornly.

"There's no such thing as sea sperpents anyway," said Spurtle. And then he added, "Aaaargh!" Because at that instant a great snakey head on the end of a long, snakey neck reached lazily out of a wave, plucked him from the walkway, and vanished with him back into the sea, leaving nothing behind but a waft of fish-stinking breath to show his startled companions that they had not dreamed it.

"Spurtle!" yelled Skarper. He fell to his paws and knees on the planks, hoping he might see his batch-brother down there, clinging to a handy rock or swimming bravely in the boiling foam. He couldn't. He saw other things, though. Long, rolling, roiling things, tumbling and tangling in the waves.

"Sea sperpents, I mean serpents!" he shouted. "Loads of them! Thick as worms in a bait jar!"

Another head came rearing up and bared its sharkish teeth. They snapped shut on nothing as Skarper dodged nimbly sideways.

"Anchovies!" wailed Gutgust.

"I think anchovies are smaller, and not so bitey," said Henwyn, almost overbalancing and toppling off the walkway as he drew his sword. But the next serpent head that rose was too far away for him to strike at; it lunged at Zeewa, and Grumpling stepped in front of her and swung his axe at it. There was a thunk as if the blade had struck a tree. Blood spurted and steamed and the serpent dropped backwards, almost taking the axe and Grumpling with it.

After that, there came a lull in the attacks. The serpents, who were not fussy eaters, were busy squabbling over the one that Grumpling had killed. The waves that heaved against the cliff turned red as they tore it apart.

"Ick!" said Henwyn, staring down.

"Poor Spurtle!" said Skarper.

"Onwards!" shouted Zeewa.

Skarper heard her, but he couldn't move. He kept staring down into the tumble of foam and slimy bodies, waiting in vain for Spurtle to reappear. He had known from the outset that their quest might be dangerous, but he had not really understood it till now. . .

Zeewa took him by one arm and dragged him after her along the walkway. "Quickly," she said, "while they are busy feeding!" Skarper had the feeling that she almost welcomed the coming of the serpents, as if she was glad to have something to think about other than the danger of falling. "The road rises ahead!" she said. "Perhaps they cannot reach that high!"

Skarper doubted that; from what he'd glimpsed of the creatures, those coiling bodies were hundreds of feet long, and could quite easily reach straight to the clifftops. The mystery was, where had they come from, so suddenly and in such numbers? Surely they were creatures of the open ocean, not the Nibbled Coast?

But this was not a time for the pondering of mysteries. It was a time for not getting eaten by sea serpents. He took one last, despairing look for Spurtle, and let Zeewa hurry him on. The pathway of planks sloped steeply upwards, more perilous than ever, but his fear of it was forgotten now in his terror of the things below.

Henwyn was in the lead as the party slithered and stumbled to the top of the slope. The road ran high here, but it was still not high enough, for when one of the serpents below grew tired of eating serpent and decided to go in search of afters, its huge hissing head rose up level with Henwyn, eyeing him over the edge of the walkway. Festooned with barbels and trailing weed, pimply with barnacles, it bared its bone-saw teeth, but Henwyn drove his blade at it and it hissed with pain and fury and withdrew into the sea again.

"They're back!" shouted Henwyn, turning to his companions, but he need not have bothered – they had already worked that out for themselves. A dozen of the dreadful worms were flailing at the roadway, and Zeewa's spear and the swords and axes of the goblins shone in the dying light as they frantically fended them off.

Henwyn felt a terrible, cold fear clutch at him. Quests weren't meant to end like this, on lonely cliffs, with no survivors to tell the tale of how brave the last fight had been. Yet he could see no way out of this for any of them. The enemy was too many and too fierce, and soon it would be night, and they would have no light to see by except the corpse-lantern glow of the serpents themselves, whose eyes seemed to be faintly luminous.

Looking desperately for shelter, but not really expecting to find any, he turned to the cliff face. There, in a sort of natural alcove in the rock, he saw a door. It was such an unlikely sight in that wild place that he thought at first he must be dreaming it. He fended off another serpent attack – a slash with his sword, the hot blood freckling him, that maw full of bony daggers hissing fury as it flinched away – and looked again.

It *was* a door. A newish-looking door, made from stout timbers, with neat hinges and a handle of dark iron. He tried the handle, but it was locked, of course.

"Just our luck!" he muttered.

He threw himself against the door, but whoever it was who had decided to put a door in a cliff face on that lonely stretch of coast had been the sort of person who liked to do things properly. It did not budge an inch.

"Grumpling!" Henwyn shouted. "Here! We have need of your axe!"

The big Chilli Hat came blundering along the roadway, almost knocking Gutgust and Skarper into the sea as he barged past them. When he saw that it was only a door he was being asked to chop down, he looked almost offended. Grumpling was always happy to use his axe on anything, but he liked using it best on things which went, "Ow!" or "Argh!" Still, no serpents were attacking at that moment, so he shrugged and gave it a go.

One, two, three massive blows, and still the door held firm. A fourth, and it opened, swinging shattered on its hinges.

"This way!" shouted Henwyn, over the sea's roar and the battle's din. "There's a passage!"

"Where does it go?" asked Skarper.

"Who cares?" yelled Zeewa.

They scrambled through the doorway one at a time, Henwyn waiting until last so that he could fend off the hungry serpents with his sword. Then he followed his friends inside, into the darkness and the sudden silence, the smells of earth and the smells of stone.

"I hate caves," said Skarper. He said it in a small

voice, but the arched stone ceiling caught his words and made them echo: "*hate caves, caves, aves. . .*"

"I hate sea sperpents more," said Flegg, and for once, everyone agreed with him.

"Them sperpents ate Spurtle," said Skarper.

"Grumpling saved my life," said Zeewa, as if she had only just realized.

Grumpling looked defensive. "It wasn't on purpose."

"Has anybody got a light?" asked Henwyn, looking in his pouch and finding that his tinderbox was full of seawater, the kindling soaked.

Everybody else was in the same position. The sea had got into everything. Even the food they had carried from Clovenstone was mostly ruined.

"I hope there's something to eat in this cave," said Grumpling.

They stumbled on, deeper and deeper into the cliff, while the sounds of the sea and the angry serpents faded behind them. At last the echoes of their footsteps changed and they realized that they had emerged from the first passage into a bigger chamber. Water dripped somewhere nearby with faint, musical sounds.

"I really hate caves," said Skarper again.

"And we hate goblins!" came a voice from out of the darkness.

A light was kindled, a lantern lit. Its glow gleamed on armour, shield bosses and the blades of sharp weapons. On a ledge above the goblins' heads stood a group of dwarves, glaring fiercely down. From openings in the cavern walls came more dwarves, clutching pickaxes, swords and hammers, candles trembling on their helmets.

"Who are you?" they demanded, beards bristling with anger. "What goblin dares to trespass in the mines of the dwarves?"

Things in Tins

Dwarves and goblins were no longer at war. A truce had been arranged after the Battle of Adherak and the fall of the Giant Dwarf, and the dwarves had withdrawn quietly to their mines. But they still had no liking for goblinkind, and to find five goblins (along with two random "biglings", as they called human beings) wandering around in their tin mine as if they owned it must have come as a nasty shock.

For a long moment the two sides faced each other in the lantern light. Henwyn was afraid that they had escaped the jaws of the sea serpents only to die upon the blades of the dwarves.

Then one of the dwarves raised a sculpted steel-helmet visor and said in a surprisingly friendly and high-pitched voice, "Skarper? Henwyn? Is that you?"

"Etty!" said Skarper.

The dwarf maiden pulled her helmet right off and shook out her long, fair plaits. Round faced and rosy cheeked, she looked just as girlish as she had the previous year when Skarper had showed her around Coriander, yet she was clearly a person of importance here; the other dwarves lowered their weapons at her command, and one took the helmet from her.

"And Zeewa too!" she cried, running down off the ledge and hugging Skarper, Henwyn and Zeewa one by one, while the other dwarves looked on in embarrassment, and the goblins shuffled backwards for fear they might get hugged too. Since the dawn of time dwarves had hated goblins and goblins had hated dwarves, but if there was one thing both races could agree on it was that they didn't hold with a lot of soppy hugging.

Etty Durgarsdottir had always been a forward-thinking sort of dwarf, however, and was not afraid to adopt the customs of the biglings when she thought that they were good customs. She was the first dwarf maiden in all of dwarven history to become a surveyor rather than a dwarf-wife, and she showed her friends the silver badge of her office with pride.

"This is my first mine," she said happily. "The king of Floonhaven asked us here to help him reopen the old tin workings, and now we are digging whole new galleries and finding masses of good tin. Come, I'll show you the workface. . ."

"Did you say Floonhaven?" asked Henwyn.

"Aye. . ."

"That's where we are bound!" said Skarper. "This black-hearted villain called Prince Rhind pinched something from Clovenstone. . ."

"My scratchbackler," grumbled Grumpling.

"And we must fetch it back!" said Skarper. "It's terribly important!"

"Can't you scratch your backs with summat else?" asked Etty, then saw how very serious they all looked, and realized that they couldn't.

"Come to my house," she said. "There you can eat, and drink, and rest, and dry your wet things. Then I can set you on the dwarf road to Floonhaven. But first, I must show you my new invention!"

Etty was very proud of her new invention. When she first came to the Nibbled Coast, and discovered how much tin was left in these old Floonish mines, she had started to wonder what use it could all be put to – for dwarves do not greatly value tin, preferring iron and gold, silver and slowsilver. It was all very well shipping the ingots south for the human smiths of Lusuenn and Coriander to turn into cheap plates and bathtubs, but she was sure a dwarf should be able to think of some new and ingenious use for it. And after a few weeks of turning the problem over in her head, she had.

Unfortunately, dwarves didn't greatly value new ideas either, so none of the miners she worked with were very impressed. She was delighted to have a chance to show off her clever invention to Skarper, Henwyn and the rest of the company from Clovenstone.

They stripped off their soggy clothes and rinsed the sea's salt out of them, and hung them to dry in the mine's huge underground kitchens. Then Etty took them to her house – a two-storey cave hollowed out of the side of one of the old mines – and they sat in her parlour, wrapped in blankets and nibbling dwarven pasties, while she fetched out her new idea to show them.

It was a cylinder of tin, about as big as a beer mug, but with no handle, and both ends were sealed.

"Lovely!" said Henwyn.

"Very interesting," said Zeewa, politely.

"What is it?" said Skarper.

"I call it a tin can," said Etty. "You put food inside it."

"What sort of food?" asked Skarper with interest, licking pasty crumbs off his nose.

"Oh, soup, vegetables, sausages, pudding . . . anything you like!" said Etty. "Yes, Gutgust, even anchovies."

"How do you get the food in there?" asked Henwyn, picking up the tin can and looking at it. "There are no openings."

"You weld the lid on once it's been filled," said Etty proudly.

"Like a sort of metal pasty?" asked Skarper.

Grumpling snatched the tin can from Henwyn and bit it hard. "Ow! It's a bit crunchy."

"You are not meant to eat it!" said Etty, grabbing the tin and frowning at the dents Grumpling's fangs had made.

"'Ow do you opens it then?"

"With one of these," said Etty, and drew a small tool from her belt. "I call it a 'tin opener'. Watch. . ."

And, so saying, she cut the top off the can. There were sausages inside this one, preserved in brine, and their delicious, salty, sausagey aroma filled the little stone room. Grumpling swiped the tin back, emptied the sausages into his open mouth, swallowed the tin too, and belched loudly.

"Weren't you listening?" asked Skarper. "You aren't meant to eat the whole thing."

"The skin's the best bit," said Grumpling. "Like wiv baked potatoes."

"But why would anyone want armoured sausages?" asked Henwyn.

"Food stays fresh inside these tin cans for ages," said Etty. "The onion soup I canned six months ago is still as fresh as the day it went in. I think you could preserve things this way for years. That would be very useful for people in deep mines, where provisions are hard to come by."

"Or people on long sea voyages. . ." mused Henwyn.

"It's a very clever idea," admitted Zeewa. "How did you come to think of it?"

"It came to me in a dream," said Etty, and her eyes took on that faraway look which told her listeners that she was about to start recounting a mystical experience.

"It was soon after I came here," she said. "That was not very long after the Battle of Adherak, and I had many strange dreams around that time. I think I may have breathed in too much of the slowsilver fumes while Skarper and I were inside the Giant Dwarf, for they began to feel more like visions than dreams. Most faded as soon as I woke, but this particular one lingered in my memory.

"In my dream, I found myself in a strange land. There were tall buildings, higher even than the manhouses we saw in Coriander, and people moved around in magical carriages which needed no horses to

pull them. Everywhere there was noise, and light, and colour. Ahead of me I saw a huge building, easily as big as the High King's castle of Boskennack. And above its doors were great letters, wrought of coloured glass and lit from within by some enchantment. In the language of that place, which I was able to read in my dream, the letters spelled out: SUPERMARKET.

"In and out of that wide doorway went the people of this wonderful land. They were biglings, and most were pushing little carts of silver wire. These they filled with produce, which was piled high on all the shelves and stalls inside. I followed them in, and wandered wondering past caves of ice, and mountains of fruit and vegetables. There was more food there than I have seen in my whole life! And there seemed to be no stallholders; everyone was simply helping themselves to the stuff on display. And yet they all looked gloomy, as if visiting this super market was the most tedious of chores."

"I passed a bakery, and stalls of fine fresh fish, and went down an avenue lined with shelves. And upon those shelves, in endless ranks, I beheld tin cans. I did not recognize them as being made of tin at first, because they had been wrapped in paper, and the paper was painted with the most lifelike pictures of the food that was inside them. But when I picked one

167

off the shelf I realized at once what it was. I began tearing off the paper wrappings and studying the tins' construction, wondering at the craftmanship of the smiths who had made them. . ."

"And then what?' asked Skarper. He was the only one of the goblins who was still listening. The others had been so moved by Etty's description of all the food that they just sat there dazed, gurgling quietly to themselves.

"Then one of the guardians of the place approached me," said Etty, frowning as she tried to recall every detail of her dream. "I think she was a priestess, for she was dressed in a tabard of some fine coloured cloth, and she wore a brooch of strange design upon her breast, on which was written in gilded letters: Sharon Matthews – Junior Manager. And she spoke to me in the tongue of that country, saying, "Ere, what the blinking 'ell do you think you're doing?' And with that, my dream was over, and I awoke and found myself in my own bunk, here in the mine."

"Strange indeed," said Zeewa.

"Fentongoose says that there are other worlds beside this one," said Henwyn. "He says that sometimes the boundary between the worlds grows thin, and things may pass across it. So perhaps it was real, this super market that you saw."

"Perhaps," said Etty, her eyes still alight with the memories. "But whether it was real or merely a dream, the memory of it stayed with me. And one day when I was thinking what we could make from all this tin, my mind went back again to the super market. Our world too shall have tin cans, I decided. Except that in our world, no one seems to want them."

"But they're so useful!" Zeewa said.

Etty rolled her eyes. "Oh, you know what dwarves are like. My father Durgar and the New Council, up in Delverdale, they disapprove of everything that is not ancient custom, handed down to us from our great-great-great-great grandsires."

Henwyn had an idea. "We may soon be embarking on a sea voyage ourselves. Could we buy some of your tin cans to take with us?"

"A sea voyage?" said the goblins, horrified. After what had happened on the cliff road they never wanted to see the sea again.

Henwyn said, "Well, if we can't catch up with Rhind before he leaves Floonhaven we shall have to take ship ourselves, and go after him. And we shall need provisions, since all our provisions were spoiled by the sea."

"Or eaten by the sea sperpents!" said Flegg with a shudder.

"Like poor Spurtle," said Skarper, ears drooping again at the thought of their lost friend.

Etty frowned. "I hope you will be careful," she said. "I've talked to sea captains in Floonhaven, and they told me that the sea serpents are solitary creatures who live far out in the western deeps and keep themselves to themselves. I have never heard of so many swarming together, and so close to shore. It sounds to me as if they were conjured here by magic. This Prince Rhind must have a great and powerful sorcerer with him."

Henwyn scratched his head. "Well, he's got Prawl."

"But Prawl isn't great," said Skarper.

"Or powerful," agreed Henwyn.

"Or a sorcerer," said Skarper. "Not really. He's just a sort of . . . he's just Prawl."

Etty shook her head till her plaits swung. "It was some evil magic that called those creatures to the Nibbled Coast at the very moment you were passing along the cliff road. And what about the storm, blowing up like that at just the same instant? It is still howling about out there; listen to the water trickling down through the cliffs. Yes, it was magic, all right. Worm magic and weather magic. And someone must be at the root of it."

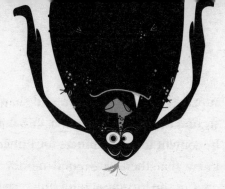

Floonhaven

A few miles away, at Floonhaven, Prawl was thinking the exact same thing. He did not know anything about the sea serpents, of course, but he had seen the storm, which struck the coast just to the east of the little town. It had been a sudden storm, and strangely *focused*, so that although it howled and raged against those eastward cliffs the sky above Floonhaven stayed clear, and the fishing smacks in the harbour barely stirred upon the calm mirror of the sea. And Prawl could not help noticing that those angry-looking clouds, spitting rain and lightning at the cliffs, were the exact same blue-black colour as the pebble which Ninnis the cook had given him: the pebble she had had him toss into the sea just before the storm began.

It made him wonder about Mistress Ninnis. She was a cheerful soul, and her apple turnovers were simply

171

superb. But didn't it seem odd that someone with the second sight and the power to conjure storms should be content to cook dinners for Prince Rhind? Everyone knew that there was good money to be made these days in the fortune-telling line (especially if you really could tell fortunes).

He would have liked to have properly looked inside that little leather bag which dangled from her belt. He would have liked to examine some of the other ingredients which Ninnis kept, bagged and bottled, in her wagon. He would very much have liked to have read the huge old leather-bound book she often consulted, with those strange runes embossed upon its cover, over which she had pasted a brown paper label bearing the handwritten word RECIPES.

But it was too late by then. The cart and horses had been sold, and King Floon's men were busy loading the contents aboard the *Swan of Govannon*. Prince Rhind was determined to leave with the tide that very evening. As soon as Prawl told him that the goblins were still behind them he had flung himself into the business of lading the ship and getting himself and his companions aboard.

He had tried telling King Floon about the goblins, hoping that he might turn the people of Floonhaven against them just as he had the farming folk of Ulawn, but King Floon had only said, "So the goblins are coming, are they? I shall be glad to see them. Excellent fellows nowadays, from all I've heard. I'm very partial to that cheese of theirs."

"Oh yes!" agreed Queen Harlyn. "My brother, Lord Ponsadane, told us how bravely they fought the Giant Dwarf at the Battle of Adherak. And Henwyn of Clovenstone is very handsome, they say."

"It is such a pity that you are in so much haste to leave," King Floon protested. "We had been hoping that you might stop with us at the castle. We had prepared a feast, with dancing and jugglers and a roast pig with an apple in its mouth and all that sort of thing. Perhaps we could invite Henwyn and the goblins to join us, if they arrive in time?"

"Nothing I'd like better," said Rhind, "but, alas, our quest must come first. We mean to raise Elvensea, and we must do it while the moon and stars are right, the tides just so. Give our love to Henwyn and those peculiar friends of his!"

"We must hope they don't get too badly delayed by that storm," said Ninnis, and looked towards the east, where the blue-black clouds still hung above the Nibbled Coast and reached tongues of lightning down to lick the cliffs.

*

Safe inside the dwarven mines, Skarper and the others put their dry clothes on again and loaded their packs with Etty's tin cans.

The tins were heavy, and when Etty called Skarper aside and said she had a gift for him he was not sure that he could carry it. But the thing she gave him, wrapped in soft cloth, was small, and weighed almost nothing. It was a silver chain, delicate but very strong. Hanging from it was a dark stone, smaller than a hen's egg, and criss-crossed with threads of bright ore.

"It is slowsilver," she said. "It is supposed to bring good fortune. My father gave it to me, but I am quite safe here in my mine, and you, setting off over the wide sea. . . I think you will have more need of it than me. You can wear it around your neck, beneath your tunic."

Skarper was not sure what to say. He was a goblin, and had a goblin's love of shiny stuff, but he knew that this amulet was worth more than money to Etty.

"I am sorry about poor Spurtle," Etty said, while he stood there wondering whether he should refuse it.

"Oh, all goblins die sooner or later," he replied, trying to sound careless. "Hatchlings are forever falling off the towers at Clovenstone, or blowing each other up, or getting squashed. It's amazing Spurtle lasted as long as he did, really."

But he was sorry, too. It was not just Clovenstone that had changed since the Keep fell. The goblins themselves were different; they were finding ways to deal with other goblins that did not just involve hitting them. The downside of that was, they cared about each other more, and the loss of one of them hurt the others. Losing Spurtle had felt as bad as losing Princess Ned.

And then he realized that that was why Etty wanted him to take her lucky stone – to try to stop him ending up like poor old Spurtle. So, although he didn't put much faith in amulets, he looped the silver chain over his head.

"Thank you," he said. "And when I return from over the wide sea, I shall bring it back to you."

"Skarper," she said, "you are the sweetest of goblins."

"Shhhh!" said Skarper. He didn't want one of the others hearing that. Sweet is the last thing a goblin wants to be.

One of the first improvements that Etty and her friends from Delverdale had made when they took over the old Floonish mines was to dig a long tunnel linking them to the harbour at Floonhaven. It was too flat to run one of their cunning gravity-assisted railways along, but there were carts, and a small stable of diremoles

175

to pull them. Into one of these carts climbed Henwyn, Zeewa and the goblins, wrinkling their noses at the mole's earthy stench, and trying not to remember how frightening those vast underground beasties had been when they had faced them in battle.

But this diremole – whose name was Butterscotch – seemed peaceable enough. She was a sleepy creature, and in place of the spiky armour of the fighting moles, she wore only the harness which the cart was hitched to, and a big candelabra like a rack of antlers strapped to her blunt velvet head.

A small ladder ran up the side of the harness. Etty climbed up it and perched on the mole's back. She poked the mole with a spiky-ended stick which she kept up there for the purpose, and they were off, trundling along the smooth floor of the tunnel while Henwyn tried to explain the difference between stalagmites and stalactites.

They had little idea how much time had passed while they were inside the dwarven mine. It was only when they emerged on a green hillside above Floonhaven that they realized a whole night had passed. The last stars were fading from the sky, the sun was showing signs of getting up, and far, far out across the calm and pearl-grey sea a single white sail shone.

"Prince Rhind?" asked the Floonish harbour

master, opening the door of his cottage at Henwyn's knock and blinking in surprise to find a diremole and a cartload of goblins parked at the end of his garden. "Oh, what a shame, you've just missed him. The *Swan of Govannon* set sail late last night, before the tide turned." He pointed westward, where that pure white sail was just vanishing into the faint band of mist where sea met sky.

"Bumcakes!" said Skarper.

"Bother!" said Henwyn.

"Anchovies!" grumbled Gutgust.

"We must go after it!" said Zeewa.

The goblins all looked aghast. Set out across that heaving, serpent-haunted wetness in a boat? They didn't even feel it was a good idea to be standing on this harbourside.

They breathed sighs of goblinny relief when the harbour master spread his hands and said, "Go after it? I'm sorry, but you can't. There are no sea-going ships in Floonhaven at present. Only our little fishing boats, which aren't big enough to carry all of you, let alone go setting out so far across the sea. None of them could catch the *Swan* anyway."

"So that is the end of our quest," said Henwyn. "Rhind has beaten us, and all we can do is wait to see what evils he unleashes with the Elvenhorn."

177

The others weren't listening. They were staring at some fisherfolk a little further out along the harbour wall, who were winching a strange object out of one of the little boats.

A sofa-shaped object, its flowery cushions dark with seawater.

"Spurtle?" Skarper whispered.

"Spurtle!" Henwyn shouted.

They ran to where the fisherfolk were untangling the sofa from their nets. "'Twas floating off Brisket Point," a fishwife said. "I wonder where it come from?"

"It's Spurtle!" shouted Skarper, furiously plumping the sofa's cushions. The fisherfolk looked on as if they thought he was mad. But after a moment the sofa coughed, shuddered, shrank, and turned into a very wet and rather tattered-looking goblin.

"Spurtle! You're alive!" laughed Henwyn.

"Well, of course I am," said Spurtle, shaking vigorously to get the water off. "That's the great advantage of being a were-sofa. I transformed into my sofa form when that sea sperpent ate me. They may eat goblins, but they don't like furniture, and it soon spat me out."

"He didn't choose to turn into a sofa," said Flegg. "It just happens when he's scared."

Spurtle glowered at him. "Then," he said, "I swam to safety."

"I don't know about 'swimming'," said one of the fisherfolk. "He was just floating around in the sea when he got caught in our nets."

"Well, swimming or floating, we are glad to see you, Spurtle," said Henwyn.

"We are!" agreed Skarper.

"Anchovies!" said Gutgust.

"So how's the questy thing going?" asked Spurtle. "Have I missed much?"

Their smiles faded. "It's over," said Skarper.

"You mean we've got the elf hooter back?"

"No," said Henwyn. "Rhind has it still. He is sailing to Elvensea, and there is no way that we can follow him."

"Perhaps there is," said Etty. "Come, we'll go and see King Floon. I'm sure he'll be able to help. He's a nice old king."

Indeed he was. "Prince Rhind told us you'd be coming!" he chuckled, welcoming his visitors, and ordering his servants to fetch the leftovers from last night's feast. There had been rather a lot of leftovers, because the Woollenfolk had had to leave so early, and King Floon was sure they would do pretty well as breakfast. "Such a pity you missed them," he said.

"A pity indeed," said Henwyn, and told him the whole story.

"A thief? Rhind? Really?" Floon was astounded.

"But he was so well spoken!" said Queen Harlyn. "And *so* good looking and nicely brought up."

"It just goes to show," said Floon. "A fair face may hide a foul heart, and a lordly manner may conceal a nasty, thieving nature that will snitch your Elvenhorn before you can say 'boo'. It's valuable, is it, this horn thingy? I saw it hanging round Rhind's neck, but I didn't realize it was anything special. Looked a bit tatty, in fact."

"It's good fer scratchlin' yer back," said Grumpling.

"Also for raising the lost land of Elvensea from its centuries-long slumber beneath the Western Ocean," said Skarper.

"Yes," agreed Queen Harlyn. "Rhind mentioned something about that. But if that's his plan, well, that's a good thing, isn't it? The elves were beautiful and wise, with lovely singing voices. We could do with a bit of their wisdom about the place again. Couldn't we?"

"Fair face may hide a foul heart," Henwyn reminded her. "Fentongoose and Doctor Prong, who are very wise, reckon that there could be a dire danger at Elvensea. Best to leave it where it lies, they say. But Rhind does not know that, and it is our fear that he may unleash this ancient evil by accident."

"That's why we must go after him," said Zeewa.

"An' chop him into little bits," added Grumpling.

"Not necessarily," said Henwyn. "Perhaps if we warn Rhind of the peril, he'll realize his mistake and give the Elvenhorn back."

"An' *then* we can chop him into little bits," insisted Grumpling, who was very reluctant to abandon the chopping-Prince-Rhind-into-little-bits part of the plan.

"But your harbour master told us there is no ship in Floonhaven which can carry us where the *Swan of Govannon* has gone," Skarper said.

"No, indeed," said King Floon. Then he brightened. "Well, perhaps there is! Captain Kestle does not sail much nowadays, but that old ship of his is still sound, I believe? It is moored upstream a way, behind the town. Come, we shall hurry there at once, and see if he will agree to take you!"

When kings say things like, "Hurry," and, "At once," they do not mean quite the same things as common folk. It took an hour or more for King Floon to get ready, with his royal walking garb and his procession of servants carrying flags and provisions for the journey; another hour to make their slow way through the town and into the woods behind it. And when they finally went down through those woods and saw the River Floon glittering through the trees and the old ship moored at the quay there, they knew that all hope of catching up with the swift-sailing *Swan of Govannon* had gone.

The ship was as unlike a swan as anything could be. Squat and black she was, with a ramshackle house of tarred timbers built on her deck and a rust-coloured sail furled on her single mast. The only thing Skarper knew about ships was that the pointy end was called the prow and the blunt end was called the stern or the mainbrace or something, but both ends of this ship were blunt, rounded like the toe and heel of a shapeless old shoe. Weeds had grown up waist high between the stones of the quay, and the whole place seemed long deserted, but the ship was still afloat, and from the iron chimney of her deckhouse came a faint dribble of woodsmoke.

"She is called the *Sea Cucumber*," said King Floon. "A fine vessel, though less modern and more traditional than Prince Rhind's. Old Captain Kestle took long voyages in her once – sometimes went as far as Porthquidden, I believe. He is a proper old sea dog."

"Go away!" snapped a voice from inside the deckhouse when the servants had cleared a way through the nettles and brambles for the king and called out to tell Captain Kestle that he had visitors.

"He doesn't *sound* like a dog," said Spurtle.

"Come, Kestle," said the king. "These good people seek passage on your ship!"

"I'm retired," said the voice. "I'm old and I'm tired and I'm grumpy, and I've retired from the sea."

"Oh look here, Kestle," said the king, "I am your king! This is a matter of importance. I'm ordering you to take these passengers!"

The door of the deckhouse creaked open just a tiny crack. An eye glistened like a pickled egg, peering out at the little crowd upon the quay. "You're king on the land, Floon," said the voice, coming from somewhere just below the eye. "I live on the water, and no man commands me, only the winds and the tides."

"Please!" said Skarper, stepping out cautiously on to the rickety gangway which was propped between the shop and the quay. "It's very important! We have to catch up with Prince Rhind!"

"Goblins, are you?" A beardy, scowling face appeared around the eye as the deckhouse door opened a crack wider and let a little sunlight in.

"Some of us. Also Henwyn of Clovenstone and Zeewa of the Tall Grass Country, two human beings."

There was a snort, and the door shut with a snick. "I don't carry goblins. Goblins is stone-born; creatures of the earth and the land. They don't know anything of the sea and her ways."

"That's why we need your help, old man!" shouted Zeewa.

"Get you gone," Kestle called back tetchily. "I haven't the time to sit here talking."

A little shuttered window in the side of the deckhouse opened, and he flung the remains of last night's supper at his visitors: an old brown apple core and a plateful of tiny fish bones with the heads and tails still attached. Skarper and the others scattered backwards and stood picking the bones out of their hair and clothes.

"Bumcakes," muttered Skarper.

"Bother," said Henwyn.

"Anchovies!" said Gutgust.

"Eh?" The window opened again, and Kestle stuck his head out. It was an ugly head and had looked better when they could only see a part of it through the crack in the door. "What's that you said?" he demanded.

They all looked blank.

"Anchovies?" said Gutgust.

"So goblins *do* know something of the sea!" said Captain Kestle. It was pure luck, but those fish he had just thrown at them had been anchovies. And now that he was leaning out of his stuffy little cabin, breathing the clean sea air, the notion of another voyage suddenly seemed more appealing. He had let himself believe that he was too old for sailing any more, but he could hear the waves beating on the sandbar at the river's mouth, and feel his tired old ship stirring under him as the tide began to turn. And if this rag-tag gang of goblins and landlubbers really wanted to go to sea, well, someone had to take them. . .

"I've got no crew, of course," he said doubtfully. "You'll have to help me sail her."

"Of course!" said Henwyn.

"Zeewa once made the crossing from Musk," said Skarper, "finding her own way by the stars. Gutgust can act as chief anchovy-spotter, and the rest of us will haul on whatever ropes you want us to."

"And we can cook for you," said Henwyn. "Etty here has supplied us with a wide range of foodstuffs, ingeniously tinned."

"And where is it that you hope to sail to?" asked Kestle.

"We want to catch the *Swan of Govannon*," said Henwyn. "I don't suppose there is much chance of that in this old ship, but we must try."

"The *Swan*?" Kestle spat contemptuously downwind. "I saw her in Floonhaven yestereve. A frail, pale toy I thought her, more suited to a child's bathtub than the open sea. My *Sea Cucumber* shall overhaul her in no time. But we must leave sharpish, while the tide is with us!"

*

Sea captains are not like kings. When they talk about doing something sharpish, sharpish is what they mean. Henwyn, Zeewa and the goblins had scarcely scrambled aboard with their heavy packs before the *Sea Cucumber* was moving away from the quay, out into the open river, where the ebbing tide caught her and drew her faster and faster towards the harbour and the sea beyond. Kestle's gruff voice could be heard bellowing briny curses at his new shipmates as they struggled with ropes and tackle and unfurled the sail. It hung limply at first, dropping a few startled moths and spiders who had been living happily among its folds. Then, as the ship passed the tiny stone-built lighthouse on the end of the harbour wall, an east wind found her, the sail filled, her head swung towards the Western Ocean, and white water began to show under her forefoot.

Etty, the king, and a host of Floonishfolk lined the harbour wall, waving hats and handkerchiefs and calling out, "Good luck!" and "Come back soon!" But it was doubtful that anyone aboard the *Sea Cucumber* could hear them. The wind was singing in her rigging, the foam went rippling down her sides, and she was bound for the high seas.

All at Sea

The seas that lapped the shores of the Westlands were wide and dangerous, and few ships crossed them. Most captains preferred to stay within sight of shore, edging from one harbour to the next, and anchoring safe when nightfall came or dirty weather threatened. Especially nowadays, with so much old magic stirring, and mermen, sea serpents and sirens added to the ordinary dangers posed by storms and shoals.

Only a few were bold or foolhardy enough to venture out across the wide ocean. Captain Kestle had been one of the brave ones, always eager to see what lay over the curve of the world. When he was a younger man, he had travelled to all sorts of strange lands. He'd sailed so far, in fact, that he believed he had been everywhere, and that was why he had anchored up in the River Floon and tried to put his wandering years behind him. He could not see the point. Why go somewhere twice? He had seen everything, or so he'd thought.

But sea-going goblins – this was something new! And this lost land young Henwyn told him of – Elvensea. . . He had heard of it, but only as a legend. He'd never be able to set foot on it, of course, not if the goblins' quest succeeded and it stayed drowned beneath the waves. But perhaps he would be able to look down upon its spires and streets through the water.

"I was born in the Autumn Isles," he said, pointing south-west to where the rocky hills of Hoonish, Wedge and Far Penderglaze showed like dim blue cut-outs in the haze. "The old folk there told tales of Elvensea. Of how the elves retreated there when men and dwarves and goblins came to live in all the other lands. And then, when Elvensea was sunk, they went into their ships and sailed away across the sea to find new lands for themselves, beyond the sunset."

Far Penderglaze fell behind them, and the *Sea Cucumber* sailed on, while her new crew practised knots and baled out the water which seeped in through the old ship's timbers to slosh about her hold, and her captain fixed his gaze on the far horizon and imagined the proud towers and shady streets of Elvensea.

*

A hundred miles ahead, the *Swan of Govannon's* captain had his eyes on the horizon, too, but he was not thinking about Elvensea. Prince Rhind had been careful not to tell him or any of his crew where they were going. "Sail west," was his only order, "along the path of the setting sun."

"But where are we going, Your Highness?"

"Nowhere."

"So how shall we know when we get there?"

"Because I shall tell you."

The captain of the *Swan* was called Woon Gumpus, and he was the other sort of sea captain – the foolhardy sort.

He had not been a captain at all until a few months earlier. He had worked at a bank, high on one of the steep hills of Coriander, counting the gold and silver that Coriander's merchants brought back from their journeys to Musk and Barragan and Tyr Davas. The little window of his counting house had looked out over the blue waters of the bay, and he had often sat there watching the ships come and go, their coloured sails as bright as petals. How he had longed to leave his stuffy little hole and sail away with them! The sea, the sea! That was a man's life, all right – far better than counting coins.

So when his auntie died and left him her fortune,

he gave up the banking life at once, and spent the whole lot on the *Swan of Govannon*. He had consulted a seeress called Madam Maura, and she had peered into the depths of her oracular bathtub and told him that sea cruises would be all the rage in future. Great white ships would be built, she said, and people would sail off in them, not with any destination in mind, but simply for the joy of sailing. There would be swimming pools on board, and games of deck quoits, and entertainment in the evenings.

Most people scoffed at Madam Maura's visions, but Woon Gumpus saw at once that she was on to something. He had his shipwrights fit a copper tank into the *Swan*'s deck, which the grumbling crew filled with water every morning in case the passengers wanted to bathe. He had a court laid out where they could play quoits, and hammered metal hoops into the deck to make a croquet pitch. He had no luck persuading any of Coriander's minstrels to come along as on-board entertainment, but luckily he had a passable singing voice himself, and he could sing "The Ballad of Eluned" and "I Left My Heart in Up-Brundibar", while accompanying himself upon the hurdy-gurdy.

The only thing he didn't have, in fact, were passengers. He had found it impossible to find anyone willing to sail with him. He had been starting to think that people were right to dismiss Madam Maura as a loopy old hedge witch who had spent too long breathing in the fumes of her own bath salts. But then Prince Rhind's envoys had arrived, clad in the rich felts and ceremonial knitwear of the Woolmark, looking for a ship – and Woon Gumpus had known that this was his chance. It was true that he had never imagined sailing far beyond the Bay of Coriander, but how hard could it be to sail the Western Ocean? You just had to point the ship west and let the wind do the work, didn't you? And when Prince Rhind and his companions had had enough of sailing around out there, and had seen some mermaids and sea cows and whatever other novelties the Western Ocean had to offer, why, he'd just turn round again and wait for a wind to blow them back to shore.

Easy, thought Woon Gumpus smugly, and began to sing another of his party pieces, "The Cabbage Picker's Love Song".

"Shoals to starboard, cap'n!" roared a sailor, from the crow's nest high on the mainmast.

"Eh?" said Woon Gumpus, who had just been getting to the good bit. "What?"

"Dirty big rocks, your honour."

"Oh!" Woon Gumpus squinted into the bright

sunshine reflected from the waves. Ah, yes, those were rocks, all right. Black, barnacled boulders, each the size of his old counting house, lying in wait there in a swirl of foam to rip the bottoms out of unwary ships. "Go right! I mean port! I mean starboard!"

He was always getting port and starboard muddled. To be honest, he got left and right muddled, too. But luckily the helmsman had already swung the tiller, and the *Swan of Govannon* went gliding past the reef as gracefully as – well, as a swan.

Oh, yes, thought Woon Gumpus, sailing was easy. This was the life, all right!

Prince Rhind was contented, too. So was his sister Breenge. They had come safely through goblin country, the Elvenhorn was theirs, and in a few more days they would reach Elvensea and the ending of their quest. Until then, they planned to while away the time lounging in the sunshine on the *Swan's* decks, swimming in the little pool, playing games of quoits and deck-croquet, and wondering what Ninnis would produce for supper. The only thing they had to worry about was the danger that the captain might to try to entertain them with another of his dreadful songs.

"But if he does," said Breenge, "you can have him clapped in irons and let the first mate steer the ship instead. You are a prince, after all."

Down in the *Swan's* galley, among the pots and pans and the smell of the simmering stew, Mistress Ninnis was not so happy. Peering into the little crystal ball she kept hidden in her second-best saucepan, she had seen Henwyn and the others boarding that old ship at Floonhaven.

Curse them! She had thought her storm and the sea worms would have finished them, or at least finished most of them, and frightened the others into giving up their quest. Her crystal had shown her those plankways on the cliffs and they had been quite bare of goblins. So where had they gone to, if not into the sea and the bellies of her worms?

And then she had seen who stood waving beside the king of Floonhaven as the goblin ship set sail – a small, stocky person, long blonde plaits blown out horizontal by the breeze that filled the ship's sail. A dwarf maiden! And there were dwarf mines in those cliffs. So the dwarves had taken them in! She had not seen it sooner because dwarf mines were full of magic; the old smithy magic of Dwarvendale, which Ninnis's powers were not strong enough to see through.

Not yet, at least. Not until foolish Prince Rhind delivered her to the shores of Elvensea, and the powers of the elves became hers.

She undid the little bag on her belt and felt inside, but there was nothing there that she could use to harm the goblins. That dried sea-worm larva had been her last; the storm pebble too. All she had left were a few seeds, a jewel from a toad's head and a clothes peg. The seeds and the jewel were earth magic, no use at sea, and the clothes peg was not magical at all.

"But never mind, Ninnis," she muttered to herself. "They'll not catch this fine ship, not in that old black washtub of theirs. By the time they find us we shall be at Elvensea, and I shall have a thousand new spells to fling at them."

She wrapped the crystal up, put it back in her second-best saucepan, and replaced the lid. She checked the bubbling stew, said under her breath, "A little more sage, I think. Now where did I leave that? In my pack, I suppose, which is in my cabin. . ." And Prawl, who had been watching all of this through a tiny gap between the planks of the galley door, drew quickly back into the shadows of the passageway outside as she left the galley and went bustling off to her quarters.

He did not like what he had heard. He did not like it one bit. It was starting to seem to Prawl that he was not dealing with a cook at all, but with something far more worrying: a sorceress.

He waited until she was out of sight, then carefully lifted the latch on the galley door and went inside. The floorboards creaked, but who would notice a creaking floorboard with the ship at sea and so many other creakings, squeakings and flappings of canvas going on?

He could tell that Ninnis did not mean to be gone long, because she had left her big book open on a worktop near the galley stove where that huge pot of stew was bubbling. Wiping the steam from his spectacles, he drew the old book closer to the light of the stove and peered at the pages. And what did he see there? Those crabbed lines of ancient letters marching across the parchment like squads of broken spiders. . . Those mysterious diagrams, spirals overlaid on triangles overlaid on crescents and pentangles and shapes for which he knew no names. . .

One thing was for sure. It was not a recipe for fish stew.

"This has gone far enough!" said Prawl to himself. He quickly let himself out of the galley. "Prince Rhind must hear of this," he said.

Behind him, in the empty galley, a bitter new smell began to mingle with the scents of the stew. Prawl had left the old book much too close to the heat of the stove. The edges of its thick pages were starting to crisp and curl, and the ink on the diagrams was bubbling.

Prawl did not realize that he was being watched as he scurried up the *Swan of Govannon's* elegant companionways, out on to the deck. Ninnis, coming back from her cabin with the sage, had heard those creaking footsteps in her galley. Hiding outside, she saw him leave, and she whispered a spell.

Prince Rhind was standing in the little white castle at the ship's prow. He was gazing at the sea ahead, which was turning golden now as the *Swan of Govannon* sailed towards another sunset, and wondering what awaited him in Elvensea. Behind him, Breenge wallowed in the copper swimming pool, wearing a felt bathing dress that made her look like a seal.

Prawl, coming from the back of the ship, had to walk past Breenge to reach the prince, and he was slightly bashful about doing so. He hesitated a moment, wondering what one should say to a princess of Tyr Davas in her bath. Should he pretend he hadn't seen her? But that might seem rude, and also unlikely – it was hard to miss someone as large as Breenge, especially now that she was swimming on her back, kicking up those frothy fountains of white water with her feet and singing shepherds' songs from her homeland.

He decided that he should just nod politely and

hurry on up to the forecastle for a word with her brother. But as he strode past the pool he realized that something strange was happening.

It began with an itching in his ears. Then he noticed that the ship was growing larger. The gunwales, which had come up only to his waist before, were suddenly high above him. The masts, no thicker than trees when he came aboard, suddenly had the girth of castle towers. Not only that, his clothes seemed to be growing, too; his robe expanded until it was more like a tent, and a big tent too, engulfing him and hampering his movements. He waded and floundered through its folds of felt.

"Sorcery!" he realized.

He kicked his way out of the robe and hurried on along the wide wooden plain of the deck. Although the sea was calm, the deck seemed to be tilting at a strange angle, as if it were rising towards him. He could only cross it by putting his hands down and going on all fours.

"Prince Rhind!" he shouted. But all that emerged was a plaintive little squeak. The prince, deep in his thoughts, did not hear it. But Breenge did. She stopped splashing and bobbed over to the side of the pool. When she peered over the edge, the first thing that she noticed was Prawl's shabby old robe lying crumpled on the deck. Really, she thought, who would have imagined that sorcerers would be so untidy? But before she could complain, or call for a sailor to pick up the robe and deliver it to Prawl's cabin, she noticed something else.

Hopping about on the deck, just at the foot of the steep stairs which led up on to the forecastle, was the dearest little white rabbit.

Breenge hauled herself out of the pool. (The water had started to grow unpleasantly hot anyway, making her feel as if she were a lobster being slowly boiled alive for someone's dinner.) She wrapped a towel around herself and went to scoop up the rabbit, which made small frightened noises and rolled its eyes at her as she cuddled it. "There, there," she cooed. "Don't be frightened, little bunny. How on earth did you get aboard?"

Ninnis, watching from the far end of the ship, smiled a smug little smile to herself. "That's the last time you'll try to make trouble for me, Mister Prawl," she said. "And now Breenge will love you, just as you always wished."

But Prawl had made more trouble than she had realized. Instead of following him up on to deck to watch and gloat as her rabbit spell transformed him, she should have gone down into the galley. If she had, she might have seen her spellbook smouldering there

beside the stove, and had a chance of
saving it before it burst into flames.

But she hadn't, and she did not realize the danger
until she noticed the steam wisping up off the surface
of the swimming pool, which was directly above the
galley. Then she guessed, and went running back
below, but it was already too late. When she flung the
galley door open, air rushed in and fire rushed out. A
tawny torrent of flames, playful as a young lion, pawed
at her pinafore and singed her eyebrows off.

"Fire!" screeched Ninnis. The sailors heard her, and
took up her cry. First they ran for buckets and hoses.
Then, when they saw how far the blaze had spread,
they ran for the boats.

"Fire! Fire!"

Prince Rhind and Breenge stood on the forecastle,
Breenge holding the rabbit, all three of them wondering
what to do. After a while Woon Gumpus appeared
too, clutching his hurdy-gurdy and blinking at them
through a mask of soot. "It seems that a small fire
has broken out," he shouted, over the noise of the
crackling flames, which had burst up through the deck
and were gathered around the mast, leaping up to lick
at the sails like wolves nipping at the toes of a tree-
bound traveller.

"What shall we do?" asked Breenge.

"Oh, it is nothing to worry about," said Woon Gumpus. "We are at sea, and it stands to reason that that is the safest place to have a fire. All this water will soon put it out."

"Then why are your sailors scrambling into those little boats?" asked Breenge. "Why are they launching them? Why are they rowing away so fast, and shouting things like, 'Save yourselves, mateys, 'tis all over with the barky'?"

"Oh, you know these seafaring types. Superstitious and easily spooked. They'll soon have the flames out."

The main sail caught fire with a massive *woof*, and transformed into a blinding golden rectangle of flames, like the window into a furnace. Everyone on the forecastle took a step back as the heat scorched their faces. Through the rippling air above the deck, through the smoke, the rising and the falling sparks, Ninnis came scampering to join them, patting at her skirts to put out the fires that had started there.

"Are there. . . Are there any more of those little boats?" asked Prince Rhind.

"Um . . . no," admitted Woon Gumpus.

The Fire in the West

The *Sea Cucumber*, meanwhile, was still barging her way steadily through the waves. Henwyn and the goblins had spent the first part of the voyage being noisily seasick over her sides, but slowly they had grown used to the pitching and swaying of the ship. Slowly, too, their fear of sea serpents had faded, but they still kept a sharp lookout. Captain Kestle might say as often he liked that sea serpents were solitary creatures, almost never seen, but Captain Kestle had not had dozens of them biting at his bottom on that lonely walkway. When they weren't busy being sick or helping him to sail the ship, the goblins stared out at the sea, sharpening their weapons and daring the serpents to appear.

None did. A day and a night and another day passed, and all they saw was a pod of playful porpoises which swam alongside for a while.

Then, on the second evening, the sea people appeared. Skarper was the first to spot them: three riders, mounted upon the big fronded seahorses of the western deeps, surfing on the crest of a foaming wave.

"Sea people?" said Henwyn, when he heard Skarper's shout, and he and Zeewa ran to the side to look. The other goblins gathered there too, and even Captain Kestle ambled over to see, enjoying their amazement, although he'd met the sea people often enough before.

"They aren't much like their pictures in the books," said Skarper, joining him.

"Those pictures was drawn by folk who'd never been to sea, I daresay," Kestle said. "Those books were written by men who'd never voyaged further than a waterfront tavern in Porthquidden."

The sea people were indeed a bit of a disappointment. No golden hair blown backwards on the breeze; no combs or mirrors, or fair voices singing. Mermen and merwomen alike were brownish, scaly, finny creatures, and they carried spears made from narwhals' horns and the business ends of swordfish. Their voices were as hard and clanging as the calls of gulls when they hailed the *Sea Cucumber*.

"Hello, old man! Hello, ugly goblins! What are you doing, so far from home, so far from shore? Why do you venture out upon the sea, which does not want you and does not like you?"

"I've as much business here as any of you," Captain Kestle shouted back. "Don't you know me?"

They came nearer and circled the *Sea Cucumber*, looking up. Their golden eyes were flecked with darkness, like the eyes of fish. "Old Kestle," they said. "So it is you! We thought you'd gone to the dry land and put down roots. That would have been wiser. The sea will eat your silly ship. You'll sink to the bottom and we'll take your nice pewter buttons and all your goblins' swords and axes too."

"The sea folk value metal," said Kestle to his passengers. "They cannot forge their own, of course, because it's so difficult to get a fire lit down beneath the sea. But don't worry; they know we are too strong for them. They rob wrecks, but they seldom attack sound ships."

The sea people circled once more, calling out their taunts and empty threats. Then they grew bored, and sank beneath the waves again, speeding off towards the west.

There was no swimming pool aboard the *Sea Cucumber*, unless you counted the eight inches of salt water which swirled about in the hold, and which the goblins kept on falling into when they were trying to bale it out with leather buckets. The dinners, cooked by Skarper and Henwyn, were odd affairs, because the tins of food that Etty had given them didn't have pictures on them to tell you what was inside, like the tin cans in her dream, only dwarf runes, which nobody on the *Sea Cucumber* could read. The first night they had sausages and custard; the second, beef and apricot stew, with some crabs which Spurtle and Flegg caught by trailing their tails over the side.

As for the on-board entertainment, there was only Henwyn. Henwyn had come by the idea somewhere that when people were off on quests or long journeys they liked nothing better than to sit around after a hard day's questing or journeying telling stories and singing songs. The fact that he was the only one who believed this never discouraged him, and he was always ready to start a rousing sing-song, even though nobody else ever joined in.

"Tonight," he said, picking bits of crab shell out of his teeth, "I shall sing you 'The Ballad of Prince Brewyon'."

"Washing up to do," said Spurtle, scampering off towards the galley with the supper dishes.

"My turn to bale the hold," said Zeewa, hurrying below.

The other goblins made excuses too, except for Grumpling, who never bothered making excuses but just left anyway.

Skarper went scrambling up the mast into the crow's nest. "I'll see if I can see any more of those sea people," he called down as he climbed. And there he sat, swaying to and fro in the gathering twilight, high above the ocean, while the plump sail spread beneath him and the sounds of canvas and rigging and waves almost drowned out Henwyn's voice from down below as he began his song.

Skarper could not see any sea people, but he soon noticed something else. Due west, dead ahead of the ship, an orange tongue of fire had appeared, as if someone had built a big bonfire out there on the horizon.

He found a useful rope and slid back down it to the deck. Captain Kestle was standing at the helm, tapping his foot to the rhythm of Henwyn's song.

"What's that?" asked Skarper, pointing to the flame in the west. "Is it a lighthouse? Is there land out there?"

"None that I ever heard of," said the old seafarer.

They watched the fire while it slowly sank and dimmed and went out. There was a stain on the sky where it had been, as if a patch of smoke hung there.

"I'd say a ship has caught fire, and burned," said Kestle.

By this time the other passengers had realized that something was happening, and were beginning to gather. Even Henwyn stopped his singing and came aft to stand with them and peer at the distant smoke, which was almost invisible by then against the deepening dusk.

"Was it the *Swan of Govannon*?" he asked.

"I know of no other ship in these waters," said Kestle.

"Good!" said Spurtle. "Then the fire has done our work for us. That'll put an end to Rhind's mischief, and the Elvenhorn will be back in the deeps where it belongs. Can we go home now?"

"But what about Prawl?" asked Skarper.

"And what about Prince Rhind, and his sister, and their nice old cook?" said Henwyn. "I wanted their quest to fail, but I did not want them all drowned!"

"What about my scratchbackler?" growled Grumpling.

"If the fire did not catch hold too quick, there's a hope they got off safe," said Kestle. "We should be in the waters where they foundered by sunrise. We must keep a good look out for their boats."

*

Dawn came, and the sides and rigging of the *Sea Cucumber* were lined with watchful goblins, but they saw no sign of any boats. All they saw was some flotsam riding the grey waves – charred spars trailing blackened snakes of rope; a few drifting timbers. One of the timbers came from a ship's stern, and on the blistered paintwork a name was still visible. As they had thought, she had been the *Swan of Govannon*.

They had almost given up hope of finding anyone alive when Zeewa sighted a larger fragment, not far off. It was a floating portion of the forecastle, and it was bristling with people. The people seemed to be hopping or dancing around, and the sounds of shouting came faintly across the water.

"It is them!" said Henwyn.

"But what are they doing?" asked Skarper.

"Anchovies!" roared Gutgust.

"The sea people are attacking them, that's what!" said Spurtle, who had borrowed Captain Kestle's telescope.

He was right. A dozen or more of the people of the sea were riding their seahorses in rings around the wreckage, waving their swordfish blades and narwhal horns.

Prince Rhind had been very brave. When the Swan's mainmast had collapsed in a flurry of sparks and the ship had begun to founder, he had wrapped himself in Breenge's wet towel and gone racing down to the cabins. He had saved the Elvenhorn, his sword, and Breenge's bow, and also his splendid armoured coat, which shone silvery bright in the dim morning light as he perched on the highest point of the floating forecastle, waving his blade at the people of the sea and shouting his war cry – the long, quavering, "Baaaa!" of the men of Tyr Davas, which had struck terror into the hearts of so many sheep rustlers down the years.

The sea people shouted back, but they dared not go close enough to test their swords against Prince Rhind's. A few had tried, and Breenge had shot their seahorses from under them. Woon Gumpus had found a length of charred plank that he was waving like a club, and Ninnis whacked her wooden spoon on the webbed hands of the unseahorsed riders as they tried to grope their way aboard the wreckage.

What Rhind didn't realize was that it was his armour which had attracted the sea people in the first place. They had been happily ransacking the wreck of the *Swan* way down on the sea floor, until the glimmer of those silver-bright scales caught their eye, glinting through the wave tops. How could they resist such shiny splendour? So they kept circling and circling, too scared of Breenge's arrows and her brother's sword to

actually attack, but waiting for the moment when the forecastle finally sank and they could help themselves to that wonderful metal vest.

The goblins, watching the battle from the *Sea Cucumber* as it swung towards the wreckage, understood what was going on at once. They loved shiny things themselves, and many a war had been fought in the corridors of Clovenstone over mail shirts far less fabulous than Rhind's.

"Take off your armour!" Skarper shouted, as Kestle steered the *Cucumber* nearer.

"What, so you goblins or your mermen friends can shoot me down?" Rhind shouted back.

"Oh, do be polite to them, Rhind," Breenge told him. "We need them to rescue us!"

"We can't shoot you!" Skarper yelled. "Goblins are rubbish shots and we haven't got bows anyway."

"I reckon I get him with a spear from here," said Grumpling. "Why's we got to rescue them anyway?"

"Because they are fellow mariners, in peril on the sea," said Henwyn.

"And because if you got him with a spear he'd fall in the sea and sink like a stone in all that armour, and then how will you get your scratchbackler back?" said Skarper. "Look, there it is, a-dangling round Rhind's neck." He cupped his paws around his mouth and yelled at Rhind again, "Take off your coat of scales! That's what the sea folk want! Let them take it, and save yourself!"

Reluctantly, Rhind took off his armour. He lifted it high above his head and threw it as far as he could from the wreckage. It hit the waves with a white splash and sank, and the sea people followed it down, shouting, "Mine! Mine!" and "I saw it first!" until the water swallowed up their voices.

Then Captain Kestle took the *Sea Cucumber* closer until it bumped against the wreckage, and the stranded Woolmarkers and Woon Gumpus scrambled aboard up ropes and ladders that the goblins dangled over her side.

They were a sorry sight, these shipwrecked woollen-folk, charred and sodden, dazed with weariness after their night adrift. At least Rhind had salvaged enough of his princely good manners to say, "Thank you for rescuing us, Henwyn of Clovenstone. Decent of you."

Henwyn just said, "I think you have something that belongs to us?"

"Belongs ter me," snarled Grumpling.

Rhind looked grim, but he took the baldric from around his neck and handed it to Henwyn with the Elvenhorn dangling.

"So is my quest to end here?" he asked.

"Too right it is," said Grumpling. He snatched the horn and shoved it down the back of his armour for a good old scratch. "Ahh," he said, "Nuffin' sorts out them flea-bites like my own scratchbackler!"

"And where is Prawl?" asked Henwyn, looking at Rhind's bedraggled followers. "I cannot see him among your number. Did he stay behind at Floonhaven?"

Rhind and his companions looked at one another. In all of the excitement, none of them had spared a moment's thought for Prawl.

"I think he was aboard the ship," said Breenge. "His cloak was aboard, anyway. It was kicking about on the deck. I noticed it, just before the fire started."

"The poor gentleman must have gone down with the ship," said Ninnis, wiping away a tear.

"*I'm here!*" said the white rabbit, which Breenge was still cuddling. "*Oh, this is so humiliating!*" But its little rabbity mouth could not form the words, so all that came out was a faint squeaking.

"Your rabbit?" asked Zeewa, reaching over to tickle it between its long ears.

"I found him aboard the *Swan*," said Breenge. "He must have stowed away. I call him Fuzzy-Nose."

"*Oh good grief,*" said the rabbit, but of course nobody understood it.

"He squeaks a lot, don't he?" said Flegg.

211

"There's good eating on a rabbit," said Spurtle, and licked his lips.

"Oh, there is no need to eat Fuzzy-Nose," said Henwyn, before they did something unfortunate. "There are much better things to eat in Etty's tin cans. Probably. I'll open a few, and cook up some breakfast."

"And I'll help you, my dearie," said Ninnis, who was still all smiles and rosy cheeks despite her sufferings, and seemed to have overcome her sadness at the loss of Prawl.

"And we'll turn back to the Westlands," said Skarper, "and leave Elvensea where it lies." But when he looked up at the sail he saw that it was hanging limply, and that the long red pennant that had fluttered out so proudly all the way from Floonhaven now dangled lifelessly. "The wind has deserted us," he said.

"Then how come we're still moving?" asked Zeewa.

It was true. *The Sea Cucumber* was still moving westward just as fast as she had when the wind was blowing her, and the white water still rippled and chuckled under her forefoot. In the west, directly above the Cucumber's brow, a strange disc of clouds hung in the sky. They were the sort of clouds that might hang above a lonely island, but there was no island to be seen.

"This is not natural," said Kestle. "We must be

caught in some current, but one I've never heard of. I shall consult my charts."

"I shall assist you!" said Woon Gumpus, who had been feeling embarrassed about the loss of his ship and hoping that none of his passengers were going to ask him for a refund.

Kestle looked him up and down. "Very well. Glad to have another seafaring man aboard. These goblins are good lads, as goblins go, but t'aint the same as a crew of real sailors."

"Oh no, indeed!" said Woon Gumpus, hurrying after him into the deckhouse where Kestle kept his charts. "And if it would help you to think, I could play you something soothing on my hurdy-gurdy. . ."

Raising the Land

There was nothing much that mere landlubbers could do while those two men of the sea held their conference around the chart table. So Henwyn and Ninnis set about cooking a breakfast, and then everyone set about eating it, and all the while the *Sea Cucumber* kept ploughing westward, although there was still no breath of wind. And by the time breakfast was finished and the clatter of cutlery had died away, a new noise could be heard. It was a rushing, roaring sound, like a far-off wind, or the world grinding round upon its axis.

The sound stirred strange memories for Henwyn. That dream which had come to him while he was drowsing in the mantrap tree had faded as soon as he awoke, but now it came back to him.

"There is a hole in the sea!" he shouted, just

as Kestle and Woon Gumpus emerged from the deckhouse to see what was causing the noise.

"Stuff and nonsense," said Woon Gumpus. "There are no holes in the sea, my dear boy. It is not a piece of cheese. I expect you are thinking of the land – there are holes in that, in places."

"He means a whirlpool," said Kestle, tugging worriedly at his whiskers. "Look yonder!"

They looked. Ahead of them, beneath that strange swirl of cloud, a dark patch had appeared upon the ocean. As the *Sea Cucumber* surged towards it, the watchers on her deck could see that it was a deep hollow in the surface of the sea.

"There *is* a hole!" said Skarper.

The wreckage of the *Swan of Govannon*, which was far lighter than the *Cucumber*, was drawn ahead of her, and vanished over the edge.

"A whirlypool!" wailed Spurtle.

"All the waters of the world are draining away down it!" gasped Henwyn.

"And we shall be taken with it," said Breenge, "like bathwater twirling down a plughole."

The goblins knew little of baths or plugholes, but they could all see the danger. When Kestle bellowed, "To the boat! Start rowing!" they jumped to obey him, and for once not even Grumpling grumbled. They threw the *Sea Cucumber's* boat overboard, Skarper attached the rope which Kestle threw them to her stern, and they started rowing with all their goblinny strength, trying desperately to drag the ship away from the brink of that terrible hole.

But it was useless. They pulled on the oars with all their might, but the whirlpool pulled harder. Soon the passengers on the *Sea Cucumber's* prow could look down into its depths. There, far below, ringed by the whirling walls of water, weed-draped turrets jutted from a pother of foam.

"Drowned Elvensea!" cried Prince Rhind, over the water's roar. "It is there! It is real!"

"And drowned is what we'll be too, if this whirlypool drags us down there," said Henwyn.

Just then, he felt someone tug at his belt. He looked round. Prince Rhind's cook, Ninnis, was staring up at him, and her usually jolly face was hard and grim. "If you would live, Henwyn of Clovenstone," she said, "if you would save your friends, you must sound the Elvenhorn."

"Eh?" said Henwyn, who had forgotten about the Elvenhorn in all the excitement. The last time he saw it, Grumpling had been scratching his back with it.

"*One blast to part the waters, one to raise the drownéd land,*" said Ninnis, in a chanting way. "*And one to wake*

216

the sleeper there," she added in an undertone.

"Eh?" Henwyn wasn't really listening. "Fentongoose said that to sound the horn may bring dire peril," he said doubtfully.

"What peril could be more dire than this?" urged Ninnis. "Did your goblins and that pretty Muskish girl follow you all these long leagues just to be smashed and smothered in the sea?"

She had a point, thought Henwyn. The *Sea Cucumber* was teetering on the very rim of the whirlpool now. The boat full of goblins which was supposed to be towing her had been dragged over already, and swung there on the taut towrope while the goblins clung to it and the fierce waters spilled over them.

Henwyn leaned over the *Sea Cucumber's* side, shouting down, "Goblins! Are you all right?"

"No!" said Grumpling.

"Bumcakes!" said Skarper.

"I'm being sick EVERYWHERE!" said Spurtle.

"Skarper!" Henwyn hollered. "Sound the Elvenhorn! It's our only hope!"

Skarper heard him. He let go of his oar and let the whirlpool take it. He scrambled through the foam-filled boat to the thwart where Grumpling sat, and snatched the Elvenhorn from around Grumpling's neck. Before Grumpling had a chance to say, "Oi!", he put the horn to his lips, and blew.

The sound was louder than it had been when Prince Rhind blew it, back on the hills in front of Clovenstone. It was a full, rich, throaty sound, not at all kazoo-like any more, as if being brought so close to Elvensea had given it more strength somehow – or maybe it was just that the sea had washed some of the dust and earwigs and Grumpling's skin-scrapings out of it. At any rate, its note rang high and clear above the thunder of the circling waters. . .

And the waters heard. The mad, rushing movement of the doomed ship slowed. The steep sides of the whirlpool shallowed. The goblins in the boat and the humans on the ship peered down and saw that Elvensea was drowned again, and that the hole in the ocean was healing. Within a few moments the ship was on an even keel again, and the goblins were sloshing water out of their swamped but floating boat. The waves were still confused and choppy, but the whirlpool was gone.

"The Elvenhorn does not work!" said Rhind. "The second blast is supposed to raise Elvensea, not sink it again!"

"It must be broken," agreed Zeewa.

"Maybe Skarper didn't blow it properly," said Breenge.

"I blew it brilliantly!" said Skarper, scrambling back aboard with the other soggy goblins as their boat came bumping against the *Cucumber's* side. "I got rid of that whirlypond thing, didn't I?" He was rather pleased with the way things had gone, and thought the humans ought to show a bit more gratitude.

"Gimme my scratchbackler back," snarled Grumpling, grabbing at the Elvenhorn.

"Wait!" said Ninnis.

Since when had a simple cook had such a commanding voice? They all fell silent. Even Grumpling stopped, one paw outstretched to take the Elvenhorn.

Into the silence that the healing of the whirlpool had left there crept a new sound. A rumbling of a different sort. A sound that you felt in the soles of your feet as it came trembling through the old ship's timbers. It was the sound of the earth flexing its muscles, of vast masses of rock shifting like sleepy animals, deep beneath the sea. It was the sound of magic.

Around the *Sea Cucumber* the water was growing paler. From deep blue-grey to light it turned, filling with foam as swarms of bubbles came wobbling up from below. The clouds above thickened and spun, sparking with lightning.

"Land ho!" shouted Woon Gumpus suddenly,

pointing off to starboard.

"Land!" cried Breenge, pointing in another direction.

"Land! Land!" the goblins yelled.

All around the ship, like breaching whales, the tops of towers were rising from the waves. The white sea gushed from their gutterings and windows as they rose; gargoyles spewed long arcs of foam. Up, up went the towers, with the rumble of their rising so loud now that everyone aboard the *Cucumber* clapped their hands over their ears to block it out.

The ship lurched.

"The ship's run aground!" shouted Rhind.

"The ground's run a-ship!" shouted Skarper.

The deck tilted steeply as the ship lay down on her side and the water drained away around her, leaving her marooned in a cleft between two towers.

And still the land kept rising, and Skarper, clinging to the *Sea Cucumber's* rigging, started to see how the towers and rooftops which he had seen peeking up at him from the depths of the whirlpool formed only the topmost tip of Elvensea. It was a tall, thin island, shaped like a witch's hat, and on every inch of it the elves of old had built their towers and streets and palaces, their delicate arbours and walled gardens and pillared halls.

Taller and taller it grew, until, at last, quays and

220

harbours emerged from the surf which frothed around its sides. Only then did the upheaval end. The mountain of ruins stood steaming in the sunlight that shafted down through the thinning clouds. Torrents of water fled foaming down its streets and stairways, back into the sea. Stranded silver fish flip-flopped on pavements which had not seen daylight for a thousand years. And the *Sea Cucumber* lay wedged five hundred feet above the waves, her empty boat swinging on its towline like a clinker-built pendulum, while her passengers gazed about in disbelief.

"It is as high as Clovenstone Keep!" said Skarper.

"Clovenstone was just a copy of Elvensea," said Breenge. "Ninnis told me once. She said the Lych Lord and his fellow sorcerers envied the elves, and set out to create something that would rival Elvensea. And when they failed, in angry jealousy, they sank Elvensea so that no one could see how poorly Clovenstone compared."

"That's not what Fentongoose said," said Skarper.

"If we want to know the truth about this place," said Henwyn, "I think Mistress Ninnis is the person to ask."

"Ninnis?" scoffed Rhind. "My cook? What would a cook know about anything? Well, except cookery, of course. She does a lovely rhubarb crumble."

"Where is Ninnis?" asked Breenge.

"And where is the Elvenhorn?" asked Zeewa.

"It's here," said Skarper, holding up the soggy baldric – and realized that it wasn't. The baldric hung empty; de-horned. He looked at Grumpling, but Grumpling looked just as mystified as he did. Well, mystified at first, then very angry.

"Is you tellin me you lost my scratchbackler AGAIN?"

"There she is!" shouted Spurtle.

He was pointing upwards. There, on one of the stairways which spiralled around the flanks of Elvensea like the tendrils of some lovely climbing plant, a tiny shape was toiling upwards. It was Ninnis, her travelling cloak fluttering about her like black wings. When they called her name she looked down at them, but she did not stop climbing.

"Where is she going?" asked Prince Rhind. "It's nearly lunchtime, too!"

"She has more important things on her mind than your lunch, Prince Rhind," said Henwyn. "I believe you have nurtured a viper in your bosom."

"I haven't got a bosom," said Rhind, who was sensitive about his figure.

"It's just an expression," Skarper explained. "It's the sort of thing you say to people who bring a sorceress along on quests with them instead of a cook."

"Ninnis isn't a sorceress!" said Breenge. "Is she?"

"Think about it," said Henwyn. "That storm and those serpents. The way Rhind knew that we were following you. Ever since we left Clovenstone I've had the feeling that some fell magic was being used against us. Only I told myself it couldn't be, because the nearest thing Prince Rhind had to a sorcerer was that numbskull Prawl."

"There there, Fuzzy-Nose," said Breenge to her rabbit, which was wriggling furiously in her arms.

"But why would a sorceress pretend to be a cook?" asked Rhind.

"Maybe because she wanted to go where you were going," said Skarper. "Maybe because she knew something about Elvensea and wanted to get its secrets for herself."

"Oh, this is flapdoodle!" blustered Rhind. "Ninnis makes sauces, not sorceries! Stews, not spells! Meringues, not magic!"

"Then why is she climbing off up there alone with the Elvenhorn?" asked Zeewa. "She must be looking for. . . Oh, I don't know. The citadel or the keep or the great hall or the throne room, or wherever the heart of this place used to be. And when she finds it she will sound the horn a third time. . ."

"And wake the sleeper," said Henwyn.

"Who's the sleeper?" asked Skarper.

"I don't know. Something Ninnis said. 'One blast to part the water, one to raise the drownéd land, one to wake the sleeper there.'"

"Some blimmin' old elf, I expect," said Spurtle. "Probably be even more trouble than blimmin' dwarves."

"But that is wonderful!" said Breenge. "I mean – isn't it? The elves were kindly folk, and, if one still sleeps here, he will be grateful to us for rousing him."

"It's not us he'll be grateful to," said Henwyn. "It's Ninnis."

They thought about that while, from the turrets and buttresses which overhung the stranded ship, statues of the elves gazed down on them. They did not look kindly. There was a coldness in those stern and handsome faces of stone, as if the sculptor who carved them had captured something of his sitters' hearts along with their features, and their hearts had not been kindly hearts at all.

"We must stop her," said Skarper.

"Anchovies!" said Gutgust firmly, and although nobody knew what he meant, as usual, he seemed to speak for all of them. They took their swords and axes, Zeewa her spear and Breenge her bow, and swarmed to the ship's sides, dropping down into the streets of Elvensea.

Found in Translation

Giants are like foals at first. They wobble on their long new legs like trainee stiltwalkers, teetering and stumbling. That was one reason why Fraddon had decided to take Bryn home. There was so much that the new giant didn't know. Safe within the Outer Wall, he would have a chance to practise things like walking, and there would be no danger of him sitting down on someone's house, or trampling their fields. People hated it when giants did that, and Fraddon still remembered the villages he had accidentally flattened when he was new, and the angry mobs which had chased him with pitchforks and burning torches – quite harmless to a giant, but awfully embarrassing. He did not want young Bryn to make the same mistakes. And so he led him back across the hills to Clovenstone.

The people of Oethford and Stag Headed Oak, who

had spilled from their cottages to watch the giants go by, scattered in panic as Bryn veered towards them, throwing out his arms for balance, coming within a whisker of stomping their villages flat. But Fraddon guided him safely past, and by the time they reached Westerly Gate, Bryn was learning how to steer that towering body of his. Most of the soil and stones had fallen off him along the way, and the massive footprints he had made in the marshy meadows by the Oeth filled quickly with water, and became the best duck-hunting country in the Westlands.

Fraddon planted the mantrap tree in a shady place he knew among the ruins, and found some clothes for Bryn. They were old clothes of his own, much patched and rather mildewed, which he had set aside when he grew too small for them. Bryn was almost too big, but he squeezed into the patchwork breeches, and thought he looked splendid.

Then Fraddon set about teaching his new friend the ways of the world. Don't pick people up to get a closer look at them, Bryn; they don't like it. And that thing where you lift the roofs of their houses like lids? They really hate that! And do watch where you're putting your feet. . .

There were a few disasters, which was only to be expected, with someone as new and tall as Bryn about

the place. He meant well, but he was clumsy. Quite a few of the old ruins of Clovenstone were knocked down once and for all as he blundered enthusiastically about the place. The boglins who lived in the marshes were horrified when he reached down into the mere beside their king's hall and pulled out the Meargh Dowr, the slimy dampdrake that they worshipped. It curled around Bryn's forearm like a snake and breathed its wet breath in his face and made him sneeze, while the boglins did fierce war dances around his feet and pincushioned his toes with spears and blowpipe darts which he didn't even notice.

Patiently, Fraddon persuaded him to put the Meargh Dowr back. He had forgotten what a handful young giants could be. But he was enjoying having Bryn there, all the same. It did him good to see that huge, inquisitive figure peering into the windows of Clovenstone's towers, or lying down to get a proper look into the shadows under the trees. He had been like that himself once, full of wonder at the wonders of the world. But he had grown used to them; he had stopped thinking of them as wonders and started to take them for granted. Having Bryn beside him made him see them all afresh and wonderful again.

The goblins were uneasy, of course. It wasn't that they didn't *like* Bryn, just that – well – he was so big.

They had based their idea of giants on Fraddon, who was not much taller than a really tall tree. Bryn was as tall as a small mountain, and they were worried he would step on them. Also, there had been an unfortunate incident a few days after he arrived, when he opened the cheesery like a lunch box and ate all of the latest batch of Clovenstone Blue.

As for Fentongoose and Dr Prong, it was a wonder that they could concentrate on their studies at all with all the giant-wrangling going on. It was unnerving to be sitting reading in a tall tower, on top of a high crag, and suddenly look up to find that a colossal eye was peering in at you. But somehow they managed to keep working, and whole gangs of goblins were kept busy in the bumwipe heaps, searching for any scroll or document which might shed light on the mysterious history of Elvensea.

"It is almost," said Dr Prong, "as if someone has deliberately removed all papers which contained a reference to the drowned land."

On the morning that the travellers reached the whirlpool and Elvensea rose from the deeps, Fentongoose was working alone. Dr Prong had stayed with him until long after midnight, then given up and gone off to bed, but Fentongoose had kept going. He had strained his old eyes by candlelight to read the broken-spider alphabet of the old chroniclers until the candle was replaced by something brighter and he looked up to find that the sun had risen.

"Well bless my beard," he muttered. "Is that the time?"

He closed his weary eyes for a moment, then opened them again and looked at all the scraps of ancient parchment scattered on his table, and at the slate book which was acting as a paperweight – and that was when it hit him.

"Prong?" he said, forgetting that Dr Prong had gone to bed.

"Prong!"

He ran out of the library, up the winding stairways, out along the battlements of the Inner Wall. "Dr Prong?"

Dr Prong's room was next to Henwyn's, in one of the cabins of Princess Ned's old ship, which was balanced on the top of Blackspike Tower. A porthole opened and Prong's grumpy, nightcap-crowned head poked out. "Well, Fentongoose, what is it?"

"That word, Prong! The one we couldn't translate? The one we thought meant 'cushion'?"

"Yes, what of it?"

"It doesn't mean cushion!"

"Well, we both know that, but—"

229

"It was carved quite unusually, that word, by whoever scratched the tale of Elvensea's fall on that old slate. The downstrokes were too shallow, and the accents were in the wrong place."

"So. . . ?"

"So we thought those two runes were 'soft' and 'chair', adding up to 'cushion'. But we were wrong! The rune that we thought meant 'soft' actually means 'fire'. And the one that we thought meant 'seating accessory' actually means 'lizard'."

"Fire lizard?" asked Dr Prong. "Well, what on earth is 'fire lizard' supposed to mean? I have never heard of a 'fire lizard'. Unless it means. . ."

"Exactly!"

"Oh no!"

"Precisely!"

"Oh, oh, oh. . . Bless my beard!" said Dr Prong. (And Dr Prong did not even *have* a beard, which gives you some idea of how worked up he was.) "Oh, Fentongoose! You really mean it? *Dragons?*"

The Streets of Elvensea

"Dragons!" shouted Grumpling, before they had gone more than a few paces from the tower where the *Sea Cucumber* had come to rest. He snatched his axe down from his shoulder, and the others scattered in panic. But when the panic faded they could see no dragons, just an ornate sculpture on a pedestal: two dragons with their wings spread wide, carved from the same pale stone as the buildings around them.

"Grumpling," said Henwyn, "that's a statue."

"What's a statchoo then?" asked Grumpling, creeping towards the pedestal with axe raised, never taking his eyes off the stone reptiles. "Is it a sort of dragon?"

Henwyn shook his head. How could you explain the difference between statues and real things to someone who was still a bit vague about the difference between *drawings* and real things?

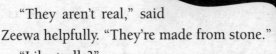

"They aren't real," said Zeewa helpfully. "They're made from stone."

"Like trolls?"

"No, like ornaments. Decorations."

"That one's watching me."

"No, it's just carved to look as if it's watching you."

"Well, I'll wipe the smirk off its face!" shouted Grumpling. Agile as a monkey he somersaulted up on to the pedestal and smashed both dragons to pieces with a few blows from the iron-shod haft of his axe.

"There!" he said. "They won't be breathing fire on us an' stuff."

"Right," said Prince Rhind. "Now that your pet gorilla has made that statue safe, we should press on. Ninnis must be right at the top of the island by now."

Henwyn nodded. "But someone should stay here to guard the ship. Just because Grumpling's dragons were stone doesn't mean there won't be dangers here." He turned to Captain Kestle and Woon Gumpus. "Captains, will you wait here for us?"

"Oh, gladly!" said Woon Gumpus, who did not like these haunted, weed-strewn streets at all.

"A good plan," agreed Kestle. "We'll stay near the ship, and pick you up should this strange old place decide to slide back down beneath the waves. And while we wait, perhaps we'll think of a way to get the old ship down again if the waters don't rise, eh, Gumpus?"

"Oh, oh, ah, yes!" said Woon Gumpus, rather startled to find that Captain Kestle thought he was the sort of person who could solve problems like that. "Perhaps we could find ropes and blocks and tackles and things like that in these old buildings."

"A splendid idea, Cap'n Gumpus!"

"Oh, was it? Good!"

So the two sea captains turned back, and the rest of the company moved on, up the streets which curled around the flanks of the tall island. The only sounds were the trickling water and the crisp noises of the seaweed as it dried in the sun. Also, Grumpling's cries of "Dragon!" and the crashings and clatterings as he hammered another statue to pieces. But soon even he had to accept that these stone dragons were no threat to him. Even if they had been, he could not have smashed them all.

For they were everywhere. Carved above doorways and flying along the pediments of the lovely old buildings were dragons. Twining up the carved stone banisters of the elegant stairways, dragons. Crouching on pedestals, spreading their bat wings to shade the squares beneath them, stone dragons.

"These old elves really had a thing for dragons," Skarper said nervously.

"Maybe it was a sort of collection that got out of hand," said Henwyn. "My auntie Gratna mentioned once that she liked badgers, so her husband gave her a carving of a badger next time her birthday came around, and then other people started giving her badgers too, wooden badgers, stone badgers, knitted badgers, sewn badgers, every birthday and every midwinter. She's got nearly two hundred now. They're a proper chore to dust, and she never really liked badgers *that* much to start with."

"Who does?" panted Spurtle, climbing after him up Elvensea's steep streets. "Horrible black-and-white bandits. They's the ones that nick all your shiny stuff and fly away with it to line their nests."

"That's magpies, not badgers," said Flegg.

"Magpies, badgers, they're all in league together," said Spurtle darkly.

"Anchovies," said Gutgust, wisely.

"Well," said Zeewa, "at least there aren't any *elves* around."

Far below them, the lower levels of Elvensea reeked and crackled with drying weed. There was weed here on the heights as well, festooning the outer walls and stairways. But as they climbed higher, they reached streets and buildings which must have been protected by powerful magic when the island sank. There were no barnacles on these walls, only wonderful tapestries, which did not even seem wet, and painted scenes of wide landscapes through which elves strode or rode. There was beautiful furniture in the wide rooms, fine carpets upon the floors, and tables laid as if for elven banquets. But there were no actual elves. Skarper had half expected to find them sprawled about asleep on the fine tiled floors or plump, claw-footed furniture, but of course they had gone, slain by the Lych Lord, or fled away upon their ships into the west.

"Grumpling?" shouted Henwyn. "Oh, where's he gone?"

They looked for the big goblin, but could not find him, although when they shouted his name his voice could be heard, replying tetchily, "I'm over 'ere!" Elvensea was a maze, far more complicated than Clovenstone. Henwyn felt sure there was some pattern to the way the curving streets and ramps and stairways interwove, and he felt that if he could spend about six weeks mapping and exploring there was a chance he might work out what it was. But they didn't have six weeks, or even six minutes; they had to find Ninnis.

Soon after that, they found that they had lost Flegg too. But nobody really minded getting separated from Flegg, while Grumpling, with his shining axe, seemed like just the sort of person you needed to have with you when you were exploring mysterious magical islands.

It was no use, though. "Grumpling, if you can hear me, work your way back to the ship!" shouted Skarper. "We'll meet you there!" Then they hurried on: him and Henwyn, Rhind and Breenge, Zeewa and Spurtle and Gutgust, higher and higher.

They passed signs of war and destruction – charred buildings, and places where walls had collapsed across the streets. And everywhere were those carven dragons, every scale and prong of their fierce bodies perfectly shaped by the elven stonemasons.

"Were there really such creatures once?" asked Breenge, as they started up a stairway walled by the long, curving tail of a particularly huge dragon. Unlike the pale dragons below, this one was black, carved from some dark and shining stone.

"Oh yes," said Henwyn. "The Lych Lord kept a few at Clovenstone. They could fly over a battlefield and breathe down fire upon his enemies."

"They all died as he lost his power, though," said Skarper. "Good riddance, too. Nasty, dangerous things."

The black tail broadened, and met a black body shaded by the dragon's folded wings. They were approaching the top of Elvensea. Above them a wide doorway let into a building with a shining golden dome. The black dragon's long neck bordered the stairway; its vast face, carved in a crocodilian smirk, rested on the pavement outside the building.

As the companions hurried up the stairs, they could hear voices above them. One voice in particular.

"Give me back my scratchbackler!" it said.

"It's Grumpling!" said Henwyn. "He's beaten us to the top! He must have found a quicker way up."

"Well, I wish he'd told us about it," panted Skarper.

They ran up the final few steps and pushed open the huge golden doors of the domed building. It was dark inside, a darkness woven with sunbeams which slanted through small high windows far above. They stood blinking in the doorway, and as their eyes adjusted they saw before them a forest of slender pillars. In the centre of the hall a circular pool had been sunk into the floor. There was something in the pool that was not water, shining with pale light beneath a layer of mist. But the most noticeable feature of the place was Grumpling. He looked bigger and grimier and spikier than ever, there among the delicate pillars. He had his axe in his paws, and he was brandishing it at Ninnis, who stood with her back to one of the pillars, the Elvenhorn clasped in her hands.

"Ninnis!" shouted Henwyn. "Give us the Elvenhorn!"

"Never!" shouted the cook, in a voice that was all cracked pride and scratchy anger, nothing at all like her usual one. "Do you know how long I have waited to undo the spells and wake the power of this place, Henwyn of Clovenstone?"

"Grumpling will start chopping bits off you if you don't," warned Skarper.

"He will never reach me," said Ninnis proudly, and she lifted the horn, making ready to blow it. "When the third blast is sounded the last of the curses which your Lych Lord wove around this place will be snapped. The sleeper will wake, and the power of Elvensea shall be mine."

"Oh no it won't!" shouted Flegg, leaping so suddenly out of the shadows behind Ninnis that Henwyn gave a yelp of surprise, and Breenge nearly dropped her rabbit. Flegg's knife flashed in the sunbeams.

"No!" shouted Henwyn. "You mustn't stab a woman!"

"You can't attack people from behind, it isn't sporting!" yelled Rhind.

But they were too late to stop Flegg. Ninnis gave one terrible cry as the knife sank into her back. Then she fell forward, dropping the Elvenhorn. Flegg caught it before it hit the floor.

"My scratchbackler!" growled Grumpling. "Nice work, Flegg."

Flegg chuckled to himself. "You don't think I'll let you scratch your nasty old back with this after the trouble I went to gettin' it back, do you, Grumpling?" he asked. "Use your tail like the rest of us."

And he raised the Elvenhorn to his mouth.

"No!" shouted everyone else – all except Gutgust (who shouted "anchovies" but probably meant "no") and Grumpling, who was experimentally scratching his back with the tip of his tail.

"Flegg, did you not hear her?" demanded Henwyn, running towards the little goblin. "At the third blast. . ."

"'The power of Elvensea will be mine,'" said Flegg, darting round to the far side of that eerie-looking pool. A chilly light seemed to gather in his eyes. "That's what Ninnis said. I fancy a bit of power, me. Flegg, King of Elvensea, master of all that elvish magic and whatnot. Why do you fink I tagged along on your stupid quest, except to get my paws on this hooter? Once I've tooted it you won't think again about droppin' me down pooin holes or orderin me about. None of you will dare! Oh no! You'll go down on your stupid knees an' beg me for mercy. Flegg the Conqueror! Flegg the Magnificent! Flegg, the Master of the World!"

Grumpling stopped scratching his back, lifted his axe, and leaped clear across the pool, ready to slice Flegg in half. But Flegg was too fast. He nipped nimbly out of the way and, while still in mid-nip, blew upon the horn.

The third blast filled the pillared hall like a thunderclap. Everyone covered their ears, except for Breenge, who covered her rabbit's ears and winced as the deafening brassy note rolled around and around the building, and spilled out through the doors and windows into the heavy, waiting air of Elvensea. The mist in the strange pool writhed and whispered. Some of the pillars trembled, vibrating with the sound. Cracks spread across the ceiling, and huge pieces of stonework came crashing down. One landed squarely on top of Grumpling, smashing him flat in a cloud of dust and swearing.

And then the sound faded, and the stones stopped falling, and all was quiet again.

"Well," said Skarper, "I don't see any sleeper waking up."

Flegg sneered at him. "He won't be up here, will he? He'll be in one of them fancy palaces down below. He's probably puttin' his socks on now and coming up to see who's woke him, so he can thank me in person." He went out through the doorway on to the sunlit pavement, looking down at the thousand towers of Elvensea, the glitter of the blue sea far below. "Well, come on sleeper!" he shouted. "Old elf king or whatever you be! Let's be having you! Wakey wakey!"

The stairways below remained deserted. No elven army issued from the weed-wigged buildings. Looking down, Skarper could see the faces of the sea captains looking up at him from the stranded *Sea Cucumber*, but nothing else moved.

And then something did.

That carved black dragon's head, resting on the pavement, very slowly opened one eyelid. A red-gold iris like a ring of fire twitched to focus upon Flegg. A pupil narrowed to a black slit in the sunlight.

Skarper pointed a helpless paw.

"Dra-Dra— It's a dra—"

Lizard-fast, the huge head lunged. Flegg turned just in time to see it coming. "Eeek!" he said – and vanished into a huge red mouth which slammed shut on him with a squelchy crunch.

"—gon!" said Skarper.

The dragon let out a long rasping breath, flexing its nostrils, baring its teeth, as if after its long sleep it was reminding itself how all the deadly mechanisms of its body worked. Its wings rose and flapped like black tents. Its tail dragged rattling over the tiled roofs of buildings. The Elvenhorn clattered to the pavement, rolled away, and went tumbling off down the stairs. But by that time, Skarper and the others were all back inside the pillared hall, and swinging shut the golden doors to hide themselves from the dragon's dreadful gaze.

"It wasn't cushions, that word in the old text," said Zeewa, in a small, quivery voice. She had come to the same conclusion as Fentongoose, but she had come to it the hard way. "It was dragons!"

"Do you think all the dragon statues are going to come to life?" asked Rhind. "I mean, there were hundreds of them!"

"I think they were just statues," said Henwyn. "This black one looked different all along. It was never a statue. It must have been a real dragon that went to sleep here when Elvensea sank."

"Well, it's awake now," said Skarper. "And who knows how many others are waking up too, and thinking about breakfast?"

"Oh, that is the only one," said a smug voice behind them. "The last of the dragons of Elvensea. But one dragon will be enough!"

They turned. Ninnis, who they had all thought Flegg had killed, was rising to her feet again.

Except that she was not Ninnis any more, or at

least, not the Ninnis that they knew. Her shabby pinafore and homespun dress were turning into garments of some rich fabric soft and dark as smoke, spangled with jewels that shone like evening stars. And her round brown face was growing longer and paler, and her blackbird eyes larger and greyer, and her sparse hair ripening thick and butter gold. A proud and haughty queen of Elvensea she seemed, and she smiled coldly down at the frightened band of humans and goblins who stood before her, and said, "Which of you was it who blew the horn?"

243

Hellesvor

The air in the hall crackled with magic. It made Skarper's nose itch. It made little sparks jump in Zeewa's hair. Spurtle gave a hiccup and turned into a sofa.

"Anchovies?" said Gutgust, who was having trouble keeping up.

With vast slithering sounds, the black dragon coiled itself around the building, pressing against the walls like an affectionate cat rubbing itself against its owner's leg. Through the little high windows Skarper and his friends saw tiny bits of it: a tail-tip like the fluke of an anchor, the ember of an eye.

"Which of you sounded the Elvenhorn?" asked Ninnis again, and she came pacing towards them with a careful, graceful tread.

"It wasn't any of us," said Skarper. "It was Flegg.

We told him not to. And now he's dead. That dragon scoffed him."

Ninnis smiled a cold smile. "A pity. I should have liked to thank him for breaking the final spell. But Mortholow was grateful to him, too, for waking her from her long nap, and she showed her gratitude in her own way."

"Mortholow?" asked Prince Rhind nervously.

"My pet," said Ninnis, gesturing with one long, pale hand at the dragon. It seemed to be sharpening its claws against the hall's walls. "My faithful steed; the hammer of the sea."

"Oh," said Prince Rhind.

"In her belly your friend Flegg will be transformed into fire; a far more glorious fate than most of you mud-born mortals can hope for."

"Ah," said Prince Rhind.

"Ninnis?" asked Henwyn. "That is . . . *are* you Ninnis still?"

"I was never Ninnis," said the elven woman. "There was no Ninnis. That was only a name I used. That was only a face I wore, so that I could go among you mud people unnoticed through all the years of waiting. I am Hellesvor, last of the royal line of Elvensea. I am the vengeance of the elves. You humans have grown sentimental about my kind. You have forgotten how, in days of old, our dragon cavalry laid waste to your shabby towns and common little kingdoms. You have forgotten the terror and the rage of elves. Now that you have raised my home and woken my dragon, I shall have to remind you."

She came closer to Henwyn, looking curiously at him. Henwyn gripped his sword, but he dared not raise it. He could feel the magic coming off her, like heat off a sun-warm stone, and he knew his blade would be no more use against it than Flegg's had been, and that if he tried to use it she would do something dreadful to him. So he stood there, and let her circle him.

"You have his eyes," she said at last.

"No, they're my own," he said. "Er. . . Whose eyes?"

"The mortal sorcerer," she hissed. "The one who called himself Lych Lord."

"Gosh, do I?" said Henwyn. "I expect it's just a family resemblance. I'm his descendent, you see. He was my great-great-grandfather or something."

"He sailed to Elvensea once," said Hellesvor. She seemed to choose her words especially for hissing; her voice was like surf sliding over shingle. "One of seven sorcerers from the east, of whom he was the subtlest. Our strength was failing, even then. Many of our kind had lost faith in me. They left Elvensea and sailed into the west, in search of new lands, not yet polluted by you grubby mortals. Only a few remained; those who were still loyal to me. Still we harried the coasts of the Westlands with sword and bow and dragon fire in the hope that we might drive your kind away and have the woods and hills and rivers for our own again. Then your great-great-grandsire and his six friends came. They tricked us. They said they sought peace, and came with gifts, but as soon as their black ship was in our harbour they struck at us with their spells. Strong, they were, stronger than we had ever imagined mortal sorcerers could grow. They toppled our towers; they tore our dragons from the sky with bolts of fire."

"I have heard of that battle," said Henwyn. "The people of the Autumn Isles saw the glow of it."

"One by one, all my warriors fell," said Hellesvor. "Gortheren, Gwaynya, Gwyngala, Moren the Fair; all fell in flames, and the sea swallowed them. And when only I was left, your grandsire turned his spells on me, and forced my dear Mortholow to the ground, and bound us both with his magic. . ." She shuddered, and it seemed to Henwyn as if he could see the memories moving behind her eyes, like cloud shadows scudding over a grey sea.

"He took the Elvenhorn," she said. "The enchanted horn that our forefathers used to raise Elvensea from the ocean, and he used it to sink our land again, to hide it in the deeps. Poor Mortholow went down with it; I saw her shining black scales dwindle, twined here about my palace, deep in her enchanted sleep. But not me. I wish I had slept too, but your Lych Lord had other plans for me. He bound me fast with chains of slowsilver and took me in his black ship back to the Westlands. He imprisoned me in one of the tallest turrets of his fortress of Clovenstone. And there I stayed, through all the centuries of his rule. I was a trophy of his first great victory."

"That must have been awful," said Zeewa.

The grey eyes turned on her, as cold as ever. "You cannot possibly imagine, little mud-born mortal. There were times when I almost wished that I had been born a mortal too, so that I could at least look forward to death setting me free.

"But as the centuries passed, so the power of the Lych Lord faded. Magic was waning from the world. There came a time when even that jumped-up mortal sorcerer could no longer work his spells. Then the armies of the kings of men assailed Clovenstone, and in the tumult and confusion before the Black Keep was sealed, I managed to escape.

"There was no point in returning to Elvensea. The spells which the Lych Lord laid could be broken only by the Elvenhorn, which was sealed up with him in his keep. I didn't think that it would work anyway, with magic in such short supply. So I fled into the wild places of the world. I wandered in those mountains where dwarves have not yet dug their mines, and in those forests where humans have not yet begun to cut down trees. And then the Slowsilver Star came, and I felt magic bloom again. My fingertips tingled with uncast spells. I had nothing of my old power, because that had come from Elvensea. I could never be more than a hedge witch in your Westlands. So I disguised myself as an old woman and went down into the lands of man and started looking for a way to get the Elvenhorn and return to my rightful home."

"Couldn't you just have come and asked for the Elvenhorn?" said Skarper.

"And then hired your own ship?" agreed Prince Rhind. "Why go posing as a cook?"

"Do you think I wished to be your servant, Sheep Lord?" hissed Hellesvor. "Do you think it pleased me to work in the kitchens of Dyn Gwlan, stewing apples and brewing soup? You mortals – your tastes are as as bland as your faces. When I set dishes before you fit for an elven king – seared crabs' hearts on a bed of rosemary, for instance, or my tagine of seahorse entrails with fried coral polyps – you turned up your lumpish, mud-born noses!"

"We are simple folk in Tyr Davas," said Breenge. "We don't like that fancy foreign cooking. You used too much garlic. We liked your rhubarb crumble though. And you did a lovely jam roly poly."

The elven queen narrowed her eyes; her thin mouth turned down so far at the corners that it looked like a childishly written letter *n*. "And how do you think I felt?" she whispered. "I, before whose dragons the armies of the kings of men had once fled in terror, when you asked me for another helping of my lovely jam roly poly?"

"A bit put out?" asked Skarper.

"It was a rhetorical question, fool."

"Oh."

"It made me curse the Lych Lord even more furiously. For not only had he drowned my home; one of the spells he laid on me meant that I could never return there – not alone. I could never order a ship or boat to Elvensea; nor could I pilot it myself, for the spell would stop me turning its prow towards the west. And so I found another way. I placed that old scroll about the Elvenhorn in the library of Dyn Gwlas, and made sure that Prawl saw it, and showed it to you, Prince Rhind. I knew your greed for gold and glory would drive you to make the journey to Elvensea, and I knew that your greed for rhubarb crumble would make you bring me with you. You would hire the captain, you would give the orders, and I would be carried here as your passenger."

"I say!" cried Rhind. "It wasn't greed for gold and glory that made me want to sound the Elvenhorn and raise this place. I did it because . . . well . . . I thought elves were nice."

Hellesvor laughed. You would think a bit of laughter would be better than an n-shaped scowl, but this wasn't a nice sort of laugh at all. It was like a cold bell clanging.

"Oh, we *are* nice," she said. "I am glad some memories of the old days, when elves were alone in the world, have echoed down even through mortal tales. We were *very* nice. We were peaceful, and gentle, and we loved nature in all its moods. But we could not share it with you mortal monkeys."

"Well, you're going to have to, I'm afraid," said Henwyn. "There's only one of you, and there are loads of us. We're just going to have to find a way to get along."

"Why?" demanded Hellesvor. "One elf is enough to destroy you all, if that elf is Queen Hellesvor and the finest sorcerers you can field against her are fools like Fentongoose and Prawl. One elf is enough to turn all your mortal cities to dust and ashes, if she is mounted upon the black dragon Mortholow. The smoke of their burning will spread across the world, and the elves who departed will see it even from their new lands across the sea, and come home to help me make the Westlands beautiful again. But there has been enough talk."

"Well, you're the one who's been doing all the talking," said Skarper.

Hellesvor ignored him. "I shall arm myself, and have Mortholow carry me east, and we shall light some torches upon the Autumn Isles and the Nibbled Coast to warn the Westlands that Hellesvor has returned!"

She turned her back on them and went striding towards the doors, and suddenly it was as if a spell had been broken. Henwyn and Rhind both lifted their swords and started after her, completely forgetting the things they'd said earlier to Flegg about stabbing women in the back. But before they could reach her, Zeewa bounded in front of them, raised her spear, and drove it hard between Hellesvor's shoulder blades.

At least, she tried to. Those jewelled black robes, which looked so soft, were harder than tempered steel. "Ow!" yowled Zeewa, dropping the blunted spear and clutching her jarred hand.

Hellesvor turned, furious, her face paler than ever. She took hold of Zeewa by her hair, plucked her off her feet and flung her across the hall. Zeewa hit the polished floor, slid for a few feet, and vanished with a cry of terror into that milky moonpool which opened in its centre.

"Zeewa!" shouted Henwyn, as he, Skarper and Gutgust ran towards the pool.

"She is gone," said Hellesvor. "Thus, in the golden days of Elvensea, did we rid ourselves of criminals and captive mortal kings." She laughed again. "I have not time to waste in killing you. In the great old days I could have sent an army of elven warriors to finish you. As it is, I must find a humbler army, but they will kill you all the same. Perhaps if you use that pretty sword of yours with skill, Prince Rhind, a few of you will survive just long enough to see my torches lit."

She opened the doors and stalked out through them into sunlight and the spiky black shadow of the dragon. Rhind and Gutgust ran to shut them, afraid that Mortholow might reach a talon in, or set her snout against the open doorway and fill the hall with fire. They did not see the dragon go creeping after Hellesvor as obediently as a puppy as she started to descend the long stairways. They did not see Hellesvor stop, and stoop to pick up a little white crab that was sidling across the flagstones, wondering where the sea had gone.

She lifted it in her white hands, blew upon it with a smile, and tossed it into the shadows under one of the dragon statues. Then, still smiling, she hurried on down the stairways of Elvensea, with the great black dragon spilling down behind her.

Back in the hall, Henwyn was still shouting, "Zeewa!" and leaning out so far over the edge of that pearly pool that Skarper was afraid he'd tumble after her.

"Didn't you hear what the elf witch said?" he asked, grabbing Henwyn by the back of his trousers. "Zeewa's gone! It's a pool of poison or something, where they used to drown their enemies."

Henwyn shook his head. "It's not poison. It's magic."

"Well, that's just as bad. She's probably been turned into a statue or an amoeba or something, and if you jump in after her you'll get changed too!"

"And we need you, Henwyn," agreed Rhind, running to help Skarper pull Henwyn away from the dreadful pool. "We need your sword. We have to stop Hellesvor before she can fly to the Nibbled Coast and light those torches of hers."

"Well, I don't see what's so very bad about lighting torches," said Breenge, who was a little wiser than her brother and guessed that neither his sword nor

Henwyn's could harm Hellesvor where Zeewa's spear had failed.

"She didn't mean torches literally," said Prince Rhind. "It was a metaphor or simile (I can never remember the difference). She means to fly that beastly dragon of hers over Choon and Lusuenn and Floonhaven and Porthstrewy and burn them to ashes with its fiery breath! That's why we have to stop her! Or die trying! It is our duty as heroes!"

He started to run towards the doors, but Skarper called him back. "Careful, Rhind! Don't you remember – Hellesvor said she would send an army to deal with us."

"She said 'a humble army'," Rhind reminded him.

Henwyn stood up, still shaky, still unwilling to admit that Zeewa was truly gone. "It does not much matter how humble they are," he said. "What do we have? Two swords, Breenge's bow, two goblin knives, and a sofa. Even the humblest army will defeat us if there are enough of them."

"Then let's not wait here to get defeated!" said Skarper. "Let's get out of here! Maybe Kestle and Woon Gumpus have sorted out a way to get the *Sea Cucumber* afloat."

There was a rattling, scraping, stony sort of noise behind him. He spun round with a squeak, afraid that

Hellesvor's humble army had already arrived. But it was only Grumpling. The Chilli Hat was harder to squash than anyone had imagined; he had been stunned when that slab of ceiling landed on him, but he was still more-or-less three dimensional, and he heaved it off himself and stood up, dusty, bloody and blinking.

"Two swords, Breenge's bow, two goblin knives, a sofa an' an AXE," he said.

"Grumpling!" they all shouted (except Spurtle, of course, who could only rustle his cushions a bit). None of them had ever imagined being pleased to see Grumpling.

Grumpling himself seemed a bit surprised by their greeting. "Well, where's this army then?" he asked, swishing his axe about in an experimental way.

"Maybe there is no army," said Henwyn. "Maybe it was only Hellesvor's ruse to keep us here while she takes flight. Our blades may not be able to harm her, but perhaps they will at least work on that dragon of hers."

"What dragon?" asked Grumpling.

Skarper realized that Grumpling had no idea of anything that happened since Flegg blew the Elvenhorn and the roof came down on him. "The dragon outside!" he said. "It wasn't stone at all, but real."

"I tole you so," said Grumpling.

"And Ninnis isn't dead, and she isn't Ninnis either – she's an old elf sorceress called Hellesvor and she chucked poor Zeewa down that hole and now she's gone to set fire to the Nibbled Coast. Clear?"

Grumpling scratched his head. It wasn't really, but there wasn't time to explain properly. Skarper ran back to the doors, opened them a crack, and peeked out. The wide paved balcony outside the hall was empty. There were a few scratches on the stonework left by Motholow's claws, and that was all. He opened the door wider and slipped outside. The others followed him. Henwyn and Rhind had their swords in their hands, Grumpling clutched his axe, and Gutgust carried the sofa. Breenge had tucked Fuzzy-Nose into the open neck of her tunic and taken her bow from her shoulder. She paused at the balcony's edge to string it and ready an arrow. Then they started down. Far below them they could hear faint scraping, slinking sounds such as a large dragon might make, squeezing through the narrow streets and colonnades they had explored earlier.

They had gone down one level, and were starting down the next flight of stairs, when Skarper happened to look over the handrail and saw that a lot of small oval buildings on the level below had started moving.

Then he remembered that there hadn't been any small oval buildings on the level below.

He was just about to point this out to everybody else when Gutgust shouted, "Anchovies!" and Breenge screamed, "Crabs! Hundreds of them!"

Grumpling on the Stairs

The crabs were the same colour as the stone that Elvensea was built from, so it was not surprising that Skarper had mistaken their shells for the roofs of small buildings. The other reason, of course, was that they were the size of small buildings. They clustered for a moment at the foot of the stairs, peering up at the people above them with their tiny black eyes, waving their feelers, and making precise little pinching motions with their claws. Then, scrambling over each other in their eagerness to attack, they began to scuttle upwards.

"A humble army indeed," whispered Henwyn.

Breenge loosed an arrow. It stuck in the shell of the leading crab, who didn't even seem to notice. Everyone turned and ran back to the level above, but the crabs moved with surprising speed, dancing along on the points of their hairy claws like eight-legged, armoured ballerinas who could only go sideways. Huge pincers reached for the companions, clopping and snicking. There was a horrible smell of rotting fish.

"It is Ninnis's joke on us," said Rhind, swinging his sword and lopping off a crab's claw. "She knows I don't like seafood!"

"We'll hold them off!" shouted Henwyn, leaping to Rhind's side. "The rest of you, find another way down!"

Grumpling shouldered both him and Rhind aside, and sank his axe through the shell of a massive crab. "This is a job fer an axe, not rubbish softling swords," he roared. "Crumble-crab armies is no match fer Grumpling the Magnificent!"

The axe swung, meteor bright, hewing through pincers and jointed legs, smashing shells, lopping off eye-stalks. Crab paste spurted high into the air.

The others fell back, slowly at first, then faster, realizing that they must use the time Grumpling was buying them to find an escape route. Skarper helped Gutgust lug Spurtle into one of the nearby buildings, despite the way the sofa kept protesting. "I'm done for!" it mumbled, in its muffled, cushiony voice. "Leave me here, Skarper! I'm no use to you. There's no room in a hard fight for soft furnishings like me. Leave me, and save yourselves!"

"You're coming with us, Spurtle," Skarper promised him. "We never know when we might need a nice sit down."

But Elvensea was playing its tricks on them again. Already Skarper had lost sight of Henwyn, Rhind and Breenge. Now he lost Gutgust and Spurtle too. He was not sure how it happened. He lingered for a moment to look back at the stairs, where Grumpling was swinging his bright axe to and fro at the heart of an explosion of shell and crab meat, and when he ran on, they were no longer ahead of him. He doubled back, checking passages that they might have turned down. It should not have been hard to spot a large goblin dragging a small sofa, but there was no sign of them. He shouted, "Gutgust!" and thought he heard a faint, answering cry of, "Anchovies!" but Grumpling was making an awful racket out on the stairs, bellowing war cries and slaughtering crabs, and it was hard to tell where Gutgust's voice had come from. Gulls had arrived, too, drawn by the smell of the crabs, and they were adding their screams to the din of the battle.

Skarper opened a door, found a narrow stairway leading down, and followed it for a way. But long before he reached the bottom he saw crabs climbing up towards him, and hastily retraced his steps, slamming the door behind him. He ran on, through glass-roofed orangeries where dead trees stood, through courts where dragon fountains had once played, through halls and chambers where Hellesvor's people must once have met and mingled and played music – an unstrung harp still stood in one, carved in the shape of a rearing dragon with mother-of-pearl eyes. Poor old elves; he almost felt sorry for them, driven out of the Westlands by noisy, messy softlings and noisier, messier goblins.

Then, stopping to catch his breath in one wide room, he glanced up at the ceiling and saw a painting there that showed a whole troop of armoured elves, riding dragons as big as Mortholow, wheeling above a blazing human town. He didn't feel sorry for *them*, he decided. Not for Hellesvor and her kind. But probably not all elves were the same, just as not all goblins or all humans were the same. Those other elves, the ones who'd gone to find a peaceful new life in the west, perhaps they'd been all right. He hoped they had found what they were seeking, out there along the sunset path.

Beyond the room with the painted ceiling was another stairway. No sound of crab claws or scrape of crabshells came from below. He started down it, but by some quirk of elvish architecture it swerved round upon itself and led up instead. He reached a small bronze door, pushed it open, and stumbled out on to the balcony outside the domed hall at the top of the island.

"We'll never get out of this place!" he wailed.

Gull shadows scattered across the flagstones, and behind them came another shadow, wider, darker. Skarper looked up.

"Oh, bumcakes!" he said.

Mortholow folded her vast bat wings and plunged towards him, and flames came belching from her open mouth.

Ten levels below, Hellesvor had been busy in her armoury. She had girded herself in shining silver-green armour, more delicate than any mortal smith could forge, yet stronger than any mortal blade could pierce. She had strapped a long sword across her back, where it would not dangle down and get in the way when she was riding Mortholow. She had found a harness made from slowsilver and dragonhide, and Mortholow, who had been waiting outside all this time, perched on a turret with her wings spread in the sun like a cormorant, came meekly when she called, and let herself be bridled.

The elves who rode dragons into battle did not saddle them, as humans saddled horses. There was nowhere on a dragon's spiny back that would be comfortable to sit, and if you did find a perch there, the creatures were so big that you would see nothing but their wings on either side of you and their long necks arching ahead. Instead, a dragon rider of Elvensea lay in a harness slung beneath the dragon's chest, rather as, in other worlds, humans hang from hangliders and kites.

Into this harness climbed Hellesvor, and at a tug on the reins (which attached to the horny spurs on either side of Mortholow's huge head) the dragon launched itself into the air and went spiralling around the flanks of Elvensea, down towards the blue waves. Each beat of her huge wings carried her clear round the island. Swinging beneath her, her hair streaming back on the wind, Hellesvor glared at the wreck of her city – empty windows and mounds of weed that disfigured the lower levels which had had no spells to protect them during their time under the sea. And what was that, that ugly black thing, like a giant's dirty slipper, caught between the turrets of the Tower of Amlowenhe? It was a ship, a horrid, ugly, shabby, mortal ship!

Hellesvor tugged on the reins again, and shouted a command as Mortholow swung towards the stranded ship. Above her head the dragon's chest glowed like the panes of a bone lantern as her inner fires ignited.

Then with a *whooof* the flames spewed out of her, enwrapping the *Sea Cucumber*, and her wingbeats fanned the blaze as she soared past it and on around the island, leaving the old ship to burn behind her; leaving Captain Kestle and Woon Gumpus (who had luckily not been on board at the time) to look up in dismay from the street below, and dodge the burning chunks of timber and spots of tar which came raining down on them.

Now Mortholow rose again, up past stairways crawling with the giant crabs Hellesvor's spell had conjured. Hellesvor saw Grumpling struggling there, at the top of the stairs on the level below the pillared hall. A burst of dragon fire blew down on him; black smoke and a smell of roast crab swirled into the air, and Mortholow went with it, spreading her wings and riding her own thermal up high into the sky above Elvensea.

And that was when Hellesvor saw Skarper, stumbling out of his little doorway and on to the balcony in front of the hall. She even heard his voice borne on the clear air. "We'll never get out of this place!"

"No, goblin," said Hellesvor, recalling all the goblins much like him who had been her gaolers during the years of her captivity in Clovenstone. "No, you will not!" And she dragged Mortholow into a steep dive and screamed, "Burn him! Blast him!", closing her eyes as the flames belched and the sparks blew back at her.

When she opened them, Mortholow was circling high again. The balcony was blackened and deserted, smoke drifted to leeward, the stones glowed red in places. Hellesvor felt suddenly sorry. Not because she'd just roasted Skarper, but because she had left that black scar upon her beautiful island.

"Come, Mortholow," she shouted. "It is human towns that should be burning, not the city of the elves!"

And she hauled on her dragon's reins and it wheeled once more around the heights of Elvensea and then went flying away towards the east, where the lands of man lay like a grubby stain along the far horizon.

Skarper heard the wingbeats as the dragon turned above the hall. He did not realize that Mortholow was leaving. He had only just survived the first attack, crashing in through the big double doors of the hall as that spout of flame hit the pavement behind him. Now he imagined the huge beast flapping down to stick its head through those same doors and breathe more fire at him. He ran into the cool shadows of the hall, and as he ran he looked back over his shoulder, expecting at any moment Mortholow's scaly snout to shove the doors apart behind him.

The doors did not open, but he did notice that his tail was on fire. What he didn't notice was the magical pool ahead of him. Not until he put down his foot expecting to find floor beneath it and found nothing but a short drop into an enchanted mist instead.

"Oh bum—" he said, falling.

The pool swallowed him, and the rest of the word with him.

Another World

"—cakes!" said Skarper.

He had landed on a floor after all. There had been a moment of silvery cold as the enchanted mist closed over him, and then a sharp thud. Now here he lay, face down on a smooth white floor that looked like marble, but wasn't cool enough for marble.

He looked up. He was in a kind of corridor whose walls were made of coloured boxes. High above him, white lights shone without flame inside more boxes on a high, white ceiling.

As he watched, a woman passed across the end of the corridor. She was pushing a small cart made of criss-crossed silver wire. Through the mesh of the cart Skarper could see bottles, boxes and – were those tin cans?

"Skarper!" hissed a voice.

"Zeewa!"

The Muskish girl was crouched close by. She looked odd and defenceless without her spear, and he remembered how she had tried to stab Hellesvor, and how she had been thrown into the magic pool.

"The pool. . ." he said. "It's not a pool at all, it's a pathway to another world. I think we're in Etty's super market."

"Or another just like it," said Zeewa.

"There can't be two super markets," said Skarper.

Zeewa wrinkled her nose. "What's that smell?"

Skarper smelled it too. An acrid, burnt-hair sort of smell, almost as if. . .

He looked round. The jaunty ginger tuft on the end of his tail was jaunty and ginger no longer. It was black, and a yellow flame fluttered from it. As he stood gawping at it, the flame spread to one of the boxes on the shelves behind him. The box was made of a sort of thick paper, decorated with pictures of small brown grating-like objects floating in a bowl of milk. It burned very well, and the flames spread quickly to the boxes on either side of it, and then up to the shelf above.

"Help!" shouted Skarper. "Fire!"

"Shhh!" hissed Zeewa, grabbing his tail and stamping the flames out while he went, "Ow! Ow!" But it was too late. The super market seemed quiet, but the woman with the cart had heard his shout. She

269

reappeared at the end of the aisle of coloured boxes, and her eyes widened as she saw all the smoke. "Fire!" she screamed. "Help! Fire!"

Zeewa let go of Skarper's tail, grabbed his hand, and set off running, dragging him after her, as a terrible noise began to fill the air. Bells rang, and weird voices wailed: *OooooOOOooOOOOO!* Up on the ceiling, lights started to flash red, and other voices boomed, "This is an emergency. Please make your way to the nearest exit."

Skarper and Zeewa didn't need telling. Frightened and alone in this strange world, they just wanted to hide, and there was no hiding in the white light of the super market. They ran past walls of jam jars, through avenues of fruit and vegetables, through an aisle of shelves that held more books than all the bumwipe heaps of Clovenstone combined. People in the strange, brightly coloured clothes of that world ran with them, or past them, or blundered in front of them, shouting, "Fire! Fire!"

Zeewa saw what she thought was a door – a glimpse of an evening sky above a landscape crowded with so many strange and unknown objects that it was easier just not to look at it. They sprinted towards it, but it wasn't a door – it was a window, filled with a sheet of glass so clear and wide that Skarper could not imagine how it had been blown, and so strong that it did not shatter when he and Zeewa slammed into it.

As they stumbled backwards, dazed, there was a weird, wild hooting from outside. It reminded Skarper of a banshee who had once roosted for a while in the ruins of the Outer Wall at Clovenstone, but even she had not been quite so loud. He stared as a huge red shape slid past outside the window. He had heard tell of carriages that moved by themselves in other worlds – he had even ridden in the Lych Lord's old Rolls Royce Silver Shadow, although it belonged to Carnglaze now and was pulled by horses in the normal way. But surely there couldn't be a carriage as big or as red as the thing which was rolling to a stop on its huge black wheels outside the super market? And what were those lights on its back, flashing blue, blue, blue? And who were these warriors, helmeted, visored, jumping down from its opening doors?

He clutched Zeewa's hand; she clutched his paw. They shrank back together into the shelter of a large cardboard cut-out of a celebrity chef. Skarper would rather have been back in Elvensea, facing the fire-breathing dragon.

"Oh no!" said Breenge.

"What is it?" asked her brother.

"I have lost Fuzzy-Nose! I had him with me on the stairs, but he must have fallen out of my tunic somewhere in these silly corridors! I must go back and look for him!"

Henwyn could barely believe it. They had spent ages hunting for a way down. Now, at last, they had found one: a tight corkscrew of stone stairs descending on the opposite side of Elvensea from those other stairs where Grumpling was holding off the crabs. And now they were here, Breenge was refusing to go down them. "He's only a rabbit!" he said, pushing her as politely as he could towards the stairs. "You and Rhind go down. I'll meet you at the bottom."

"You're going back?" asked Rhind. He looked as if he were afraid that Henwyn was about to out-hero him, and for a moment Henwyn was worried that he was going to refuse to go down the stairs, too.

"I have to fetch Grumpling," he said.

"Do you?" Rhind looked doubtful. "He's never been a friendly fellow. To be honest, I wondered why you brought him with you. He never seemed to like you much."

"Nor I him," Henwyn agreed. "But he is my companion, and it would be wrong to leave him behind. You and Breenge go on. I'll fetch Grumpling and be right behind you. And I'll look for Fuzzy-Nose on my way."

"We'll see you at the ship," said Rhind.

"And if we see that dragon, we shall find out how it likes the taste of the arrows of the Woolmark," promised Breenge.

They started down the stair, and Henwyn turned back through the maze of buildings. He was very afraid that he would lose his way again, but either his sense of direction was improving or some spell that had confused him when he entered was losing its power, for he went back with barely a wrong turning to the stairway where Grumpling had made his stand against the crabs.

As he neared it he began to notice the smell of roasted crab, ominous but mouth-watering. When he emerged on to the balcony where the stairway ended he cried out in amazement at what he saw there.

All across the balcony, dead crabs were strewn. They were heaped three deep around the head of the stairs, and all the way down the staircase too. When he peered over the balustrade Henwyn could see scores of them scattered on the streets and roofs below. There seemed to be not a single live crab left in Elvensea, apart from little ones, which had appeared out of the weeds to feast upon the bodies of their outsize cousins.

At the top of the stairs, and on the balcony, the mounds of crab carcasses seemed to have been swept by a wildfire. They were blackened and still smouldering. Saffron flames licked up here and there from a still-burning shell. A haze of dirty smoke hung in the air. Of Grumpling, there was no sign.

Then one of the crabs stirred and shifted, its cracked shell creaking. Henwyn sprang back, readying his sword, but the creature was long dead. It rolled on to its back, legs in the air, and out from under it came crawling Grumpling.

He had paid dearly for his victory. Dark goblin blood spilled from a dozen wounds. One eye was swollen shut, or perhaps gone entirely, Henwyn couldn't tell. And the fire had charred him too, burning his hair to stubble, blackening his face.

"That bloomin' dragon!" he croaked. "I dealt with the crabs all right, but that dragon cheated. It was flying about up there an' I thought it was another statue till it came swoopin' down an' burped fire all over me. Bloomin' dragon."

"Oh, Grumpling," said Henwyn, catching him as he collapsed – or trying to, for Grumpling was very heavy. "Statues don't fly!"

"Well, nobody tole me that," the dying goblin grumbled. His surviving eye swivelled round to glare at Henwyn. "I never liked you, softling. Only reason I came on this stupid quest is cos Flegg said we'd have a chance to get my scratchbackler back, an' maybe get rid of you, an' then I'd be King of Clovenstone. Cos that's what I oughter be. I'm the biggest an' toughest and most magnificent of all the goblins."

Henwyn looked about him at the mounds of dead crabs, and at the notched and buckled blade of the axe still clutched in Grumpling's massive paw. He felt almost as sad as he had when Princess Ned died. He had never imagined feeling sad for Grumpling.

"You are," he said. "You are bigger and tougher and more magnificent than any of us, and I am going to make sure that everyone knows it. Ballads shall be sung about Grumpling the Great, and how he Held the Stair at Elvensea. I shall make sure everyone knows of your bravery. If we get back to Clovenstone, I shall try and get a statue done of you."

"A fat lot of good that's goin ter be ter me," said Grumpling, grumpily. "Just get rid of that bloomin' dragon, softling."

And with that he died, and Henwyn knelt there for a moment with him, and then remembered that there was a dragon and a mad elf witch to deal with, and laid Grumpling's axe across his chest, and left him there, and ran back to the other stairway where he had bade farewell to Rhind and Breenge. And as he ran he thought, *I wonder what's become of Skarper? I hope he's all right. But I expect he is – Skarper usually finds a way to be all right.*

275

Fire Warriors

Outside the super market window, the warriors from the red carriage assembled their battle gear, unrolling long leathery-looking hoses, taking down canisters of silvery metal from cupboards in the carriage's side where axes and other devices were also stored. Their captain moved across the pavement outside the super market. He was acting as warriors act in every world, proud of his power and his big voice, ordering people to move back and make way.

Peeking from behind the cardboard cut-out, Skarper thought that it was little wonder the elves had sent people to this world as a punishment. He could see nothing outside the window but walls and roofs and strangely dressed people and little brightly coloured carriages. There were a couple of trees, but they were sad little things, growing through holes in a plain of

276

stone, their trunks imprisoned inside wire cages. It was not an elfy sort of place at all.

"Skarper!" said Zeewa. "Get down!"

The warriors were coming inside the super market now. Skarper could hear the tramp of their big boots even over the racket of the bells and banshees. Three of them came right past the place where he and Zeewa crouched. They shouted things to each other, and into crackly boxes strapped to their tunics. They did not seem frightened of the fire. They strode towards it, two of them hefting those shiny cylinders. There were short hoses attached to the cylinders' tops, with nozzles at the end. They reminded Skarper of the contraptions which the dwarves used to shoot flame at their enemies. But that couldn't be right, could it? Were the warriors planning to fight the fire with more fire?

He supposed that, in this strange world, anything was possible.

As the warriors stomped past him and vanished up the aisle where the fire had started, Skarper nudged Zeewa. "Come on, let's follow them!"

"Why?"

"Because I want to see what they're doing. And anyway, where the fire started is where we came through from Elvensea. If we're going to go back, that's where we need to be."

"Do you think there will be a way back?"

"Maybe," said Skarper. He fingered the amulet around his neck. "Etty gave me this stone. It's full of slowsilver, and I can feel it kind of *pulling*, wanting to get back to the Westlands. It doesn't belong in this place any more than we do. Maybe if we can find the place where the wall between the worlds is thin, it will pull us through with it."

Carefully, holding the cut-out celebrity chef in front of them like a shield, they crept after the warriors. It was raining now in the aisle where the fire had started; indoor rain sprinkling down from the ceiling. The rain had stopped the fire from spreading, but some of the boxes which Skarper had set light to still burned merrily, giving off smells like burnt biscuits. One of the warriors set down his silver cylinder, raised the nozzle on the end of its hose, and sprayed a hissing cloud of white smoke at the flames. For a moment Skarper could not imagine what he was trying to do. Wasn't there enough smoke already? Then he saw that wherever the white smoke touched, the fire withered and went out.

"Look!" he said. But Zeewa was looking at something else.

At the far end of the aisle, beyond the warriors, strange things were happening to the smoke. It was not so much swirling as whirling, forming a spinning ring a bit like an upright version of the whirlpool that had first bared Elvensea. In the centre of the ring was a milky mist, and through it, very faintly, shapes could be glimpsed: the tapering pillars and cracked ceiling of Hellesvor's pillared hall.

"It is the way home!" said Zeewa.

"And it's shrinking!" said Skarper.

He was right. The ring was slowly diminishing in size. It had filled the aisle when they first saw it; now it was not much larger than a door.

He felt something tug at his neck. Etty's stone was floating, straining at its cord in its eagerness to pass through the smoke and return to its own world.

"Quickly!" said Zeewa. "Before it is gone altogether!"

The warriors had noticed the smoke ring now. The one with the smoke squirter had stopped squirting and was staring at the strange portal. His comrade beside him stared too, and spoke quickly and urgently into the crackle box on his shoulder. The third man stood a little way behind them, holding his own smoke squirter ready. He was the only one to look round as the cardboard cut-out chef came scuttling towards him from the other end of the aisle.

"Delia?" he said, in a surprised way. And then added, in a still more surprised way, "Ooof!" as Zeewa's fist lashed out from behind the cut-out and caught him on the chin. He crashed backwards against more shelves of food boxes, and Skarper reached out a hairy paw and snatched his smoke squirter. The other two warriors sprang aside as Zeewa, Skarper and the cut-out dashed past them and dived into the heart of the smoke ring. . .

Which closed behind them with a faint "pop".

"Trick of the light," the warriors said to each other later, when the fire was out. "Reflections on the smoke. Kids mucking about."

"Lost my balance on that wet floor," said the one whom Zeewa had punched.

But the people who worked in the super market exchanged knowing glances. It was not the first time there had been strange goings on in the cereals aisle.

They surfaced through the white mist in Hellesvor's pool: Zeewa, Skarper and the beaming cut-out. They left the cut-out bobbing there and scrambled out.

"Where is everyone?" asked Zeewa. "And why does everything smell of overcooked crab?"

Skarper did his best to explain, and while he did so, Zeewa helped him carry the heavy smoke squirter out on to the balcony. They looked down at the crab-strewn city, the black ribs of the *Sea Cucumber* still burning on their tower. Far, far below, tiny figures fled across an open square.

"Henwyn!" shouted Skarper. "Wait for us! We've got a thing! A thing for fighting dragons with!"

Fentongoose and Doctor Prong had a thing for fighting dragons with, too. They were not sure that it would work, but they had to do something to defend the Westlands if the goblins' quest should fail, and it was the best they had been able to come up with at short notice. It was the Bratapult, the massive old war machine from Blackspike Tower, and they had bolted it to a hastily assembled wooden hat and strapped the whole lot on to Bryn's head.

Now they clung to it as the young giant ran towards the sea. Bryn's long legs could cover in one stride the distance that Skarper and his friends had travelled in an hour. The only trouble was, the passengers on his head had a bumpy ride, and so did the various goblins and twiglings who had come along, clinging to his beard and his broad shoulders. Close behind him came Fraddon, carrying more seasick goblins, and a few huge boulders that would be the Bratapult's ammunition.

Fraddon had been unsure at first about asking Bryn to help. If there were really dragons in the offing it could be dangerous, even for a giant. For all their size, his kind were not natural fighters. Leave the little peoples to their quarrels; that was the giants' way, and

281

that was how Fraddon had thought once. But then he had made friends with Princess Ned, and with other little people, and their friendship had been good for him. He wanted Bryn to be their friend too, right from the start. And if you were friends with someone, you could not let them set off to fight dragons alone.

Besides, Bryn wanted to help. He was young and strong, and eager for adventure.

The Wastes of Ulawn were covered by low cloud that morning. The people there sensed that something was coming down the road from Clovenstone, but they did not know what. "Goblins!" they shouted, snatching their scythes and pitchforks, reassembling their barricade and gathering behind it. They had just enough time to scatter again when the huge shape of Bryn loomed out of the murk. His left foot, big as a barn, booted the barricade to pieces. Fraddon's right foot, big as a boat, hammered the pieces flat. "Terribly sorry!" called Fentongoose, peering over the edge of Bryn's plank hat.

"Whoops!" cheered the goblins, clinging to his beard.

"Happy to pay for any damage!" added Doctor Prong.

Then they were gone, giants, goblins, old men, all off along the road to the sea, leaving the Ulawn folk to stare after them and wonder about building a bigger barricade. They left the clouds behind them too, and came out into sunlight on the cliffs west of Floonhaven.

Everything seemed calm. Bright sails speckled the blue sea at the mouth of the River Floon. People were gathering on the harbour wall and the battlements of the castle to stare at the two giants. A fresh west wind blew the smells of the salt sea over them, and Bryn breathed deeply and said, "This is it? The sea?"

"That is the sea," said Fraddon. "I stepped down off Choon Head once – a little south of here – and picked up Ned's ship. I was as big then as you are now."

"There is no sign of any dragons," said Doctor Prong.

"I am delighted to say you're right," agreed Fentongoose. "The goblins' quest must have succeeded."

"But I am quite sure we heard the Elvenhorn sound," said Doctor Prong.

"You are quite certain it was the Elvenhorn? The wind can make strange noises sometimes, blowing round the towers of Clovenstone. Not to mention the goblins' tummies. . ."

"Look!" shouted one of the goblins just then. "What's that?"

"Fire!" said Fentongoose. "There is fire on the Autumn Isles!"

Out there at the edge of sight, where the islands lay like ghosts of islands on the Western Ocean, a tower of smoke was rising. A black speck rose with it.

"A butterfly?" asked Dr Prong, hopefully.

"A bird?" said Fentongoose, as the speck grew larger.

"A bat, a very large bat, perhaps the lesser-spotted Barraganese fruit bat. . ." pondered Doctor Prong.

But they both knew what it really was.

So did the goblins. "Dragon!" they shouted. "Dragon!" And the giants took up the cry in their sky-wide voices, and so the bad news of the dragon's coming spread to Floonhaven. The people there abandoned their boats and nets, their crops and cottages, and ran up the hill to the king's castle to seek shelter. Out on the sea the ships scudded for shelter too. Goblins crowded on to Bryn's hat, heaving the boulder which Fraddon passed them up into the cup of the Bratapult, while Fentongoose trained his telescope on the approaching dragon and Doctor Prong called out helpful things like, "Don't shoot till you see the reds of its eyes!" and, "Remember, short, controlled bursts!"

And all the while the dragon came on.

Henwyn was standing at the foot of the tower where the *Sea Cucumber* had come to rest when Skarper and Zeewa finally caught up with him. Breenge and Rhind sat nearby on Spurtle, who was still in his sofa form. They were all looking up at the charred black skeleton, which was all that remained of their ship.

"We are stuck here, then," said Skarper.

"Poor Kestle!" said Zeewa. "Poor Woon Gumpus!"

"Oh, we're all right!" shouted Kestle, appearing at that moment on one of the steep roads that led down to the island's edge.

Everyone stood up (except Spurtle, of course), not sure whether to run one way and hug Zeewa, who they had thought was lost for ever, or run the other and hug the sea captains, who they had thought were burned. In the end, most of them did both, and when all the hugging and but-we-thought-you-were-dead-ing was over, Woon Gumpus said, "When Captain Kestle's ship was burned by that dragon, we decided that we must find another."

"We must!" agreed Henwyn. "Mortholow is flying towards the Nibbled Coast even now, and Hellesvor means to burn every town she sees there. We must find a ship, and go to help!"

"It is my fault that this peril has been unleashed upon the world," said Rhind. "I shall slay that dragon, even if it means my own death."

"And I shall stand beside you, brother!" said Breenge bravely, although she was still a bit sniffly about losing her rabbit.

"Well then," said Woon Gumpus, "you will all be glad to hear that we have just the ship for you! Come and see!"

They hurried down towards the sea, with Spurtle rolling ahead on his swift casters. As they went, Kestle explained, "There are harbours all around the shore. The ships in most of 'em have rotted away to nothing, but we found one which must have been protected by some spell."

"Just like the palaces on the heights," said Henwyn.

"Perhaps it was Hellesvor's own ship," said Breenge.

"I can't say who she belonged to," said Kestle, "but they were lucky to have her. She's a beauty!"

The ship was full of seawater of course, and lay low in the water like a floating log. But even landlubbers like Skarper and Henwyn could see how fine she was. A sleek arrow of a ship, made from the smooth white wood of some tree they could not name, her hull tapering to a high, carved prow shaped like a dragon's head, her stern to a fish-like tail. Even her sails and rigging seemed to have survived the time beneath the sea; like the tapestries in the halls above, the white ropes and furled red cloth did not even seem wet.

She was a wonderful find, and it was easy to see why the two sea captains were so pleased. But as Skarper and the others fetched pots and buckets from the harbourside and started scooping out the water, Henwyn looked worriedly towards the east. A pall of smoke hung on the sky there, larger and darker than the stain that had led them to the wreckage of the *Swan*. It came from the Autumn Isles, he guessed. By now, the shadow of Mortholow's wings must be falling upon the Nibbled Coast, and her fiery breath kindling the thatch of Choon or Floonhaven. And even in an elven ship, even with a west wind in her sails, the Nibbled Coast must be a day and a night away at least. By the time they reached it there would be nothing but smoke and embers.

"We shall be too late!" he said. "We shall be too late to help, too late to save anyone!"

The others understood. "But what else can we do?" asked Zeewa. "If we cannot help them, at least we shall avenge them."

"No," said Henwyn. "By the time we reach the Nibbled Coast, Hellesvor will have flown on. She will be far inland, burning Clovenstone, or Adherak, or Tyr Davas. Our only hope is to draw her back to us. We must make her leave off her attack upon the lands of men, and fly back here to Elvensea."

"But what would bring her back?" asked Rhind. "She thinks her crab-army killed us. She thinks Elvensea is deserted. Why would she return?"

"She will come back when the Westlands are black and dead," said Henwyn. "She will come back to see if her plan has worked, and if the smoke of the fires she kindled has called the elves back here from across the ocean. But what if we kindle a fire of our own, to call her here? If she wants her people to return to Elvensea, she would not want to see it burn."

"Set fire to Elvensea?" said Skarper. It seemed wrong, somehow, to think of destroying all this beauty. But it was only stone, after all. Only empty buildings. It was not worth a single cottage in Floonhaven or Porthstrewy.

"Would it even burn?" asked Woon Gumpus. "It's all wet and seaweedy."

"These lower levels are," said Henwyn, "but up above we saw rooms full of tapestries and fine furniture. Musical instruments. Papers. Books."

"A treasure trove," said Rhind.

"Kindling for a mighty bonfire," said Skarper.

And somehow it was decided, without anyone saying another word. They left Gutgust behind to help the captains empty out the elven ship, and the rest ran back up the winding roadways and the stairs, seizing burning brands from the wreckage of the *Sea Cucumber* as they went. Back into the labyrinths of the elves' high palaces they ran, and in each room and corridor they scattered fire like golden flowers.

Fire on the Nibbled Coast

Low over the blue swell flew Mortholow. Foam from the rippling waves flecked Hellesvor's face where she hung in her harness under the dragon's breast. Behind her rose the smoke of the Autumn Isles. The settlements there were so tiny and so scattered that she had not had the patience to burn them; she had just had her dragon start heath fires on the heathered tops of Grundy and Far Penderglaze, then soared on. Ahead of her lay the Nibbled Coast, the ugly white towns of the mortals littered in every bay and cove like tide-wrack, waiting for the cleansing dragon-fire.

But what was that? Northward, where the coast faded into mist, two man-shaped things too massive to be men. Hellesvor hauled on a rein and Mortholow obeyed her, veering towards the huge figures. Giants? She took the dragon higher, wondering. Elves had no argument with giants. But the Clovenstone goblins had counted a giant among their friends, if the stories of the fight at Adherak were true. Was this him? And if so, who was the other?

Up on Bryn's hat, Fentongoose said, "Ready, take aim . . . not yet, Yabber – oh bother!"

The first shot from the Bratapult flew so wide of its mark that Hellesvor didn't even realize it had been a shot until it crashed into the sea, far to the south of her. Then she understood. She tugged on the reins again, and Mortholow shrieked and folded her wings, diving towards the giants on the cliff.

"Left seven degrees," Doctor Prong was shouting, up on Bryn's hat. "Right just a whisker . . . elevate. . ."

"What does elevate mean?" Bryn wondered.

"Up a bit!" shouted Fentongoose.

Bryn tilted his huge face a little more towards the sky, and frowned as he saw the dragon plunging towards him like a black dart. With a clunk and a twang the Bratapult released its payload. The boulder went tumbling towards the oncoming dragon, and the dragon backed in mid-air and flapped wildly sideways to avoid it, missing it by a wing's breadth.

"Yay!" cheered the goblins on Bryn's hat.

"Reload, you fools!" yelled
Fentongoose. "Fraddon!"

Fraddon passed a boulder to Bryn, who reached up with it so that the goblins could guide it into the cup of the Bratapult. But the dragon had recovered, and was rushing down on them again. Fraddon hurled another boulder at it with his hands, but that missed too, and before the Bratapult was ready Mortholow swept past Bryn's head and let out a great gust of fire.

"Ow!" said Bryn.

Yabber released the Bratapult. The boulder sprang out and struck Mortholow's tail, making the dragon squeal in pain and slide away downwind. But Bryn's hair was burning like a gorse fire, and the platform on which the Bratapult had been mounted was starting to burn as well. Blazing chunks of it went tumbling down into the sea as Bryn stepped from the cliff, patting with one hand at his blazing hair while the other snatched uselessly at the dragon like a cat trying to catch a bird.

"Abandon giant!" shouted Fentongoose, as the sea surged around Bryn's knees. Goblins hurled themselves from the blazing platform and cannonballed into the water, surfacing to shout, "Help! Help!" as they remembered that they did not know how to swim. Fentongoose plunged after them yelling, "Stay calm, I'll save you!" and then remembered that he didn't, either. Doctor Prong dived in and struck out for the shore doing a scientific doggy-paddle of his own invention. Fraddon lashed at Mortholow as the dragon soared past him, swerved, and dived at Bryn again. More fire. Twiglings fled rustling through Bryn's beard. They were terrified by the flames, and so was Bryn. He floundered deeper into the sea, and the waves he threw up washed over Floonhaven harbour wall, sinking fishing boats and flooding seafront cottages.

"The sea!" shouted Fraddon. "The sea will put it out!"

Bryn did not hear him, so he took off his own hat, filled it with water, and flung it in the young giant's face. Bryn was so startled that he lost his footing and fell backwards, arms outstretched, throwing up a wall of foam that set the bobbing goblins shrieking even louder. Steam burst up with the foam; singed strands of Bryn's woody hair littered the waves. Fraddon turned, scanning the bright air for dragon wings.

High above, Hellesvor laughed her cruel, cold laugh. She had forgotten how clumsy and how helpless mortals were, and how pleasurable it was to destroy them. How quickly fear would spread across the lands of men when they heard that even giants were powerless before the fires of Mortholow!

She was just circling above the battle, waiting for the steam to clear and wondering whether to attack the old giant or finish off the young one first, when she happened to glance west. There was the smoke from the heath fires she'd lit in passing on the Autumn Isles. And there, beyond them, like a beacon on the world's edge. . .

"No!" she said.

"No!" she screamed.

Was it her own folly? Had the fire she'd poured down on that ugly old ship or on the goblin on the stairs spread? No, it couldn't be that. The mortals had survived somehow, and they were bringing ruin to her island, just as they brought ruin with them everywhere they went.

Mortholow was eager to attack the giants, claws extended, teeth bared; her saliva spattered Hellesvor's face like hot rain. But giants would wait. With a complicated elvish curse so rude and magical that it stunned a passing gull, Hellesvor wrenched her dragon's head towards the west.

Below, goblins were washing up on the beaches, or scrambling on to Bryn's chest, or into fishing boats which brave Floonish folk had brought out to rescue them. They ducked as the batwinged shadow of the dragon swept over them, then began to cheer as they saw it speeding away, dwindling back into the west where it had come from, no bigger than a fruitbat, a

293

bird, a butterfly.

"We won!" the goblins shouted. "We saw it off! We did it! Goblins is brilliant!"

But Fentongoose and Doctor Prong suspected dragons weren't beaten that easily. So did Fraddon. When he waded through the sea to help Bryn up and the young giant asked hopefully, "We won, then?" Fraddon shook his head.

"We fought bravely," he said, "and at least we saved Floonhaven from a burning. But that elf witch and her dragon were more than a match for giants and goblins. It's not us she's fleeing from. There must be other poor souls out west somewhere who she feels even more inclined to roast."

The Flames of Elvensea

Just as the water had rushed down the sides of Elvensea when it rose out of the ocean, so now the fire rushed up. Streams and rivers of fire; waves of fire that broke in sprays of dancing sparks; geysers of fire that spouted high into the air above the island. White stone turned black; lovely statues shattered and tumbled; scraps of burning tapestry rode the thermals like dazzling birds.

"It's such a shame," said Henwyn. He had begun to regret his bright idea almost as soon as the first fires were lit. How Fentongoose would have loved all those old scrolls! How Carnglaze would have wondered at the statuary and hangings! And now it would all be ash. "If only Hellesvor had been a bit more reasonable. If only we could have made peace with her. Elvensea for the elves, the Westlands for mortals."

"You saw her eyes," said Zeewa. "Sometimes there is no peace to be made."

Breenge said, "This place could be repaired, I suppose, if the elves ever come back across the sea."

"You know what I think?" said Skarper. "I think maybe those elves cleared off because of Hellesvor, not us. Maybe it was her and her wars and her dragons that made them leave here and go looking for a new land to live in. You couldn't blame them, could you?"

"I certainly wouldn't want to share an island with her," agreed Rhind.

They were standing on a wide battlement that jutted like a ship's prow from the flank of Elvensea, just below the levels they had burned. From there they had a good view of the eastern sea, of the harbour below them where Kestle, Gutgust and Woon Gumpus were readying the ship, and of the roaring flames above. At first the heat of the blaze had been almost too fierce, and they had thought about going further down, but a lower vantage point would allow less warning if Mortholow came. Now, quite quickly, the fires were dying down; the flames had devoured everything that would burn among the old palaces, and they could not feed on stone alone.

"I hope it works," said Henwyn.

Skarper wondered what had happened to the magic

pool. The dome of Hellesvor's hall had split open like an egg, letting out smoke and flames. Would some of the smoke find its way through the mist and into the super market, setting off the fire bells again? Or would the fire just melt the mist, and the portal into that strange world be closed for ever? It was a pity, he thought. He would have liked to explore there, and try some of the food on the super market's shelves. It had been a long time since breakfast, and the memory of the way those burning boxes smelled made his mouth water.

The sun was warm, the fires were warmer, and the thought of all that lovely food was so pleasant that Skarper was almost asleep when Zeewa suddenly shouted, "There!"

And suddenly, luring Hellesvor and her dragon back did not seem like such a good idea. There it was, like a jagged black crack in the eastern sky, growing larger as they ran to the edge of the battlement to watch it come.

"Breenge!" said Henwyn.

She fitted an arrow to her bow.

"Zeewa!" he said.

She raised a bow too; a recurved bow of smooth white wood that they had found for her in Elvensea's armouries before they set fire to them.

"Skarper?" asked Henwyn.

Skarper heaved his smoke squirter up on to the wall, pointing its nozzle towards the approaching dragon. They had not dared to test the squirter in case it was a one-time-only sort of weapon, so it was decided that Skarper should operate it, as he was the only one who had clearly seen it being used. It had a label on it like a tin can, with some useful pictures showing how it worked, but now that the time had come Skarper couldn't help but worry that the thing might have been broken during its journey between the worlds. Or maybe it ran on some super market magic that just wouldn't work here on the Western Ocean. . .

Morthalow was so near now they could hear the whoosh and crack of her leathery wings. She was so close that they could hear Hellesvor's voice, wild and angry as the crying of the gulls. "Verminous mortals! Mud folk! Filth!"

It was only a few hours since they had seen the dragon, but somehow in that time they had managed to forget how big she was. How colossally, unreasonably enormous. How red her eyes, how wide her wings, how sharp and bright her claws. . .

"Skarper, now!" shouted Henwyn.

With a flap of her wings the dragon came almost

to a halt in mid-air, her huge head reaching down towards the battlements. Still not quite close enough, thought Skarper, to be in range of the smoke squirter, so he scrambled up on to the wall with it. He could see clear down Mortholow's throat into the furnace of her belly. He saw the flames ignite down there, and come roaring up towards him. He pressed the trigger of the squirter as shown in the instructions, and the white smoke of the other world burst out with a hiss nearly as fierce as the noises the dragon was making. As it struck Mortholow's nose the dragon flinched away, swallowing the fire she had been about to belch out. The white smoke had formed like frost upon her face.

The dragon screeched and fell sideways, away from the battlement. Breenge and Zeewa loosed their bows, one arrow missing its mark, the other thudding between the scales of Mortholow's flank and sticking there. Her tail lashed around like a whip, and Skarper, who had been balancing precariously on the battlement with the smoke squirter when it hit him, was suddenly reminded why balancing precariously on battlements is Not A Good Idea.

It was a sheer drop, all the way to some sharp-looking turrets down at the water's edge. As he toppled he looked back in horror at his friends. Henwyn had flung his sword aside and was reaching out to catch him, but all he caught was the smoke squirter. The slippery cylinder slid through Skarper's fingers and he fell, arms flailing, a scream fighting its way up his throat . . .

. . . and then turning to a little squeak of surprise as his grasping paws grabbed hold of something.

That was lucky, he thought. But it wasn't really, because the something was Mortholow's tail.

The enraged dragon wheeled again above the battlement, Hellesvor jerking like an armoured doll in her harness beneath it as she struggled to control the creature. It snorted fire at the group on the battlements, but Henwyn raised the smoke squirter again and Mortholow swerved away, wary of this magic from another world. Breenge already had another arrow ready, but before she could loose it Henwyn shouted, "No! You might shoot Skarper!"

"Help?" suggested Skarper, as he flew past them, clinging desperately to Mortholow's tail. But he wasn't really expecting them to help him. What could they do but stand and stare as the dragon went roaring up into the sky above the island, and he went with it?

A tail seemed a dangerous place to be – it kept lashing about, as if Mortholow could feel him there and was trying to throw him off.

He started to climb, using the spikes on her spine as handholds. The Western Ocean tilted beneath him. He was so far above it that he could see the Autumn Isles and the Nibbled Coast – he could probably have seen all the way to Clovenstone if he'd had time to look. But he hadn't; he was climbing an angry dragon, and just ahead of him he could hear an even angrier Hellesvor shouting as she jerked at the reins.

"What is wrong with you? Go down! Down! You are one of the great drakes of Elvensea. You need not be scared of a bottle of smoke. It is mortal trickery, no more. Go down and burn them!"

She does not know that I am here, thought Skarper. *She thinks the dragon is wriggling like this out of fright or stubborness. She doesn't know it's trying to flick me off.*

Just then, as he reached the place where her tail joined her body, Mortholow gave a fierce jerk and dislodged him. He slithered down her side and saved himself by catching hold of Breenge's arrow, which stuck out like a little handle between the black scales. Black blood spattered down his arm as his weight began to drag the arrow free, and the dragon twitched like a pony stung by horseflies. She lashed her head back, trying to bite at Skarper, and her crocodile jaws went "clop" a few inches from his ear. He flung himself sideways as the arrow popped out, and seized one of

301

the straps of the leather harness from which Hellesvor dangled.

The elf witch noticed them. She twisted her fierce white face towards him and her eyes went wide and then narrow as she realized she had a stowaway. She reached for the sword whose scabbard was strapped across her back, its ornate hilt jutting over one shoulder. Before she could draw it, though, the maddened dragon made a move so violent that Hellesvor's sword hand had to dart back to the reins.

Skarper saw his chance. It wasn't a very good chance, but it was the only one he seemed likely to get. He scrambled along the straps of the harness, seized the sword, and drew it from its scabbard himself.

Hellesvor shrieked in fury and took both hands from the reins to snatch at him.

Mortholow made another lunge with her head, determined to rid herself of this irritating creature on her belly. She almost bit Hellesvor instead; her sharp teeth struck sparks from the elven armour.

Skarper, who had been dangling with one paw from the harness while he tried to raise the sword high enough to stick it into Hellesvor, lost his grip and dropped on to the dragon's snout. The long neck lashed again, almost flicking him off, but he clung on grimly, glad of all the spines and spurs which dragons seemed to think were necessary facial features. Still clutching the sword, he scrambled up the long nose, over the ridge of the eyebrows, out on to the long neck, just behind the head. Mortholow could not bite him now, and he was out of Hellesvor's reach as well. He turned to wave at the furious elf woman, making her more furious still and almost dropping the sword in the process.

She snatched the flapping reins again. "Your friends shall burn," she said, "and then I'll deal with you! Dive, Mortholow!"

Mortholow seemed to understand. She folded her wings. The air began to rush past Skarper's face. The wind pushed its thumbs into his eyes, just as it had on that long-ago day when he was flung from Blackspike Tower. Between the dragon's horny eyebrows he saw Elvensea grow larger and larger, and his friends on the battlements there, looking up.

He did not think that arrows or even a smoke squirter were going to harm this dragon much. But elven steel might. He edged a little further down Mortholow's neck, going, "Ooh!" and "Ow!" as he eased his bottom over her spines. Taking a firm grip with his knees and his scorched tail, he raised the sword two-handed.

Just before the blow fell, Hellesvor realized what he

was doing. "No, you fool!" she shouted.

For once she sounded not just angry, but afraid.

The sword slashed down. It was heavier than Skarper had expected; also, sharper. It cut through Mortholow's bony scales like a cheese knife slicing Clovenstone Blue. Black blood spurted, flames flared, and the dragon's head, wearing a look of extreme surprise, tumbled away from her still-flapping body.

Skarper was so surprised that he dropped the sword. He stared at the lopped-off head as it tumbled away. He realized, numbly, that he had become one of those rare heroes whose names are remembered for all time, because they have slain a dragon.

What separated him from them, of course, was that they had all had the sense to slay their dragons while the dragons were *on the ground*.

Mortholow's enormous wings had ceased to flap. Like a stone, like a broken statue of a dragon, she plummeted towards Elvensea.

"Oh, bumcakes," said Skarper, as he fell towards certain death. "Not again!"

The Final Act

On the battlements of Elvensea, Henwyn and his companions cheered as they saw the dragon start to fall. Then their cheers faded, as they realized that she was going to fall on them.

They scattered towards the landward end of the battlement, but could not go far because of the still-burning fires there. Henwyn ran back to fetch the smoke squirter, which he had set down beside the parapet after Skarper fell. He snatched it up, and ran to join the others cowering in the smoke with just seconds to spare.

The immense, scaly carcass landed on the battlement with a thump that cracked the paving and sent chunks of the parapet tumbling down the sides of Elvensea. Black dragon-blood spattered the stonework, and hissed in the burning buildings.

Skarper, clinging tightly to Mortholow's neck, cautiously opened one eye and then the other, and checked to make sure that he was still all there. He was. The dragon had broken his fall. But when he looked for Hellesvor he saw only the crumpled struts of the harness protruding from beneath the wreck. The elven woman had been crushed under her own dragon. Which seemed to Skarper to serve her right.

And then, while he was still getting used to the idea that he was not dead after all, his friends came running to help him down, and tell him what a hero he had been.

"The bravest thing I ever saw!" Breenge was saying. "The way he leaped upon that dragon's tail. . ."

"It was all part of his plan, of course," said Henwyn, who knew it hadn't been but was pleased to see the proud Woolmarkers praising his friend.

"The way he climbed its body, and used the elf witch's own blade to behead it!" agreed Rhind. He shook Skarper manfully by the paw and said, "I am sorry I doubted you, goblin. You are worthy of your place in the Hall of Heroes!"

"My what?" wondered Skarper, who was still feeling a bit dizzy.

"The Hall of Heroes at Boskennack," said Henwyn. "Didn't you know? By ancient decree, anyone who slays a dragon is summoned to join the company of heroes there, and aid the High King in keeping the Westlands safe."

"What, with Lord Ponsandane and Kerwyn of Bryngallow and all them idiots?" asked Skarper.

"They are not idiots," said Rhind. "They are the bravest men in all the Westlands. But none so brave as you, Skarper of Clovenstone!"

Skarper would have told him a few home truths about Kerwyn, Lord Ponsandane and the rest, but just at that moment there was a leathery rasp from behind him. One of Mortholow's wings, which had settled like a tent across the wreckage of her body, was moving. Everyone stood and stared at it, as it was drawn aside, and out from the shadows behind it, battered and dented and slick with dragon blood, came Hellesvor. Her armour of elven steel had saved her, and while the mortals talked she had managed to free herself from beneath her fallen steed.

Too angry to even speak, she stood and hissed at them, and raked them with her wintry eyes.

Rhind sprang forward, raising his sword. She smashed him aside with a blow from her armoured fist. Henwyn swung his sword at her and she caught it in her gauntlet and snapped it, leaving him blinking at the useless stub. Breenge and Zeewa loosed their bows, but she made a snake-quick movement of her head and the arrows slid past her, their flight feathers flicking her face. She snatched the bows and shattered them, flung Breenge and Zeewa aside and stalked on towards Skarper, who ran towards the edge of the battlement, and then could run no further. The parapet had collapsed when Mortholow fell, and he teetered among the rubble there, dislodging small shards of stone and watching them fall end-over-end down on to the rocks and roofs below.

"Goblin," said Hellesvor, finding her voice at last. "Meddling, stupid, ugly goblin. Not even a mortal man, and yet you have laid all my hopes in ruins."

"Sorry," said Skarper.

Hellesvor picked up Prince Rhind's sword and swished it through the air. Severed sunbeams flicked from the bright blade. "At least," she said, looking down at him where he cowered there on the battlement's brink, "at least I shall have my revenge. Prepare to—"

And then, out of the smoke at the battlement's landward end, a tiny shape came running. A tiny, furry shape, long ears blown backwards with the speed of its coming. The movement caught Hellesvor's eye. She turned her head, and gasped.

"Fuzzy-Nose!" cried Breenge, delightedly.

The rabbit jumped on to Prince Rhind, using his plump stomach as a trampoline to bounce itself up on to the ruined parapet. From there it launched itself at Hellesvor, somersaulting past the sword she held and landing with a furry thump in her face. She stumbled backwards, batting at the rampant rodent with her free hand while it scrabbled its paws at her eyes and nibbled at her nose with its long front teeth. With a cry of fury she caught it by the ears and flung it away from her. But while she had been struggling with it, Henwyn had run to fetch the only weapon left – the smoke squirter. As Hellesvor recovered and swung back towards Skarper, Henwyn came at her, emptying the white smoke into her face.

"Argh!" and "Ack!" choked Hellesvor, her eyes and mouth and nose full of the choking, freezing vapour. She still swung the sword, she still kept staggering towards Skarper, but she could no longer see where she was going. Skarper curled himself into a tight little ball there at the battlement's edge, and she bumped into him, tripped, and went tumbling over.

Henwyn threw aside the empty smoke squirter, and he and Skarper peered over the edge. Hellesvor's silver armour flashed and flickered as she fell, struck a rooftop, slid, hit another, slid some more, and went whirling clean off the edge of Elvensea, vanishing at last with a white splash into the deep blue water just off shore.

A sort of shudder ran through the stone of Elvensea; a sort of shiver, swiftly stilled. And then there was only the smoke, and the whisper of the dying fires, the call of the gulls and the lonely distant murmur of the surf.

"Is she dead?" asked Skarper.

"I think so," said Henwyn.

"I thought elves are immortal?"

"But not indestructible," said Henwyn. "And even if she does still live, that armour will carry her down into the deep. And she has no dragon any more, no sword. We have defeated her."

"Fuzzy-Nose defeated her," said Breenge, scrambling up and running over to where the rabbit had fallen. It was dazed, but it wriggled and twitched its nose as she picked it up. "Oh, Fuzzy-Nose, how brave you are!" said Breenge, kissing it. And whether it was the kiss that made it happen, or maybe Hellesvor's magic had all died with her, there was a sort of flash, a popping sound, and suddenly Breenge was not holding a soot-stained rabbit any more, but staggering under the weight of a large, nude, and very embarrassed sorcerer.

"Prawl!" everyone shouted.

310

"Eep!" said Prawl, as Breenge dropped him in surprise.

Henwyn handed him a cloak. Prince Rhind woke up and said, "What? Where's Prawl come from? Where did Hellesvor go?"

"Into the sea," said Zeewa. "And we should go too; back to the Westlands, in case Elvensea decides to sink again."

Henwyn did not think that Elvensea would sink. He had a feeling that it was here to stay. The fires were failing now, and as his companions went down the winding paths to where the new ship waited, he went upwards, through the burned and blackened palaces. The hangings and fine furniture were all gone to ash, but here and there, on flat, empty places which the fires had not touched, he saw a blush of green, as if seeds that had slept a long time in the soil were waking and stretching up to feel the sunlight. Perhaps those were the real sleepers of Elvensea, he thought; the trees and grasses that would make it green again.

And what about the elves, the ones who had fled, rather than stay with Hellesvor and wage war against the coming of the mortals? Were they still out there somewhere, in some unknown land across the Western Ocean? He walked through the ruins of the pillared hall (there were still a few wisps of mist in the enchanted pool) and stood outside it, looking westward where the sun was sinking, wondering. Some of the hall's shining dome had melted in the fire's heat and spilled down its walls, coating them with metal. The metal was black with soot and ash, but when Henwyn rubbed his hand across it the black came away and the space he'd cleared blazed brightly with reflections of the sun. And he thought, *After we leave this place, the rain will wash it clean, and the sun will shine upon these heights, and maybe one day some elven ship, venturing from those far lands of theirs, will see the gleam, and know that Elvensea is risen again. And maybe the elves will come back here, and maybe they'll be a bit friendlier than Hellesvor was.*

He found a roof slate, fallen from some lesser building, and with the stub of his snapped-off sword he scratched a little stone book of his own. *Greetings, elves,* he wrote. *Hellesvor wanted war, and we defeated her, but if you come to the Westlands, the men and women and goblins and dwarves and giants who live there will welcome you in peace. Henwyn of Clovenstone. P.S. Sorry about the mess.*

He left it in the hall, beside the magic pool, and went running down to join the others. He hoped the elves would come back some day. He had a feeling that they couldn't all be like Hellesvor. They were just a different sort of people, after all, and most people are all right, really.

5 Homeward Bound

The white ship sailed like a dream, her sails filled by a kindly wind that blew her across the calm blue sea.

"A fine ship," said Captain Kestle, standing at the helm. "She needs a name, though. I was thinking of *Sea Cucumber the Second,* but there's nothing cucumberish about her."

"What about the *Swan*?" asked Henwyn. "She is more like a swan than even Captain Gumpus's old ship."

"But not the *Swan of Govannon,*" said Woon Gumpus, thinking sadly of his lost ship. "There was only one ship of that name, and she is gone for ever."

"Then she is the *Swan of Elvensea,*" said Captain Kestle. "A lovely name for a lovely vessel. If only I had somewhere to sail her to!"

"To sail anywhere would be an adventure, in a ship

like this!" said Woon Gumpus. "Look here, Kestle, you know all about sailing these things, which strings to pull and how to avoid large rocks and so on. And I can find you passengers! There are rich folk in Coriander and Porthquidden and Choon who will pay good money to sail in an elven ship. We'll show them the night forests of Musk, the deserts of Barragan. We'll visit the sea people. We'll show them Elvensea itself. What do you say?"

"I'll have to think on it," said Kestle gravely. But there was a look in his eyes which made everyone feel sure that he had thought about it already, and that his answer would be yes.

Breenge and Prawl seemed to have come to an agreement, too. At first Breenge had been rather disappointed to find that her cute rabbit had really just been Prawl all along. But he had retained a few of Fuzzy-Nose's rabbity ways, such as a tendency to twitch his nose, and a liking for salad – and she began to decide that he was still quite cute, in his way, even in human form. And he had saved her life, after all; he had saved everyone's lives, hurling himself at Hellesvor like that.

"Oh, Breenge," he said adoringly, as they sat together on a little sofa in one of the new *Swan*'s cabins.

"Oh, Fuzzy-Nose!" she replied, with shining eyes.

"Oh, yuck!" said the sofa, tipping them both on to the deck and squeaking away on its casters to another cabin. Spurtle might have had the outward form and semblance of furniture, but he was still a goblin through and through, and if there's one thing goblins *hate* it's romance.

The *Swan of Elvensea* soon carried them to Far Penderglaze. Black badges of scorched gorse on the island's summit showed where Mortholow had passed. They passed the rest of the Autumn Isles, and swung north-east to Floonhaven. There, upon the cliffs, they saw the two tall figures of the giants waiting to greet them, and they were amazed, because they had not known till then of Bryn's discovery. At first they were inclined to be afraid of him, because he was so very big, but as they drew nearer they could see that the other giant was Fraddon. Fraddon was waving happily at them, and Bryn, who was so big that they could not stop staring at him, walked out and stood with one foot on the end of either wall of the harbour, beaming down at the pretty white ship as it passed beneath him.

"He is as big as I was, when I was young," shouted Fraddon, introducing the young giant to his friends aboard the ship. "But twice as strong, and thrice as brave! He kept the dragon from burning this town, and many another, likely! What of the dragon, by the way? Have you news of it?"

"It is dead!" shouted Henwyn. "Skarper killed it"

"Shhh!" said Skarper, because the others had been teasing him all the way from Elvensea, calling him Dragonslayer and asking him if they could come and visit when he was living at the Hall of Heroes.

"Skarper has killed the dragon!" roared Fraddon, and before the *Swan of Elvensea* had even tied up at the quay the news had spread through the streets of Floonhaven. Bells were ringing, bright flags were unfurled, and the sounds of cheering voices echoed across the water, so loud that, far offshore, the people of the sea popped their ugly heads above the waves to see what was happening.

Half of Clovenstone seemed to be waiting on the harbourside as the *Swan's* passengers came ashore: Fentongoose, Doctor Prong and dozens of goblins, all with their own tales of the battle to tell. Then Etty and some of her miners appeared, and Skarper was able to give her back her father's amulet and tell her how it had helped to pull him back through the wall between the worlds from the super market. And finally King Floon and Queen Harwyn descended from their castle to invite everyone inside, and to declare a feast and holiday in honour of Skarper the Dragonslayer. Long into the night the lamps burned and the laughter echoed, and Henwyn, Zeewa and the others grew quite tired of telling their stories of the quest.

Towards the end of the evening, Skarper noticed that Henwyn was missing from the feasting hall, and went to look for him. He went outside into the summer night. The battlements of Castle Floon seemed low and humble and sort of cosy after the heights of Elvensea, and the moon made a silvery pathway on the sea.

Henwyn stood there, looking out over the harbour and the sea beyond. Skarper went and leaned upon the wall beside him, and they stood there together for a while in silence, until Skarper noticed another solitary figure leaning on a lower balcony, also staring out across the sea.

"Is that Prince Rhind?" he asked softly.

"Yes," said Henwyn. "He is sad because his quest came to nothing. He did not raise the elves, only Hellesvor and her dragon, and you slew that. He so wanted to be a hero, poor man!"

"Like you did, when you first turned up at Clovenstone," said Skarper.

"Yes," said Henwyn, and sighed. "We are more alike than I wanted to admit, Prince Rhind and I.

318

I did nothing on this quest either. Telling the story of it made me realize how useless I have been. I got eaten by a tree, and led you all on to the sea cliffs. It was Grumpling who saved us from the crabs. It was you who slew the dragon."

"It was your idea to burn Elvensea."

"But that is hardly something to be proud of!"

"Well, it was you who defeated Hellesvor."

"That was Prawl. Even a rabbit was more use than me."

"Without you," said Skarper, "we wouldn't have had a quest at all. We'd have stayed in Clovenstone arguing and eating and burping and stuff, and Rhind would have raised Elvensea and Hellesvor would have burned half the world down, probably. Cos goblins are a bit rubbish sometimes, though we mean well. So we need someone to give us a shove and make us do things."

"That was Princess Ned's job," said Henwyn.

"Well, now it's yours," said Skarper. "If you don't do it, some other big lunk like Grumpling will come along and start organizing us all. And you're the Lych Lord's heir, after all, so it's only right you should give us goblins a helping shove from time to time. A friendly kick up the tail, as it were. And I'll help."

"You'll be in Boskennack," said Henwyn. "When

the High King hears of your dragon slayery, he will send for you, and you will go to dwell in the Hall of Heroes."

"They don't have goblins in the Hall of Heroes," said Skarper. "You're stuck with me."

But a few days later, when the long line of happy, full-bellied, hungover goblins was weaving its way back across the heathland west of Clovenstone, they saw a cloud of dust upon the road ahead, and as it drew closer they saw the glitter of armour and bright horse-trappings in its heart, and pretty soon it turned out to be a band of riders bearing the banner of the High King, and led by their old friend Garvon Hael.

"Well met, my friends!" called the old warrior, reining in his horse and smiling down at them (and up at the giants). "News of your high deeds has come to Boskennack. The people of the sea told it to the fishermen, who told it the High King. I am come with his thanks."

The goblins all looked proud. There had been a time, not so long ago, when important people like High Kings had thought of goblins as a bit of a menace, if not downright evil.

"Also, a command," said Garvon Hael. "By the ancient custom of these lands, any man who slays a dragon is rewarded with a seat at the High King's right hand, a place in the Hall of Heroes, and the hand in marriage of a princess of the royal line (subject to availability)." He paused a moment, smiling at Skarper. "Skarper, I am to take you back with me to Coriander. You shall live at Boskennack henceforth."

Skarper felt as dizzy as he had when he stepped off that crashed dragon at Elvensea. To be summoned to the Hall of Heroes was the greatest honour that could be bestowed upon a warrior of the Westlands. He thought of all the treasure there, the shining things with which he could fill his new nest. He thought of all the food – for the kitchens of Boskennack were famed far and wide. He didn't like the sound of marrying a princess, but probably most princesses wouldn't like the sound of marrying a goblin, so he expected he'd be allowed to skip that bit. It would be brilliant!

And yet his heart did not leap up, as he knew it should. He thought of Clovenstone: the weed-grown ruins, the damp rooms and draughty windows, the pervading smells of cheese and goblins. He thought about blackberrying in the ruins with Henwyn or Zeewa – there would be big, juicy blackberries at the end of a summer like this – and how sad it would be if he never got to prick his paws again on Clovenstone's fearsome bramble patches, and sit down afterwards with his friends on some patch of overgrown lawn to eat berries and talk of this and that.

"I'm only a hero by accident," he said.

"That doesn't matter," laughed Garvon Hael. "So are most heroes! You cannot refuse this summons, dragonslayer." And he gestured at a riderless horse that one of his companions held by the reins. Its stirrups had already been shortened to fit Skarper's short goblin legs.

"The thing is. . ." said Skarper, looking round, wondering how he should say goodbye to his friends, and how long it would be before he saw them again. "The thing is. . . It wasn't me who slew the dragon. It was Prince Rhind!"

There was a bit of commotion among the goblins at that. Cries of "No!" and "What?" and "Was it?" and, "Anchovies!" Prince Rhind shook his head disbelievingly.

"It's true," said Skarper. "Rhind got knocked out by Hellesvor, and it's blurred his memories a bit. It was him who chopped the dragon's head off, fair and square. He's the one who belongs in the Hall of Heroes, not me."

"But the sea people said—"

"They must have been lying," said Henwyn. "Or perhaps they got the wrong end of the stick. At any rate, Skarper is right. It was Rhind who slew the dragon. Wasn't it?"

"Yes!" said Zeewa, cottoning on. "Yes!" said Breenge and Prawl. "Yes," said Spurtle (who was back in his own shape now). "I suppose it must have been," said Rhind.

There was a gleam in the grey eyes of Garvon Hael that suggested he did not believe this for a moment. But he understood why it was being done, and so he nodded, and said, "Rhind of Tyr Davas, welcome. Are you ready to ride with me now?"

And Prince Rhind, blushing and shaking his head in amazement, but beaming too, said to Skarper, "Are you sure?"

Skarper nodded.

"Then yes!" said Rhind. And goodbyes were said, and he mounted the horse (whose stirrups had been lengthened again). Horses were found for Prawl and Breenge too, who were to go with him, and once all were mounted, the riders from Boskennack turned south again, for the High King had been keen to bring the dragonslayer to the Hall of Heroes before the story of his victory grew too old.

"Prince Rhind will fit in well at Boskennack," said Garvon Hael, before he spurred his horse and followed them.

"Oh, he is very brave, really," said Henwyn.

"I am sure he is," said Garvon Hael. "But if we ever find that we have need of true heroes, we shall send word to Clovenstone."

The goblins shouted, burped, hallooed. But Henwyn said, "Oh, we aren't heroes, not really." And Skarper said, "We just sort of muddle along."

And then they went on their way, goblins, giants and humans, laughing and singing under the summer sun, muddling along through the lengthening shadows and the lanes where the blackberries were ripening, home to Clovenstone.